PRIDE AND MODERN PREJUDICE

AJ MICHAELS

Dreamspinner Press

Published by
Dreamspinner Press
5032 Capital Circle SW
Suite 2, PMB# 279
Tallahassee, FL 32305-7886
USA
http://www.dreamspinnerpress.com/

Pride and Modern Prejudice
© 2014 AJ Michaels.

Cover Art
© 2014 Anna Sikorska.
Cover content is for illustrative purposes only and any person depicted on the cover is a model.

ISBN: 978-1-62798-709-7
Digital ISBN: 978-1-62798-710-3

Printed in the United States of America
First Edition
June 2014

CHAPTER ONE

THE GYMNASIUM practically hummed with applause, and Liam Bennet felt relief, solid palpable relief, easing his muscles for the first time in weeks. He smiled, thanked his fellow classmates, and left the podium.

His best friend Charlotte slipped him a high five on the walk back to his seat. He listened to her graduation speech, which wasn't so much *inspiring* as it was littered with Steve Jobs quotes. She had a lifelong devotion to the Apple pioneer. When he passed, she had missed school for three days.

Liam looked around. The graduating class of Longbourn Academy was tiny, barely above two hundred. And he could not *wait* to get away from these people. He couldn't wait to leave Longbourn County in general, to escape this bumbling, gossiping small town outside of Philadelphia, the nosiness of the neighbors, his mother's melodrama, all of it.

"Not that you'll ever be *completely* free," his older brother Jamie had told him earlier that week. "But at least I limit my familial interactions to winter and summer breaks now."

Liam found his older brother's face in the crowd. Jamie grinned his megawatt smile and stuck both of his thumbs up. The rest of his family was huddled on the bleachers. His mother was crying. His father was beaming proudly. Mason's nose was buried in *The Hitchhiker's Guide to the Galaxy*, which he had *refused* to leave at home. Ben and Nate were texting… each other.

The ceremony dwindled to an uneventful close. As all of his classmates filtered out of the building, Liam had the sudden sensation of time slipping from him. But then he was tackled by his brothers and promptly forgot all about his sentimental lapse.

After his parents treated him to dinner at his favorite Italian restaurant, Liam spent the evening with his older brother.

"Hi there, graduate. How do you feel?" Jamie asked when Liam entered the room.

"Remarkably the same. Maybe 2 percent nostalgic."

"I remember that feeling. It'll go away."

Liam snorted and sat on the edge of his bed. "I get to spend all my time with *you* now! Pause for ecstatic reaction."

"Yeah. About that—I don't have a lot of time this summer. I got an internship with Bingley Corp," Jamie said casually.

Liam glanced up. "What? That's huge! I thought you said the position was filled when you called."

"Well, it was. But I have a friend, and he pulled some strings for me...."

Liam narrowed his eyes. "Which friend?"

"Um." Jamie laughed and rubbed his jaw, looking anywhere but his brother's face. "You know that graduate student who hired me to do about fifteen hours of code last semester?"

"Yeah. Charlie, right?"

"That's him."

"What does he have to do with Bingley Corp?"

"His father is CEO," Jamie muttered quickly.

A beat, and then laughingly, "Charlie *Bingley*? Oh wow. You whored yourself out."

"Shut up, I did not."

Liam could not stop laughing. "I didn't realize he was a graduate student at your school. I'm pretty sure I've seen that guy in *Forbes* at least twice in the last year." And he had, most recently in their "30 Under 30" issue. "Hang on, I probably still have it."

Liam crossed the room to his bookshelf and thumbed through his magazines, all organized on the two bottom shelves in alphabetical and chronological order.

"You are freakishly OCD about your magazines," Jamie said. "The entire room is a shithole but *no*, god no! Don't touch the magazines."

Liam ignored the quip and pulled out the December issue he had been searching for. He spent a couple of moments flipping through it before he stopped on a page. Charlie Bingley smiled warmly at them from his glossy photo, his dark blond hair disheveled in an irritatingly perfect and probably stylistic way. He wore black frames and a navy sweater, with the mint-green collar of his button-down sticking out past the neckline.

"Your type, no doubt about it."

"He is not," Jamie mumbled, unconvincingly.

Liam smiled to himself. Jamie had a type. Of a *man*, no less. He would have never seen it coming years ago, but his big brother had come out last summer and freed himself from four years' worth of suppression and mixed feelings. It made sense to him in hindsight.

"Why?" Jamie had prompted his brother at the time.

"I don't know," Liam had replied. "You're just so graceful. And you turned down Jessica Cartwright, the hottest girl in high school. Plus, you were just really into *Spring Awakening*—please stop laughing at me."

Liam was supportive. Jamie was his favorite brother; how could he not be? Their mother had been quiet, but ultimately accepting. Their father had been just as quiet but not quite as accepting.

Liam read on.

Charles Bingley IV, 27 years old, founder and co-owner of Nerve, a multimedia social networking site. You may recognize the legendary last name. Yes, like the Carnegies and the Vanderbilts before them, the Bingley family is renowned for their contributions to the steel and railroad industries. But it is young Charlie who is making headlines now with his newest endeavor, Nerve. Bingley brings to the table a sharp education, a zest for learning, and a killer sense of humor. He had our staffers in stitches during our phone conference—

"Starting to sound like an online dating profile, if you ask me." Jamie laughed. "He's much better than they describe. Sure, he's loaded, but he's so *nice* and humble. It's kind of unreal."

Liam shot him a knowing glance and turned the page.

Bingley is currently completing his Master's degree at Oakham Mount University, outside Philadelphia. He shares half of his profits with his Nerve co-owner, William Darcy.

"Are you done reading? Because I have a second point."

"By all means," Liam drawled sarcastically, spreading out on the bed. He interlaced his fingers behind his head.

"Charlie—well, the company, I guess—is throwing a launch party this coming Saturday. He rented out the Netherfield House for the year."

Liam lifted his head. "What, that rotting mansion in the center of your campus?"

"It is an architectural *gem* and it has since been *renovated*," corrected Jamie. "And yes. Go with me. I'm nervous as all hell. I have trouble socializing."

"Since when?" Liam laughed. The idea was ridiculous. Jamie Bennet had a crest of auburn hair and bright eyes, easy banter, and an uncanny ability to be friends with *everybody*. He had been captain of the lacrosse team in high school, had been crowned Prom King, and had been voted Best Smile and Most Likely to Succeed.

It was sickening.

Liam was different. He was a clever young man but occasionally too confrontational to curry favor with the entire student body. Likeable, sure. But he made a *lot* of people's shit lists.

"I've been freezing up since I met Charlie. He just unsettles me," Jamie sighed, already on edge. "I have to rehearse everything I want to say in my head before I *actually* say it. It's exhausting."

"Well, that's just because you like him," said Liam.

Jamie looked down. "Dammit."

Liam's phone buzzed, and he drew it out of his pocket with a sigh. Jamie tilted his head, and his younger brother answered, "Angela King. My prom date, remember?"

"She's *still* bugging you?" Jamie laughed. "Prom was a month ago. Poor girl."

"I guess she read into it."

"Did you kiss her?"

"No. We're friends," said Liam.

"Poor girl," Jamie repeated.

CHAPTER TWO

HE FELT really underdressed.

Weren't launch parties supposed to be casual? Weren't today's billionaires and entrepreneurs supposed to be shockingly laid-back? Mark Zuckerberg wore those I-don't-give-a-shit Adidas flip-flops all the time, didn't he?

No, Charlie Bingley arrived at the Netherfield House wearing a tuxedo. A blonde, sneering waif of a girl was tethered to his side, clothed in a dramatic, backless black gown that seemed more appropriate for the Met Gala.

"These people go all out," Liam muttered under his breath. Jamie shrugged. Both held flutes of champagne, untouched.

"I told you to dress up," his older brother insisted. "The invitation said black-tie."

"I forgot, okay?" Liam grunted, annoyed. "It's like everyone is forgetting that we're on a college *campus*; I saw three guys hauling keggers down the street. I'll stick to my jeans."

Jamie sighed.

Liam stuck out like a sore thumb among the expensive cocktail dresses and fine, tailored suits, but he embraced his worn jeans, blue polo, and gray hoodie. In a weird way, it was attracting more people than usual. An hour passed and he could *not* get a red-haired girl named Andrea off of his arm.

"It's funny because they think I'm downplaying the wealth I actually don't have." Liam grinned at his brother. "I'm going to patent this one as The Zuckerberg Effect."

Jamie wasn't paying attention to him but was staring, besotted, at Charlie Bingley at the bar. Bingley smiled and joined their party from across the room. He brought with him the blonde girl and a tall, sullen stranger.

"Jamie, I'm so glad you could make it." Bingley smiled, all dimples. They shook hands. "Allow me to introduce my sister, Caroline Bingley. And this is my best friend and business partner, Will Darcy."

The business partner nodded curtly. Caroline looked as if she had just sucked on a lemon.

Liam shook each person's hand. "Hi, I'm Liam, Jamie's brother. How do you do?" The warmth and assurance in each handshake dissipated as he went down the line; Bingley's was the most welcoming and Darcy's felt like a cold fish slipping in his grasp.

They made idle chitchat, mostly about the launch, until Bingley asked Jamie to come with him so that he could introduce him to some of his colleagues. Liam opened his mouth and watched his only lifeline go. Suddenly, he was stuck in the middle of a ballroom with an ice queen and quite possibly a hit man.

He turned to face his company. Caroline Bingley was very pretty in a willowy, carved-cheekbones kind of way. She was staring at his shoes, and her red lips twisted into a smirk.

"Your dress is interesting," he told her.

"Westwood," she trilled back immediately. Liam arched an eyebrow.

Will Darcy was staring just past his shoulder, inspecting the crowd. He was tall, striking, and long-limbed, and he seemed to wear his tux uncomfortably. His posture was impeccable but rigid, and he seemed to be perpetually frowning. Darcy's ice blue eyes flickered to his own. Liam tore his gaze away.

Liam excused himself to the pair. "Enjoy the rest of your evening."

Out on the terrace, the air was cool.

Liam shut his eyes and gripped the marble railing, taking in a full breath. When he opened his eyes, the massive, rolling property of

Netherfield Park greeted him. Stone steps led to a garden pathway and a massive cherry blossom tree, its pale pink buds trickling down in threads. He took a seat on the first step.

Charlotte called him a minute later, and Liam didn't hesitate to answer his phone. "Hey."

"How's the big Bingley bash?"

Liam laughed. "How long have you been working on that impressive alliteration?"

"Like, ten minutes. Leave me alone. Not all of us can be English majors."

"Most of us can't afford to be," Liam said. "Mom is still convinced I'll change direction halfway into the semester. She cites you as an example all the time."

"Me? I thought your mom hated me."

"Nope." Liam mimicked his mother's tone. "'Charlotte's getting a sensible degree and you should be a computer science major too. Or else go to law school.' She's pushing that one too."

"Oh, please. What's sensible these days with this kind of economy?"

Liam smiled, grateful for her support. "I'm glad you called. Jamie ditched me."

"Sucks to be you. The real party is in my living room. You should have stayed to watch this Harry Potter marathon with me."

"Damn," he sighed, dejected.

The double doors to the terrace suddenly opened, and Liam bristled. "One second," he murmured. Behind him, Darcy and Caroline stood a few feet away.

"This party is boring me to tears," she sighed, an unlit cigarette bobbing in her mouth. Darcy obliged her with a light. "Thank you, Will. You're the only gentleman to be found for miles."

It was all Liam could do to suppress a snort.

"And your brother?" murmured Darcy, voice low.

"Charlie's too distracted by his new intern to be a gentleman." A beat. "I wonder about his taste sometimes."

Darcy might have smiled. It was tough to tell in the darkness.

"I want more champagne. Hold this." She gave him her unfinished cigarette and disappeared inside.

Liam watched, hidden by the hydrangea bushes that lined the stone steps, as Darcy rolled the cigarette between his fingers, paused, and stubbed it out on the marble. The orange embers faded, and black ash floated into the air.

Bingley joined him a moment later. His blazer and tie were gone, and he had pushed up the sleeves of his button-down. "Hey buzz-kill. Why aren't you enjoying the party?"

"I'm enjoying it as much as I can," replied Darcy.

"Bright and bubbly, as always," Bingley said. He leaned across the terrace railing, and Liam compacted himself into an even smaller ball, just in case. "Sorry I dragged you out tonight. I know you'd rather be at the office in a daze of Red Bull and productivity."

Darcy smiled wryly. "True. I still haven't fixed that glitch from Thursday night."

"Workaholic."

"Yes, I am. You would have never gone into business with me if I weren't. Somebody has to account for your laziness."

"Ow, *ouch*." Bingley mimed drawing an invisible sword out of his side. Liam grinned. He liked him already.

"Where's your intern?"

"Talking to our CFO. He's great, isn't he?"

"The CFO?" Darcy scoffed. "Hardly—"

"No, *Jamie*," Bingley clarified. "He's the nicest guy I've worked with in years. And he's got talent, real, genuine talent and vision—"

Darcy gave him a knowing glance. "Be careful there, Charlie."

"What do you mean?"

"You tend to pick favorites and lose professionalism quite quickly."

"I'm not even going to dignify that with a response," Bingley said, but he was laughing.

"That *was* a response."

"You're a jackass," Bingley said cheerfully. "What did you think of his brother, Liam?"

Darcy hesitated. "I'm sorry, was I supposed to think anything of him? Other than the only idiot to consciously avoid your dress code...."

"I'm sure there is a perfectly logical explanation behind his clothing choice—"

"Yes, definitely," said Darcy. "We shouldn't be surprised. This is what you get for throwing your launch party in the University District, Charlie. A bunch of know-nothing college kids are always running around, freeloading. Caroline said it herself: there's just no class, no respect."

"Now you're listening to Caroline?"

"I zone in and out when she's speaking," Darcy quipped. "Let's go find her."

They disappeared inside. Liam stood up too quickly, livid. *What an asshole*. He realized Charlotte was still on the line. "Oh my god, Charlotte, I'm so sorry—"

"Wow, Liam, your phone has amazing clarity."

"How much did you hear?"

"I picked up on Jamie's name and eavesdropped onward. Who was that man bad-mouthing you?" she asked.

Liam looked at the terrace doors, shut now. "Just some dickhead."

After a few minutes, Liam slipped back inside to find his brother. Jamie was among a cluster of professionals at the bar. "Pleasure meeting you, gentlemen," Jamie excused himself. "There you are," he said, once he had started walking with Liam into the hall. "I was wondering where you ran off to."

"Oh, just admiring the property."

"Yeah, it's beautiful. I can't believe Charlie is lucky enough to stay here."

"You mean rich enough," Liam corrected. He beamed at his brother. "Mom will be proud of you."

Jamie sighed gravely.

Caroline, Darcy, and Bingley joined them shortly afterward. Soon the four of them were engrossed in conversation, swapping stories about the company. Liam listened in silence and smiled politely on occasion, if the gesture was warranted. Mostly he admired the chandelier overhead, which was disgustingly opulent and dripping with excess crystals.

"I don't miss home much," Bingley was saying, "but if I have to go back, it's not that far. Our headquarters are in Manhattan."

"Well, I'm glad you like it here." Jamie smiled.

"I do; it's a really pleasant campus. So much nature." Bingley smiled back. "And there's a lot to do in town. The park is wonderful. I went hiking the other day—"

"I disagree. I think it's such a *boring* little town. No offense." Caroline gave a honeyed little laugh and touched Jamie fleetingly on the arm. "Don't you think so, Darcy?"

Darcy lifted his shoulders almost mechanically. "I have no opinion in this matter."

"Really?" Liam asked, and all glanced up in surprise. "I think it must be so difficult for someone of your caliber to spend so much time here." He paused for effect. "You know, what with all the low-class, *know-nothing* college kids freeloading every weekend."

Will Darcy opened his mouth slightly, but no speech came.

Jamie was staring at him, puzzled.

"I'm gonna go get a drink," Liam told him casually, before turning around and walking off. He smiled to himself and took an hors d'œuvre from the tray of a passing waiter.

CHAPTER THREE

IT WAS already blazing hot for early July, and Liam almost regretted offering to help his mother in the front yard. He set down a bag of mulch, removed his cap, and wiped the sweat from his forehead.

Mrs. Bennet glanced at him from under her floppy hat and sunglasses. "Thank you, Liam. Just don't step on the petunias, you'll ruin everything."

He ignored this, seeing as he was a good two feet away from her treasured flowerbeds.

Liam watched her gloved fingers nimbly flatten the soil, arranging the flowers just so. "You know," she said, her voice light and lyrical, "I could spend hours out here. It's so peaceful. But I burn so easily, as I've told you before."

"Yes." He scratched his nose. "You told me, Mom." She had already slathered on SPF 50—twice.

Liam turned to the garage. He hoisted another bag of mulch over his shoulder and came out a few moments later. When it thudded on the ground, his mother looked up at him again. She smiled. "You pack a lot of strength for such a wiry boy. Who knew?"

"*Wiry?*" Liam glowered.

"Yeah, you know: scrawny, slight, lanky—" she elaborated.

"Yeah, okay, thanks, Mom. I understand."

"Oh, don't take offense, sweetheart. You get it from your great-grandfather Phillips. He was an acrobat for the Barnum and Bailey Circus."

He had actually been a bank teller, which Liam had found out years ago from his aunt. He didn't have the heart to rob his mother of this piece of sensationalism. "I remember." He sat down cross-legged on the grass and raised his face to the sun.

She continued tending to the flowers, digging her little shovel into the earth. "So tell me about the launch party, sweetie. Did Jamie meet somebody?"

"Yeah. A rich somebody."

His mother beamed. "*Oh?* I'll have to call him later today. In the meantime, there's always Google."

Liam grinned and shook his head, and his mother busied herself with her garden.

He looked at the street. He had lived in this neighborhood his whole life. There was Charlotte's house, just around the corner, and the Flamhaffs to his left. Liam had avoided their house ever since he puked on their driveway on Halloween of 2003.

"Honey." His mother interrupted his reverie, and Liam turned. She was holding out her cell phone. "Do me a favor and go charge this inside? It's almost dead."

He walked back up the garden trail, a winding path with weeds jutting out between the stones. Inside, Nate and Ben were sprawled on the living room couch, watching some movie with explosions and action heroes who ignored the devastation.

Liam plugged the phone charger into the outlet in the kitchen.

"Stacy Flamhaff wants to go to the movies with me," Nate was saying proudly.

Ben snorted, "You moron. You're going with a group of people."

"Yeah but it's still a date."

"She's taking her two best friends."

"Whatever. I'm still gonna get to second base," Nate said, shrugging.

"People are still doing that?" Liam asked, incredulous. "Hooking up in the back of movie theaters?"

Nate looked over the back of the couch. "I'm bringing it back in style." Ben tossed the remote at his face, and he lurched back with a yelp.

Liam rolled his eyes and walked down the corridor, stopping for a moment outside the den. The door was ajar, and he could see his father scanning the paper, his reading glasses perched at the end of his long nose. He hesitated long enough for his father to sense the intrusion.

"Son," Mr. Bennet said.

"Dad." Liam saluted him and his father chuckled. "Any good articles?"

"Not looking at the articles. I'm looking at the job listings."

"Really?" Liam leaned against the doorframe. "You sick of the office already?"

Mr. Bennet turned a page. He sighed. "I'm afraid it may be the other way around. They're laying people off left and right. Entry-level associates are cheaper to staff."

A beat. "Have you told Mom?"

"I'm not crazy, Liam. Why say the forest is on fire when you only see a tiny speck of smoke?"

"Interesting, but troubling metaphor." Liam folded his arms across his chest. "I wouldn't worry. You've been there for over a decade. You're untouchable."

"Obviously," his father assured him. "But a Bennet is always prepared."

"Is *that* how the saying goes?" Liam asked, dubious.

"No, not at all. I'm starting it now."

Liam laughed. Mr. Bennet turned back to his paper and Liam shut the door.

Upstairs, his room was cool and quiet. He powered up his laptop and enjoyed the solitude. Well, almost solitude. Mason was blasting music from his room next door—something slow and mournful and tragically indie.

His fingers hovered at the keyboard, and then he blinked and typed "Will Darcy" into the search bar without bothering to dissect whether or not he really wanted to.

Darcy didn't have a personal website. Just some press clippings and paparazzi photos, and a site or two dedicated to what appeared to be the English aristocracy. Recent news articles identified him as the cofounder of Nerve, followed by a short blurb of a biography:

Will Darcy, 23, son of Annabella Parker, a former actress from New York, and Henry Darcy, proprietor of the Pemberley estate in Derbyshire, England.

Liam sorted through the images. Many were of Will Darcy at some benefit or another, wearing variations of the same black suit, smiling politely for the camera. *But mostly dead inside.* Liam chuckled and hit another photo. The smile never seemed to touch his eyes.

He came across a photo of Darcy leaving a restaurant with a woman. His hand rested at the small of her back, an area exposed given the risqué cut of her silver dress. The caption read:

Will Darcy is caught leaving The Ivy with Violet de Bourgh, British starlet and heiress. Are things steaming up for these hot young multimillionaires? Their reps refused to confirm.

Liam closed his laptop and leaned back in his chair. "Whatever. Not like I'll ever see the bastard again."

CHAPTER FOUR

JAMIE REGRESSED to something like a shy schoolboy during the next few weeks. It was a change that lifted eyebrows throughout the Bennet household, especially when he spent half his Saturday visit skirting around the first floor with his cell phone stapled to his ear.

"Observe," murmured Mr. Bennet at the kitchen table, "as the oldest Bennet circles obliviously around his habitat, giggling because Chuck from the varsity football team has asked him out to the homecoming dance."

As if on cue, Jamie laughed at an unheard joke. His father sat up in surprise.

Liam snorted. "You're terrible." He looked back down into his cereal.

"Do you think Charlie's taking him in a stretch limo or Cadillac?" Mr. Bennet goaded, watching Jamie intently.

Jamie hopped up on the countertop and spoke into the phone. "Yeah. Yeah, that's a great idea. I've never done that before."

"Cadillac," his father declared.

Jamie looked at the both of them now and held his hand over the mouthpiece. "Did you say something?"

Liam pursed his lips, but he couldn't help it. His body began to shake with silent laughter. John Bennet cast him a sidelong glance.

It was comforting to Liam. Jamie's coming out had been so stressful. His mother, initially silent, eventually became vocal in her support; Mr. Bennet had fallen unnervingly silent at the time. Joking about it now—well, it was the best he could offer.

"Are you suddenly supportive because it's a rich guy?" Liam vocalized his thoughts. His father looked up at him, puzzled. "Charlie," Liam explained. "He's loaded."

"Whatever makes Jamie happy."

Liam smirked. "That's a very diplomatic answer, Dad."

"I'm a very diplomatic father, son."

When Jamie returned to Oakham, Liam barely heard from him for a good month and a half. So he resigned himself to hot summer days lounging at Charlotte's pool, and nights and weekends scooping ice cream at Claire's Creamery. After ten o'clock, he would come home and usually find Charlotte waiting for him on his front porch.

Tonight was no exception. Charlotte was sitting on the second step, her pale legs stretched out in front of her. She closed her book and grinned at Liam when she saw him coming up the driveway.

"You cut your hair," he observed.

Her long blonde plait had been shorn to her chin, all angled and wispy now. She brushed her bangs out of her eyes. "Do you like it?"

"You look so grown-up," Liam sighed, sitting beside her. "*Gross.*"

She hit him with the spine of her book.

Liam smiled and leaned back on his elbows. It was quiet for a little while, save for the familiar chorus of cicadas and crickets. Charlotte was hugging her knees and looking past the front lawn.

She scrunched her nose. "You smell like sweat and mint chocolate chip."

He turned. "It's sexy, right?"

"Yeah. Bottle that up and pitch it to Armani," Charlotte chuckled. "*Pour homme.*"

"You laugh. It'll be a bestseller at department stores." He lay down on the porch and covered his eyes. "Jamie's offered to help us move into the dorm, by the way."

"You make it sound like we're rooming together."

"Which would be *awesome.*"

"I know." She pouted. "I guess three blocks apart isn't so bad either."

"No," Liam replied. "Not bad at all. Maybe we're destined to be neighbors for the rest of our lives."

Charlotte grimaced. "I'm not interested in being your neighbor unless your mother is around to feed me."

He chuckled. "What did she make for dinner tonight?"

"Chili."

"Dad made it, then." Liam turned his head. "He has an old recipe. He uses unsweetened cocoa powder."

"Hmm," said Charlotte. "Does Jamie cook? Maybe I'll spend all my time at his place."

"Learn to cook, Charlotte."

"No."

"It's attractive in a woman. Leads to domestic bliss and all that," he goaded her on, smiling. "Mom can teach you all about it."

"*No.*" She thwacked him with her book again, which ultimately led to a series of mild attacks. "I'll just have the Bennet brothers feed me for the rest of my life."

"I can't cook," Liam argued.

"Bennet brothers," Charlotte was still musing as she settled her hands on her flat belly. "Sounds like a franchise."

"Bennet Brothers' Bakery."

"Bennet Brothers' Bitchin' Bakery."

"Hold on." Liam pulled out his phone. "Let me tell Jamie about our new business." Charlotte began giggling and he added, "Watch out, Charlie Bingley! You're not the only entrepreneur in town."

Charlotte grinned. She was threading her fingers through her cropped blonde hair again, perhaps relishing the lack of split ends. "Are they an item yet?"

Liam shrugged and scrolled through his phone. "They might as well be."

"Dating?"

"They spend a lot of time together outside the office. They can't chalk the whole thing up to the internship, especially when they're going to the movies together on Saturday nights."

"Yeah, but they could be doing that as friends."

"*Please.* I called Jamie, like, last Monday night, and he was in Manhattan, spending the night at Charlie's apartment."

"Hey-o," Charlotte teased. She opened her book again and muttered, "At least someone is having sex."

"Wait, not his apartment." Liam sat up. "What did he call it? His loft."

"These celebrities and their fancy-schmancy real estate." She gave a dramatic hand flourish. "Wait, is Charlie even out?"

"Yeah," Liam said. "He is. I feel like every magazine article I read about him mentions it in the first two sentences. '*Charlie Bingley, social media tycoon and—*'"

"'*Deeply fabulous homosexual,*'" Charlotte cut in.

He snorted and she stretched out next to him, the two of them laughing for a while. An hour slipped by, and then Mrs. Bennet cranked open the living room window, wearing her paisley nightgown and bright red hair rollers. "Liam, aren't you going to bed soon?"

"No school tomorrow, Mom, I graduated."

"*So?* Did you know that there is a correlation between psychological disorders in teenagers and sleep deprivation?"

"No, I did not," said Liam dryly.

"And *you*, Charlotte? Isn't your mother worried about where you are?"

"Not really." Charlotte shrugged. "She's watching *Conan*."

Mrs. Bennet sighed. "I just don't like it when you guys are walking around the neighborhood at all hours of the night. It makes me nervous ever since Betsy Flamhaff sent me that website that tracks all the sex offenders in the township—"

"We're not walking around, Ma."

"But what if you *will*?"

"I have my phone."

"Nora, leave them alone and go upstairs, please," Mr. Bennet's voice rumbled from somewhere within the house.

She hesitated and then popped her head back into the house, muttering.

"You know," said Charlotte after she was gone, "it takes a special brand of person to tolerate your mother."

Liam shrugged. "Or just really effective prescription drugs."

"Well, my mom has a nicely stocked medicine cabinet, if yours is ever running low...."

"That is quite the offer, Char; I will definitely keep you posted."

CHAPTER FIVE

JAMIE STEPPED out of oblivion. The entire family pulled together just in time for Liam's move-in day. He was grateful for the free labor. Charlotte was too. Her mother was tiny and extremely inefficient at dragging boxes.

Liam felt a pang of sympathy for his own mother, who took one look at his barren new bedroom and unleashed one great hiccup of a sob before yanking him into a hug.

He laughed, "Mom, it's okay. I'll be home a lot too."

First college-student lie of the semester.

She pulled back and smoothed his hair. "I would just feel so much more comfortable if you were in a residence hall, Liam. Are you *sure* that we can't call and find an opening—?"

Liam sighed as the week-old conversation reran itself like a broken record. "No, Mom. Charlotte and I will be fine here, really."

"It's perfectly safe, Nora." Mrs. Lucas dropped her arm around the other woman's shoulders.

"Yeah, Mom. I know plenty of people living in this building. He'll be fine," Jamie said.

Charlotte's housing plans had dropped out at the last minute when her roommate Meredith Bates had decided to room with Christine Elliot right before they were supposed to sign their contract.

This effectively boxed her out of Wesley Hall.

Gutted, Liam had sworn he wouldn't leave her alone for the first term. They found a student-approved apartment complex two miles off campus, mostly for upperclassmen and some graduate students, but they were able to coax the landlord into giving them a shot.

"You guys won him over with your responsible, reliable, young student vibes," said Mr. Bennet. He was unloading a box of kitchen appliances, and Liam rushed over to help him with the coffee machine, his baby.

"No, it was definitely the slutty sundress I wore that Wednesday," deadpanned Charlotte.

Mrs. Bennet looked mortified.

By late evening, nine pairs of hands had scrubbed every surface clean; everything was up and running, except cable, which would be installed on Tuesday. Mrs. Lucas hugged her daughter for a full five minutes. "If you need anything, Charlotte, don't be afraid to ask. I know money's tight, but I am here."

"I'll be fine, Mom. You take care of yourself."

Their families finally filed out. Charlotte went to visit Meredith, despite her earlier betrayal.

Liam fought the urge to hurl his sweaty, dust-coated self into his clean sheets, and turned the shower on instead. He was just about to pull off his shirt when someone knocked at his door.

He intuitively knew it was his mother even before he unbolted the door.

"Hi, Mom."

"One last good-bye." She smiled and stood on her tiptoes to kiss his cheek. He hugged her.

"I'm not dying, you know."

She ignored his quip. "Also, Liam. About you and Charlotte... I really can't say that I condone a *romantic* attachment between you two. You've been friends for so long, it's almost unnatural—"

"*Mom,*" Liam sighed and crossed his arms over his chest. "Seriously? We're practically siblings. You know that. We're just living together. Go back to Dad before he falls asleep at the wheel."

"Love you."

"Love you too."

And with that, he closed the door behind her.

The stillness of the apartment settled in and Liam looked around. It was so nondescript, with its white walls and its bare beds and its leaky faucet. He smiled wide.

He was already in love with the place, as only a naïve college student could be. "My very own illusion of freedom," he murmured.

CHAPTER SIX

IN THE weeks that followed, Liam took long, aimless walks around Hartford. He discovered shortcuts to campus and scoped out possible shops and restaurants for a part-time job.

It was his desire to have something *other* than cereal for breakfast that led him to Oak Café, a small but cozy corner restaurant a few blocks away from Jamie's apartment. He was charmed by the fact that they poured coffee into bright ceramic mugs. Like, ones that you could actually *wash*.

Plus, the owner seemed genuinely kind, and Liam was seduced by the rows of red velvet cupcakes and butterscotch parfaits in the display. He applied as a barista. He interviewed on a Wednesday, got the job on Thursday morning, and started his first shift on Saturday at noon.

"You're an asshole," Charlotte sighed over the phone.

"I love you too," he teased. He had just left the apartment and was walking toward the bus stop. He stopped to pull his gray hoodie over his head, then continued the conversation.

"Do you know how many places I applied to?" she asked, hardly discouraged by his subsequent silence. "Thirteen. I mean, mostly stores because I'm a retail rat through and through. Only one of them interviewed me, and I didn't even get *that job.*"

"Yeah, because you wore corduroy pants to the interview," Liam insisted, "which you might as well have borrowed from my *mom.*"

"I wish I could spear you through the phone."

"Save that determination for your next job interview."

He trained for about a week. He learned the formulas for each drink, how to steam milk properly, and the percentage of foam that should be in a cappuccino. It would have been mind-numbingly tedious if he didn't like the owners so much.

Because the truth of the matter was that the Brandons were delightful.

Callum Brandon bore a striking resemblance to Prince Charles. His ears were too big for his face, but he had a kind, crinkly smile, a thick Irish brogue, and a penchant for wearing plaid. His wife Mindy was a Philadelphian and ran a boutique near The Parkway. She worked on Tuesdays and Thursdays at the café.

The weekend of September eighth was hell. The University District was bustling from all the new arrivals; all three schools would start classes that Monday. The weather was unseasonably cold—it had been raining for days, and that morning brought torrents of freezing rain slashing to the ground, the trees glistening with premature frost.

Liam was off his game from the beginning of his shift.

The first hour, he spilled ice all over the back room floor and tripped Josie, a coworker. In the afternoon, the regulars left and twiggy students in their identical North Face jackets and Uggs chirped their aggressive, hyperspeed orders at him.

"I wanted *skim*."

"Oh, I'm sorry. I thought you said 2 percent."

"I changed my mind."

"Okay." *If you're eating five chocolate scones, though, does it really matter if your latte is skim?* He wiped his brow and set the pitcher beneath the steaming wand again.

"Do you guys have frappuccinos?" another asked.

"No, we're not a franchise like—"

"Claire, I wanted a *frappuccino!*" the brunette girl hollered across the café.

God almighty. Scream into my ear one more time. One more time, I dare you; I'll stick this steaming wand up your nose.

"How many calories are in that cupcake?" a customer inquired at the same time.

Callum opened the register next to him and laid a hand on his shoulder. "I've got it, son. Why don't you take a fifteen?" He turned toward the line. "What would you like, my dear?"

His gratitude was immediate.

Liam washed his face in the bathroom. He took off his visor and apron and let the cool water trickle down his neck. Bambi on ice skates—that's what he felt like. His reflection seemed to agree with him.

He had thinned out since he moved here. Charlotte had said it a week before, but he hadn't seen it until now. His face looked thin, his cheekbones apparent. Tired green eyes stared back at him.

Mr. Brandon called him back a few minutes later. He put his visor back on.

Liam sighed and took his place at the register, still tying his apron. "Hi, what would you like to—" He glanced up. "—*shit.*"

Will Darcy was standing on the other side of the counter, his iceblue eyes fixed on him. "That was pretty eloquent of you. Medium coffee. Black."

Liam sneered but turned toward the coffee machine. He poured a pitcher of their house blend into a cup. He felt sour.

Jamie. I have to be polite for Jamie's sake. Think of Jamie.

He handed Darcy his order. "Is Charlie in town too?"

"Yes," he replied.

Darcy was a stylish douchebag at any rate. He wore a gray peacoat, and his hair was windswept in a way that almost looked purposeful. It didn't look *boyish* and stupid like it would have on Liam; he looked like a model out of a Burberry advertisement, which was impossibly annoying.

Liam pushed aside his resentment and tried small talk again. "Charlie's in town so often. You guys might as well move your headquarters to the University District, huh?"

Darcy said nothing, leaving a pause in the conversation that seemed to last a decade. Liam gave up.

The other man opened his wallet and procured two crisp bills. "Keep the change."

"You're too kind," said Liam, brusquely. Darcy looked at him with a start, his mouth opening.

"Will!"

They both turned their heads. Bingley was walking up to the counter, holding out his phone. "Vicky's on the phone—that writer from *GQ*. She says she's been trying to reach you for hours. Hi, Liam."

"Damn," Darcy muttered, searching his pockets for his phone. "I must've left it in the car. I'm not going back out in that shit storm. What does she want?"

"Wants to know if Thursday afternoon is better for the interview."

"Morning is best. Let's do a video chat."

"In *person*, you antisocial bastard." Bingley rolled his eyes. "There are only so many interviews you can do through the computer."

"Fine." Darcy pinched the bridge of his nose.

"Can you do morning, Vic?" Bingley spoke into the phone. "Thank you. I'll see you then. Bye."

Liam stood awkwardly in front of them now, praying for a new line of customers that never materialized. Bingley noticed him again. "Liam, I didn't know you worked here."

"New knowledge is empowering, isn't it?" Liam smiled.

"That it is. How you been?"

"Pretty good. Jamie will be thrilled that you're back in town."

"Really?" Bingley asked, and Liam observed the slow smile blossoming on his face. There was no doubt in his mind now. Bingley was smitten.

"Really." Liam smiled back.

"Well, listen. Tell your brother that you're both invited to Netherfield tonight," Bingley said warmly. "My sister and Will are staying for the weekend. We'll make a dinner out of it!"

"Yeah, absolutely. I'll let him know."

He did let him know, as soon as Jamie picked him up from work.

"You smell like you've been marinating in coffee beans all day."

Liam sighed heavily and tossed his work uniform into the backseat. "I pretty much have been. Oh, and Bingley wants us to come to his fancy mansion for dinner tonight."

Jamie practically ran the red light. "You saw Charlie?" he asked, breathless.

"Holy crap—I'm buckling up now. *Yes*, Cinderella, I saw your prince and he wants you… over for dinner."

Jamie laughed and switched lanes. "I haven't seen him in two weeks now. I was wondering when he would be back in town."

"Well, he just got here and he's excited to see you."

"Are you coming? Please come," Jamie pleaded.

"*Why?* Jamie, you got this." Liam reclined in his seat and folded his hands behind his head. "I have better things to do than sit across a table from that douchebag, Will Darcy."

"He's really not that bad, Liam. When I was in New York with Charlie, he was perfectly nice to me…."

"Yeah, well he was an arrogant prick to *me*."

"What are you gonna do at home?" Jamie asked skeptically. "Watch TV with Charlotte for five hours straight?"

"Maybe. Don't judge our lifestyle choices, okay?"

Jamie snorted. He dropped his younger brother off at his apartment. Liam got his backpack and uniform from the backseat and slung both over his shoulder. Jamie rolled down the window. "Last chance."

Liam saluted him. "Have fun. You driving there?"

"Nope. The Netherfield House is like ten minutes off Lancaster Road—I think I'll take my bike."

"Be safe, brother."

Inside, the apartment was strewn with dresses, skirts, and blouses. Charlotte was in the bathroom, scrunching her blonde hair, shaking it out, and then scrunching it again. She turned. "Look who's home. I made frozen pizza."

"Thanks, honey," he said sarcastically. He flopped onto the couch. "Where are you going? I thought we were going to watch Gordon Ramsay scream at people tonight."

"Which *was* the plan," Charlotte started, slipping on a pair of black flats, "before I found out about the gallery opening in Spruce Hall. Our neighbors invited me. Want to come?"

"No thank you," Liam sighed. "Art history majors—"

"*Minor.*"

"Whatever. I'm set for the night. I've got subpar-cable programming and… the Internet."

Charlotte pouted at him and tilted her head.

"What?" he laughed.

"You're just so *sad*, Liam Bennet."

He embraced it, widened his eyes to saucer proportions, and jutted out his bottom lip. Charlotte crumbled and wrapped him in a hug. "Baby!"

He grinned wide, satisfied. "You know I'm just using this embrace as a sneaky way to make you smell like a sweaty, overworked barista, right?"

Charlotte pulled back in an instant and scowled.

When she left, Liam took a long, hot shower. He scrubbed himself clean and let the scalding water beat on his shoulders until it seemed to work out all the kinks. His phone rang as soon as he came out, and he was able to glance at the screen fast enough to see that he had already missed two calls. Curious, he answered: "Hello?"

"Hi, Liam?"

"Speaking."

"This is Charlie."

"Oh, hey, man."

"Is your brother allergic to any cold medication? Because I gave him ibuprofen but—"

"Why, what happened?"

"He was here for about an hour and then he came down with a really bad case of the chills. I've got him in the guest bedroom now; he's pretty feverish and he's beat…."

"I'll be over soon."

CHAPTER SEVEN

INDIAN SUMMER is a complete blip, Liam thought to himself, cycling uphill against the cold rain pin-prickling his face. It was drizzling again, a dampness that crept into his bones, but he pushed past it and biked the two and a half miles to the Netherfield estate, which was hidden among winding roads that crisscrossed Oakham Mount's campus.

"You must be freezing," Bingley told him when he arrived. "Did you walk?"

Liam's face was flushed from the cold. "Biked."

"Caroline, go put the kettle on for Liam."

"Do I *look* like your maid, Charlie dear?" she hummed above a magazine. Will Darcy was feeding the fire in the hearth and glanced over his shoulder at him.

"Don't trouble yourselves," Liam said derisively, tugging his navy beanie off. "Where's Jamie?"

Bingley led him upstairs to the guest bedroom, where Jamie was drifting off. He stirred when Liam sat on the edge of the mattress. "Hey." He smiled sleepily.

"The tricks you pull to make me come over." Liam clicked his tongue. "Are the meds pulling you under?"

"Yep." Jamie sniffed, pulling the comforter up to his shoulders. "I'm off to Graceland...."

"Okay, Elvis."

"Charlie has been taking such good care of me, Liam," his older brother said.

Bingley squeezed his hand; a slow smile lit up his face.

"Undoubtedly," Liam said.

"Liam, I have to ask you for a favor." Jamie turned toward his brother. "I left my inhaler in my apartment—"

Liam pulled a spare inhaler out of his backpack and set it on the bedstand. "No worries, Jamie. I figured as much. I keep one in my bathroom cabinet, remember?"

Jamie smiled gratefully and shut his eyes.

Downstairs, the Judgmental Duo was arranged in the sitting room just as they had been before. Only now, Darcy had his laptop open and Caroline was peering invasively over his shoulder. "Are you talking to Georgiana? What a *doll*—give her my love."

"I will do my best."

She straightened as she saw Liam walk downstairs with Bingley.

"I didn't know your brother is asthmatic," said Bingley.

"Jamie hasn't had an asthma attack in two years, but he becomes pretty susceptible when he's sick."

Bingley nodded, visibly concerned. He crossed his arms over his chest. "Thank you for telling me, Liam. I'll keep an eye out for him."

Liam nodded, shivered, and pulled his beanie back on his head. He glanced out the window. Bingley suggested that he stay the night, given the slippery road conditions. Jamie would feel more comfortable with him there, which Liam couldn't argue with.

"Get out of that sweatshirt; you're soaked through," said Bingley. He unzipped his suitcase, which was still propped against the grand staircase. Rifling through its contents, he swore, "Dammit. Why do I only have one sweater with me?"

"Because you left the city on a fifteen-second whim," said Darcy dryly. He sighed and closed his laptop, rising from the couch in one fluid motion. "Come. I might have something."

Liam stiffened, not keen on taking orders like a dog, but he followed him down the hall, past the billiards room.

Darcy's room was well furnished, and the bed was still made. He opened a dresser drawer and tossed Liam a T-shirt and a gray NYU hoodie, barely affording him a second glance.

"Thanks," Liam said stiffly.

He peeled off his wet clothes and shuddered again as the draft hit his bare skin. Bingley's house—his rented mansion—was frigid and beautiful, like a museum. He pulled on the T-shirt and relished its warmth. Then he turned back for the sweatshirt....

Darcy was watching him, his expression unreadable. His blue eyes flickered up, and he shifted a moment later. He shut the drawer and then left abruptly.

Liam watched him go, curious.

He should have slept soundly that night, nestled in what had to be five-hundred-count, Egyptian-cotton sheets stretched across a king-sized bed in the middle of an obnoxiously decadent guest bedroom with the heaviest red-velvet drapes imaginable—it was like being buried alive in luxury.

It made him uncomfortable. He texted Charlotte an hour after midnight, confident that she was either drinking or sitting on somebody's lap. Possibly both. His fingers moved nimbly over the typepad:

LB: I hope you're avoiding open containers. Roofies are still a thing.

He closed his eyes, and then *ping!*

CL: Thanks Mom. Date rape always seems to escape my mind when I'm having a good time, but I can always count on you to reel it on back. How's Netherfield?

LB: Creepy. My curtains block out natural light. I can probably trick my body into thinking it's perpetually nighttime.

CL: Ideal if you're a vampire. Is Dipshit Darcy there?

LB: Yep.

CL: You can take him.

LB: I like how you already hate him just because I do.

CL: Well you know what they say. The enemy of my enemy is my friend.

LB: No, Charlotte. That doesn't apply to this situation.

CL: Shit. Well, the enemy of my friend is… still my enemy.

LB: Still no.

CL: I'm just trying to be supportive.

LB: I know. I love you. Get home safe and I'll see you tomorrow.

CL: Sweet dreams. Play nice xx

CHAPTER EIGHT

NETHERFIELD WAS an entirely different creature in the morning. It was still and quietly optimistic. Light filtered through the stained-glass panels in the foyer, creating ripples of oranges, blues, violets, and reds that scattered across the hardwood floors. Liam followed the winding stairs, his bare feet padding quietly to the ballroom.

Without the clusters of suits and cocktail dresses, the tinkling of champagne flutes and jazz quartets, he took in the stretch of white marble tiles and pillars. The room was so much bigger now; it was eerie in its emptiness, but he liked it.

Since the Bennet brothers knew nothing about Netherfield, Bingley filled in the gaps of its history that morning. "It's named for Benedict Netherfield," he said, scrambling eggs on the gas stove, his hair an unruly mess and his sleeves hiked up to the elbows.

Darcy was pouring ground coffee beans into a filter. Liam watched him, noted the unnerving grace that he possessed in each movement. Everything he did was a smooth, precise, mechanical motion.

"He inherited his millions from his family's trade company and had it built in 1893," Bingley continued. "When he died three years later—" He paused to turn the stove off and unfurled his sleeves. "—his widow sold the estate to the university."

"The year keeps changing each time you tell this story," Darcy interrupted. "It was 1891 yesterday."

"Thanks for committing my mistakes to memory, Will."

Caroline, irritated at being excluded, slid off her barstool. "History is so *boring*; what's done is done," she purred, stretching over the counter and giving Will Darcy an eyeful, had he chosen to look. "I don't know how anybody studies it."

"Through textbooks, I would imagine," said Liam. "You know, primitive forms of the tablet."

Darcy rubbed his mouth to conceal a smile.

"*Liam.*" Jamie nudged him.

"Put it in a tabloid rag and Caroline will read it." Bingley was smiling and setting out plates. Jamie got up to help. "No, *no.* Sit back down before I hit you with my spatula—"

"I feel so useless, though," began Jamie.

"You're *sick.*"

"This is someone who apologizes for being sick," said Liam dryly, getting up. "Do you have any orange juice?"

"In the fridge. Help yourself," Bingley said.

"Thank you kindly."

Caroline cleared her throat, miffed. "I do *not* just read tabloids, Charlie. I read books too."

"I know, Caroline, don't be so sensitive," Bingley insisted, smiling again. "You said it yourself that you can't pass through an airport terminal without stocking up on *US Weekly, Star, Globe*...."

"Jamie, would you like some orange juice?" Liam asked his brother, pulling two glasses out of the cupboard.

"Yes, please."

Caroline tossed her blonde hair over her shoulder. "Whatever. I have *The Help* on my Kindle. Lucy recommended it to me and I *love* it. It is *excellent.*"

"What's it about?" prompted Liam.

Caroline pulled out her phone. "Maids or something," she mumbled after a while.

They settled in the living room. Jamie let out a rattling cough, and Bingley looked concerned. "That sounded shitty. Let's go get you some cough syrup or something—"

"I'm fine, seriously. Don't trouble yourself."

"It's no trouble at all. You're not feeling well and we need to fix that."

"I have an immune system made out of steel," laughed Jamie.

"Yeah, okay. I'm getting you some medicine. There's a pharmacy right in town."

"I'll pick it up on my way home."

"That's ridiculous," said Bingley. "I'll go get it for you. You're my guest and it's a *two-minute* drive—"

"I'm not that sick. If I get worse, I'll swing by later—"

"Just *go*," Liam interrupted impatiently. "Jesus, it's like you both are the resident Nice Guys in the company office and you're fighting over who should walk through the door first. It's exhausting; Jamie, please just go with him."

Jamie was blushing, which rendered him schoolboyish once more. They left the house.

Once the satisfaction of giving Jamie and Bingley some privacy wore off, Liam realized that he had shot himself in the foot when he looked up and saw he was alone with Darcy and Caroline. "Hi."

"Your brother is very sweet," Caroline said slowly.

Liam didn't know what she was getting at, so he said, "As is yours. I guess they're cut from the same cloth."

She gave a short smile. "Jamie is *so* not his type, to be perfectly honest. I think Charlie is just exploring his horizons. He broke up with his boyfriend Miles only a few months ago... *that* was a serious relationship. Love of his life, wouldn't you say so, Will?"

Darcy shrugged. He was engrossed by his laptop.

"Is that what the tabloids say?" Liam said softly, scrolling through his phone.

"Charlie falls for men often." Caroline leaned forward to rest her espresso cup on the glass coffee table. "Jamie's a sweet kid, and it would be a shame to see him hurt. I'm saying this all in your brother's best interest, you understand."

"Of course," said Liam, shoving away his disgust. He turned on the TV and changed through the channels.

Darcy was staring at him again, and he felt restless and itchy, his patience fraying. "I'm gonna get some water," he announced to nobody in particular.

In the kitchen, he filled a glass with water from the tap.

Bingley and Caroline were so completely different that one had to wonder how they were even related. *Then again, Cain and Abel were siblings too.*

A door shut gently, muffled. Liam heard chuckling and inched ever so slightly to see out of the kitchen and into a laundry room that led directly out into the garage. Bingley handed a plastic bag to Jamie. "Here you go." He was grinning. When was he not?

"Thanks again," said Jamie. "You're even more stubborn than I am."

"Whatever, it was only a few bucks."

"You didn't have to pay—"

"It was my pleasure," Bingley said softly. He looked down and fiddled with his car keys as Jamie stared at him. Fluidly, he grasped Bingley's shirt and pulled him gently forward. It was a chaste kiss, sweet and romantic.

"I'm probably gonna get you sick now," Jamie murmured.

"Worth it," Bingley replied. His hand moved from Jamie's elbow, trailing down to take his hand in his own. "I won't be in New York for too long. Don't go out with someone new." He said it lightly, but there was a hint of earnestness coloring his tone. "Please."

"When will you be back?" Jamie asked.

"In about five weeks. I'm getting an extension with my classes, because of the huge press release with the company," Bingley explained, looking down at their hands. "But I'm going to host a private party when I get back and I want you to be there."

"What, *another* one?" Jamie teased.

Bingley grinned. "Yes, another one. I donated to the university last April so the president is throwing some upscale ball in my family's honor or whatever. It's going to be pretty fancy...." He paused and a slow smile crept onto his face. *"So please don't wear jeans, Liam!"*

Liam shifted, and then called out, "I won't!"

"Liam!" Jamie chided, blushing.

"What?" He shrugged, setting the glass down. "It's *not* that I'm eavesdropping! It's just that you two are being mushy two feet from the kitchen. The fault is yours, not mine."

"God." Jamie covered his face with his hands. Bingley was laughing.

Charlotte picked them up about two hours later, showing up at Bingley's door in last night's dress, her smudged eyeliner concealed by oversized shades. "Holy hell," she chirped, whirling around the foyer. "This is beautiful."

Liam slung his messenger bag over his shoulder. He had changed back into yesterday's clothes, leaving Darcy's in a neatly folded pile at the foot of the guest bed. "You think so? Frankly, I'm a little sick of it now," he muttered.

Charlotte was introduced to everyone. And in true Charles Bingley hospitality, she was instantly invited to the private ball. "Uh, yes please." She smiled, delighted. "How do I dress?"

"Formal," Caroline purred, looking pointedly at Liam.

He crossed his arms over his chest. *This bitch right here.*

Outside, Jamie slid into the passenger seat of Charlotte's little black sedan. Meanwhile, she helped Liam wrestle his and Jamie's bikes into the trunk. He moved the clutter of clothes and shoeboxes out of the way first.

"I forgot that you use your trunk like a second closet."

"It's a practical move." She winked at him. "By the way, I see what you mean about Charlie. *Smitten*, if I may say. But his sister is going to be a problem."

"You get that vibe too?" Liam asked.

"Yeah, she was hardcore side-eyeing the shit out of my outfit." Charlotte stopped, pensive. She propped her sunglasses over her head. "Will Darcy though—"

"Bastard, right? He's chronically quiet until he opens his mouth to insult you, so don't let his mute tendencies mislead you."

"He is *so* attractive, though!" laughed Charlotte, moving her hands emphatically. "So fit and tall and handsome. You left *that* part out."

"You can do better," he said automatically.

"Oh, I'm not into jerks. I'm just an admirer of beauty in general." She shut the trunk. "I mean, not even *you* can deny that that man is ruggedly beautiful. Not pretty but just *striking*—god, I need a fan for my lady parts."

Liam was scowling, so she giggled and ushered him into the car. "I'm kidding, I'm kidding, I'm kidding." He relaxed and clicked in his seat belt. "But seriously," Charlotte said, before shutting the door in his face.

CHAPTER NINE

IT IS a truth universally acknowledged that a delicate balance must be formed between studies, work, and social life. Liam had yet to acknowledge this truth—actually, Liam had yet to *hear* of this truth.

His alarm went off at 7:00 a.m. each morning. He showered, washed up, dressed, tamed his unruly hair (what was this Darcyish art of making it look *nicely* messed up?)—then he would practice his culinary skills by whipping up a bowl of cereal and milk.

Biking was his absolute favorite part of the day. He biked *everywhere*: to work, to class, to the Laundromat, to the grocery store. His International Business class required him to dress professionally for his first presentation in October. So he did, biking uphill in his black suit and his white dress shirt, neatly pressed thanks to Charlotte, his blue tie tossed haphazardly over his shoulder.

He stopped by the campus Starbucks right next to Kennedy Hall and ignored the pang of guilt that wormed its way into his lower stomach. *The less that Mr. Brandon knows of my café infidelity, the better.*

He sampled two sips of his iced coffee before the rest emptied on some poor slob's white button-down. He had veered to the left a little too late, knocking the iced coffee out of Liam's hand.

"Oh shit. Sorry, are you okay?"

"*Damn* it," the other man emphasized, examining the stain. "I have a job interview this afternoon."

"I'm so sorry."

"Your dress shirt would be a nice replacement. Can I have it?"

Liam blanched and looked down at his own suit, the only one he had ever owned. It was a graduation gift from his aunt and uncle. "No."

The stranger laughed and shrugged his shoulders. "No worries. It was worth a shot, though, am I right?"

Liam's brow furrowed. He started. "Wait, I *know* you!"

The stranger's face was all too familiar: scraggly dark blond hair, brown eyes, and a couple lines of Buddhist scripture inked across his forearm. Liam immediately recognized him as a singer from one of the local bands back home, one that he and his brothers had met last summer at Festival Pier in Philadelphia. "I've seen your band."

"Ah, very good!" He extended a hand just before Liam identified his accent as some watered-down, British-American hybrid. "George Wickham. You've seen us play?"

"Yeah, you guys were awesome. My youngest brothers are really into Warped Tour and summer festivals, so I played the role of dutiful chauffeur. We were at Festival Pier last August. I'm Liam Bennet."

"Bennet." George rubbed his scruff in contemplation. "Oh, *those* two teenage twin pricks who waited backstage for Sheila? Classic!"

Liam felt a blush warm his face. It was true. The Moron Twins had waited backstage for autographs, only to grow impatient and attempt to sneak into the dressing room of Sheila Erikson, the band's beautiful Swedish bassist. Security had caught them in a heartbeat, and Charlotte had spent three hours sweet-talking management so that they wouldn't press charges.

"'Fraid so."

"Don't look so shameful, mate." George clapped him on the back, and Liam bristled, first caught off guard by his friendliness and then vaguely flattered. "Where are you from?"

"Longbourn, originally. I go to school at Hartford now. You?"

"Surrey, originally. I used to play gigs all over Philly and New York. It might break your heart to know that the Lemon Wedges kicked me out of their band. I am in search of new enterprises now."

"Why would they do that?" Liam asked. They were outside now, and the wind whipped his tie right past his shoulder again.

George lit the cigarette between his lips and shrugged. "Long sob story for another time." A plume of smoke accompanied his words, and Liam felt very much like he had stumbled upon some soulful hippie character from a novel—young but world-weary, poetic but broken.

"Mm." Liam nodded sympathetically.

"I like you. You look like an attorney in training." George smiled fondly, as if praising a little brother. "You should come to Militia on Friday night. Ever heard of the place?"

"What, that hookah bar on Fifty-Seventh Street?" Being a barista brought wind of the area's most popular hangouts, asked for or not.

"That's the one. I'm playing that night. Bring some friends." George laid his hand on his heart. "Drinks on me."

Liam thought better of revealing his age and nodded eagerly. "Yeah, definitely. I'll be there."

His new friend left him in a haze of secondhand smoke and warm wishes. Liam strapped his messenger bag across his chest, put on his helmet, and biked out of the parking lot.

The rest of the day was not as pleasant. He discovered that he had missed the deadline for a rough draft of an Ethics paper. His presentation, however, had gone brilliantly. His uncanny ability to engage his peers had followed him from high school to college, coasting on equal parts charm, knowledge... and maybe a small dash of pop culture.

"You referenced the diner in Stars Hollow again, didn't you?" said Charlotte dryly that night. She had her textbooks sprawled out across the living room sofa. Her hair was drawn up into a short, stubby blonde ponytail with pencils sticking out from it.

"It applied to my business model." Liam shrugged and opened the fridge. "And everybody loves *Gilmore Girls*."

"I wonder about you sometimes," she purred. "Put on the kettle, would you? I'm craving tea. There's some chamomile in the top cabinet."

"Got it." He shoved the kettle under the tap.

She cracked her neck and sighed. "Liam, I am *so* stressed-out tonight. Give me an idea for this essay. It's on global public health."

Liam pretended to snore, and Charlotte chucked her highlighter at him. He ducked gracefully. "Why is a study-abroad application prompting you on global public health? You would think you were majoring in health administration."

"Because this is how applications *work*. They throw you the least relevant essay questions ever."

"Which school?"

"King's College in London."

"Pick a closer school. Prince William is already married," Liam said, handing her a mug. "I see no other motivation for you to travel across the pond."

"Well, Harry is still single." Charlotte shrugged and blew over the top of her tea. She cocked her head at the seat cushion next to her, and Liam obligingly sat down, drinking from his own cup. "How was the rest of your day?"

"Went downhill a little after my presentation," he said. "Got glared at by Dr. Harrington when I asked for a paper extension. Spent three hours in the library grinding *out* said paper. Oh, but I got us plans for Friday night, so…."

"Where to?"

"Militia."

Charlotte wrinkled her nose. "I hate hookah."

"Yeah, me too."

They drank their tea in unison.

"Let's go." She grinned.

THEY WENT on Friday.

Liam liked Militia instantly, which was strange, because he normally didn't take to bars or lounges. But it had a dreamlike atmosphere to it, dim and muted, but welcoming. The walls were dark navy and strung with twinkling lights. And George Wickham, dressed to the nines, had a voice that suited his acoustic guitar perfectly.

"He is the lovechild of Jeff Buckley and Jack Johnson. I just know it," Charlotte mused. "I can feel it in my *bones*."

George played a full set, all covers except for an original that needed better lyrics; then he introduced himself to Charlotte and sat with them exclusively for a full half hour. "Friends," he beamed. "I'm so glad you could make it."

So many people approached him—women, men, friends, the staff, and fellow musicians. But he stayed with Charlotte and Liam, made sure that they were attended to without charge, and even asked about their hometown on the outskirts of Philadelphia.

"*Beautiful* city," George gushed, setting down his glass of whiskey. "But it's nice to get away into the suburbs. The nitty-gritty of it all. I love it."

At times, it was difficult to understand what he was talking about. Liam chalked it up to spirituality, and Charlotte pinned it on his drink.

When his gig was over, George stepped out with Liam while Charlotte used the ladies' room. George sat on the curb and removed his tie, which he handed to Liam. "You inspired me, mate. *Sartorially*."

"You know, I never really wear ties," Liam snorted. "I just had a business presentation that morning."

George shrugged and removed the pack of cigarettes from his shirt pocket. He tilted it in Liam's direction. "Good man," he replied, when Liam politely refused. "It's a terrible habit."

"Smoking? I agree."

"No, *bumming*. I hate freeloaders. Do you know how expensive cigarettes are?"

Liam laughed, and George shook his head and smiled. "Thanks for coming tonight and bringing your friend. It's nice to have some support. I play to strangers more often than not these days."

"I'd imagine hopping from place to place does that," Liam mused.

"Yes, it does. But I'm not the best at keeping touch," said George quietly. "I learned the hard way to value friendships while I still have them. Now that there's nobody left—"

"Bullshit," Liam said laughingly. George lifted his eyebrows. He continued, "Who do you call that string of people who shook your hand after your set?"

"Fans of the weary, tortured artist," George trilled mournfully, taking another drag. Liam rolled his eyes and he laughed. "Fine, fine, fine. I'm a sorry sack of shit. I enjoy it, I really do. I *enjoy* feeling sorry for myself. It gives me material for my songs."

"At least you admit it. That's half the battle right there."

"Cheers."

He liked George a lot. He was brutally honest about himself, light and carefree, and an inspired musician.

"What was that second song you played? It sounded like...." Liam trailed off, seeing as George wasn't paying any speck of attention to him. He was staring up with his eyes wide.

And then Liam blinked, startled. Will Darcy was standing before them. A group of people stood behind *him*, waiting expectantly; it was clear that he had just disbanded from a cluster of young professionals.

His body was angled toward Liam, but his icy stare was glued to George Wickham now. An inexplicable hatred radiated off him, stiffening his posture and curling his lower lip.

"Darcy," said Liam. "What brings you here?"

Darcy's eyes shifted to Liam. "I'm out with friends. I saw you and I thought I'd say hi."

An uneasy silence passed. "Hi, Will," George spoke, unsmiling. "Good to see you again."

Darcy's jaw clenched. He met Liam's eye, and for some strange, inconceivable moment, Liam got the feeling that he had done something very wrong that he didn't quite understand; it chilled him to the bone. He felt his face grow warm, and hated himself for it. *What is the evolutionary purpose behind blushing? Besides making me feel like an idiot.* Then Darcy turned away without another word.

AFTER THE group had turned down the street, Liam recovered. "What *was* that?"

George was crushing his cigarette butt into the asphalt. He sniffed. "Fancy that. We have a mutual acquaintance."

Charlotte stumbled out then, muttering curses and yanking down her skirt to a more modest length. "If I had known this thing rides up, I wouldn't have bought it from the clearance bin...." She looked up. "What happened?"

George got to his feet. He rubbed something imaginary out of his eye and said, "Well, my new friends. I'm very tired. I'll run back in for my instruments and head home. I bid you adieu. You have my number."

He walked back inside quickly, leaving Liam gaping in his wake.

"Does he really say shit like that?" Charlotte let out a hollow laugh. "Because that's going to get very annoying very fast."

Liam sighed. He pulled the silver tie around his own neck into a loose knot. "You know, Charlotte," he said whimsically, "I'm beginning to think that we're not mysterious enough for this town."

CHAPTER TEN

EARLY NOVEMBER was unseasonably cold. Liam couldn't rely on his usual warm-bloodedness to help him through the season, especially when he took out the garbage at work one evening in just his T-shirt and apron and came down with a horrible cold two mornings later.

"Thank you," he sniffed, as Charlotte lowered a full thermos of tea and two empty cups onto his bedstand. He looked at her with adoration. "Let's get married."

"Jamie made this," Charlotte clarified. "But thanks for the offer; I'll think about it."

"Fine," he said gruffly. He heard Jamie warbling a Beach Boys song and cooking in the kitchen. Oh, how grateful he was that his older brother was home today—movie marathoning and menthol and tea seemed to be the order of the day.

Charlotte sat down beside him and inspected her chipping, turquoise nail polish. "I guess marriage might be a viable option if we weren't so much like brother and sister."

"That does make it a little creepy," said Liam, burrowing himself under the comforter.

"Or if you were actually attracted to me."

"You're very pretty, Charlotte, I've told you that."

"You find lots of girls pretty." She smiled, tilting her head curiously. "But you just have no real lasting interest in anybody. You're indifferent at best."

Liam shrugged, validating her words. Charlotte laughed. "Do you know how *long* I've waited for you to fall in love with a girl just so I could make you feel self-conscious and miserable about it? I feel like I've been missing out on a blessed rite of passage."

"Sorry to disappoint you, but I'm destined to die alone." He drew the comforter over his head. "Oh god, I feel awful. I *want* to die."

"Here, have a lozenge."

"Eucalyptus? *Gross*. Never!"

"Maybe you're asexual or pansexual or something," she suggested.

Liam poked his head out from the covers. "What's that, attracted to pans?"

"*No*," Charlotte laughed. She kissed his cheek and got to her feet. "Jamie! Come in here and make sure your brother doesn't die while I'm gone."

After Charlotte left, Liam and Jamie spent upward of five hours watching movies. Liam drained three full thermoses of tea with honey and sat squirming under his quilt as Jamie watched *Trainspotting*, engrossed.

"Why does the bathroom feel so far away?" Liam moaned. His muscles ached.

"That baby is going to haunt my nightmares until I die," Jamie muttered, ignoring him. He propped his feet on top of the coffee table. "Also, I'm never doing heroin."

"I'll let Mom know. She will add it to her Why-Jamie-is-a-Godsend list." Liam propped himself up to a sitting position and blew his nose.

Jamie snorted. "Is there such a list?"

"Pinned to the fridge."

"I call bullshit."

"Call away," said Liam coolly. When Jamie pulled a sour face, Liam started to laugh. "Hey, if you wanted someone nice to talk to today, you should have kidnapped Charlie or something."

"I would if I could," Jamie assured him. "But I missed you, you asshole."

Liam beamed proudly. "You'll see your boyfriend soon too."

Jamie smiled. But he looked tense, and rubbed the back of his neck. "We're not... uh, I'm not sure that's what we are."

Liam raised his eyebrows. "Seriously? I thought you guys were exclusive."

"We are. I think. But that conversation hasn't officially happened yet—"

"Because you both are nonconfrontational weenies."

"No, we're not," Jamie argued, laughing.

"*Please*." Liam reclined again and drew his quilt up to his shoulders. "Can you imagine if you met in a car accident? You would each spend months taking the blame for it, even if it was obvious who caused it."

"Why do we have to *label* this?" Jamie argued weakly. "We both care a lot for one another and clearly enjoy each other's company. These are modern times. *You* always say things like that."

"Yeah, but...." Liam smiled slowly. "Jamie, it's the mature thing to do. You two are at a point in your life where you have to be grown-ups and clarify what the hell you're doing, or else someone gets more attached than the other and feelings get shit on."

Jamie grew quiet. "You're right."

"You have nothing to be worried about," Liam assured him. "It's very obvious that Charlie is pretty much in love with you."

A slow smile spread across Jamie's face, and for a moment, his cheeks matched the hue of his hair. "So." He cleared his throat. "What about you? Taking a date to the party?"

"Nope. I am a free man."

"Stop chasing people away and maybe you won't be." Jamie smiled. "You have to let people in."

"But I hate people." Liam frowned.

Jamie sighed and got to his feet. "Let's go get you some more soup."

Liam watched him go, uncomfortable with the sudden interest in his love life. He didn't really *need* anybody, nor had anybody caught his eye in the last few years. There were the occasional hookups, purely physical, nothing remarkable. And what was the point in being with somebody just to say that you were with somebody?

"Is chicken noodle okay?" Jamie hollered from the kitchen.

"Yeah, that's fine," muttered Liam, rubbing his neck.

Indifferent at best. Maybe because there seemed to be nobody around worth making a fuss over....

THREE DAYS passed before Liam felt well enough to go to class again. Well, one class. That was in the afternoon. *Late* in the afternoon. His Communications class was his largest, and he felt safe and lovingly embraced in its anonymity. He sat in the second-to-last row, tugged the brim of his baseball cap farther down, and doodled in the margins of his notebook.

His phone vibrated on his tiny slab of a desk; Jamie had texted him.

JB: Keep taking those zinc tablets I gave you. Cold and flu season is right around the corner and I don't want you to relapse.

Liam smiled. Dearest Jamie. His biological waste was probably composed of butterflies and sugar and rainbows....

Dr. Rosenthal struck the chalkboard with a frighteningly loud crack. Liam sat up. The crotchety professor smiled. "Just making sure the last three rows are attentive." He set down his pointer. "Your exam is *this* Thursday, ladies and gentlemen. It would be a pity to bomb it because you were too busy playing solitaire on your smartphones."

There was a low chorus of chuckles. And then Liam met her eye, two rows ahead of him to the right. The girl's face flooded with color, and she turned away instantly. He had seen her before. Numerous times. She was at the Oak Café often, and always ordered a soy chai with a shot of espresso.

And "Chai" shall now be your name, gamine-wood-nymph-fairy person. Liam turned back to his doodles.

When class let out, he took his time packing up and was one of the last to leave. To his surprise, the girl was waiting just beyond the doorway. She brightened when she saw him and then blushed all over again. "Hello."

"Hey," he said, at ease.

"I'm Ann." She extended her hand. *Whoops, there goes my brilliantly penned nickname.*

"Liam."

"I'm sorry this is kind of out of the blue, but I recognized you straightaway from the café. I was wondering—are they hiring?"

He blinked, not having expected her lyrical English accent.

"What, Oak?" Liam recovered and thought about it for a few seconds. "They might be. I work tonight if you want to stop by. I'm pretty sure the hiring manager will be there too."

She beamed. "That's great! I am *desperate* for a part-time job. I can barely afford the gas in my car."

"Nobody can." He laughed shortly.

She laughed with him. As they walked out of Kennedy Hall, he watched her carefully. Ann was a tiny, tiny girl. Very slight and pocket-size, with blue eyes and a shorn crop of dark brown hair and an easy grace about her. She was startlingly pretty, and he told her so.

"I'm not being sleazy, I promise; I just want you to know that you look very much like a pixie."

"I was actually Tinker Bell two Halloweens ago."

"You're joking!"

"'Fraid not. I went blonde and everything." A beat. "That's not true, I didn't. I'm lying to you. I just had a wig."

They spent the rest of the day together, which surprised him. It happened so naturally. They were headed for the same building; her boyfriend lived a floor below Liam and Charlotte's apartment. He learned that she was only studying at Hartford for the fall semester.

"I go back to England around Christmastime," Ann told him when they were in Liam's kitchen. He microwaved macaroni and cheese from the night before and offered her some, but she shook her head demurely. "No thank you."

"Why Hartford?" Liam asked.

"Oh, lots of reasons," Ann sighed. "Mostly just me chasing my American boyfriend of a year. Have you met Roger? He lives in C2." When he shook his head, she shrugged. "Anyway, it's a little silly. I can't say my family condones my behavior... chasing a boy across an ocean to college."

"You seem too smart for that."

"Well, my brother lives in this area. So it's that as well. He hasn't lived at home nearly half of his life and I miss him." Ann smiled. "*That's* how I'm justifying it. Do you believe me?"

Liam smiled and made her a cup of tea. "Partially."

"What about you?" she asked. "What's your story?"

"No story. Just going to college."

"On your little bicycle," Ann teased, smiling gaily.

"Are you disrespecting the bike?"

"Only a little. Don't be terribly upset."

He grinned, and they both sat at the little kitchen table, a rickety hand-me-down from Charlotte's uncle's old townhouse. It wobbled on its left front leg, so he bent down and wedged two old magazines underneath to steady it.

"Your apartment is a lot cuter than Roger's," she murmured, spreading her fingers across the lace that trimmed her placemat. "Well done."

"Blame all decorating touches on my roommate." Liam curbed her credit. "Charlotte spends half her paycheck on throw pillows and tea sets and shit like that."

"It's adorable."

"And useless," he pointed out.

"But *warm*," Ann emphasized. "I think I met your roommate in the laundry room last week. Blonde? Curses a lot?"

"Yep, that's Charlotte."

"Are you two together?"

"*No.*" Liam shook his head. "She's my oldest friend. We grew up together."

Ann wrinkled her nose. "That's really cute—it's bugging me just how cute that is."

Liam laughed. "You two will get along just fine."

They walked into town about an hour and a half later. Liam took his bike for the trip home but rolled it along beside them for the mile and a half to the café. "I'm not gonna bike and have you *walk*," he told her with a laugh. "It's just rude."

She met Mr. Brandon and applied for a position. He warned Ann that they had just hired three people and probably wouldn't be perusing applications for a month or so. Ann shrugged this off, like it was the smallest nuisance in the world. "I'll wait, then. No worries."

When his manager disappeared into the back, Liam muttered to Ann, "Wow, that means he doesn't like you. Tough break, kid."

She fixed him with a cold, withering stare. In jest or not, he was hit by a swell of déjà vu that lingered long after she kissed his cheek and left. Liam rubbed the stubble on his chin and frowned, puzzled.

WORK WAS slow and irritating. He was consciously aware of the smell of coffee grind and sweat lingering on his clothes. A customer screamed at him for selling her a brownie that had peanuts in it, even though he had had no previous knowledge of this complete stranger's allergy. She threatened to sue, wrote down everybody's names, and stalked off in a huff.

"Working in food is going to make you hate people," his coworker Megan told him wisely while they closed up shop. "Don't take it personally. It says on the package that there are peanuts inside."

Callum Brandon sighed gravely.

Still, it was enough to ruin his night. When Liam punched out and trailed to the back, his bike was missing from where he had propped it near the emergency exit. His mouth fell open. "Seriously. *Seriously?*"

Silence echoed back. He whirled around, livid. "Oh come *on!*"

Jamie picked him up half an hour later. "Buddy, it serves you right for not chaining it up."

"I *do*, Jamie. I always do!" Liam argued angrily. "This was the one time I didn't have my lock on me, okay? I didn't think that humankind would fail me *today*." He hit the dashboard. "Dammit all."

"Calm down. Shit happens," Jamie said coolly. "You can't be so explosive about it. Why don't you borrow my car until you can get a replacement?"

"That's not practical; you're always commuting to the city."

"I'll take the train," Jamie told him. When Liam gave him a look, he said, "I'm serious! I've been thinking about it. Parking is such a bitch and it might be a cheaper method."

"No, that's okay," Liam sighed and pinched the bridge of his nose. "I'll figure something out. I'm just upset. I've been so obnoxious about preventing it from being stolen, and literally the *one* night I let my guard down...."

Jamie's phone rang then, and he wedged it between his ear and shoulder while he drove. "Hello? Oh, hey Mom."

Liam looked out the window at the expanse of residential streets that looped and turned into forested areas. He listened halfheartedly to his brother's conversation.

"Wow. Eighty-seven years? Well, don't cry, Mom. That's a long life. Plus he's from Dad's side of the family...." Jamie sighed. "Yes, but—okay—*Mom*. Yeah, Liam and I will come down this weekend.... Sure, here he is."

Liam made a pained face as Jamie handed him the phone. "Be nice," Jamie murmured to his brother. "Grandpa passed away last night and she's kind of shaken up about it."

Liam sighed and answered it. "Hi, Mom."

"Liam." His mother's voice was congested and sniffley. "Did Jamie tell you?"

"He did. Is Dad okay?"

"I don't know!" she wailed. "He's shut himself up in the den again. Cold, unfeeling man! Are you coming down for the funeral?"

"Well, we only met Grandpa Lawrence like *once*, Mom. I was nine. And it's been at least five years since Dad saw him, so...." Gargled, hysterical sobs were the response, and Liam slouched in his seat, miserable. "Fine. We'll see you on Friday."

CHAPTER ELEVEN

THE FUNERAL was gloomy but eerily beautiful. There were so many flowers, so many video tributes and warm speeches. Grandpa Lawrence had accumulated quite a sum of people in his lifetime: friends, acquaintances, and grandchildren. Liam was instantly reminded of how many brothers and sisters his father had but never spoke of.

He only recognized one—Aunt Clara. She stared, face ashen, at a bouquet of lilies, as the coffin was lowered into the ground. Her oldest son, Bill, checked his phone every few minutes. Liam clenched his fists in irritation. He never liked Bill Collins. A bookish boy growing up, he had reappeared years later and blossomed into a thirty-year-old yuppie who compensated for his short stature and nonexistent chin with too much hair product and pressed suits.

They had a small dinner at the Bennet household, but nobody sat down. Dishes were stacked, and the mourners wandered around, mumbling softly amongst themselves, catching up with distant relatives who were only brought together for the happiest and most depressing occasions.

"Nothing in the middle," Liam told his brothers conversationally. "Isn't that sad? I have twenty-eight cousins, half of whom I've only seen at weddings and funerals."

"What about Tommy Phillip's graduation?" Jamie suggested. The five of them were sitting on the first few steps of the main staircase.

"That's Mom's side of the family," Mason reminded him. He loosened his tie, grimacing. Dress clothes didn't suit him very well.

"Damn, that girl is hot." Nate leered across the hall at a slim brunette who poked at her salad gingerly. She met his eye and turned away.

Ben shoved him. "You sick bastard. She's your cousin."

"Is she really?" Nate's face fell.

"Yeah, I think she's Uncle Henry's daughter," Jamie chuckled.

A beat. "Who the *hell* is Uncle Henry?"

"The dude in tweed, down yonder." Liam pointed down the hall.

Jamie snorted softly. Nate sighed, thudding his head on the wall behind him.

BY EIGHT o'clock in the evening, all but one of the guests had trickled out of the large country house. The Bennet boys stared warily at Bill Collins from across the kitchen table, tight-lipped and judgmental. Well, at least Jamie was smiling politely.

"His will—" Bill cleared his throat and delicately moved the parcel across the table. "—stipulates that whichever grandson is the first to marry… will benefit from a sizeable inheritance."

"How much are we talking about?" Nate narrowed his eyes.

"Half a million," Bill said.

A squeak came out of Mrs. Bennet, and she wheeled around to her husband and clutched his arm. "We are saved."

"Grand*son*?" Mr. Bennet asked Bill. "He excluded his granddaughters?"

"That is correct."

"Never did value the girls much," Mr. Bennet sighed and rubbed the sleep out of his eyes. He looked so tired and worn-down all of a sudden. Liam observed that he also badly needed a haircut.

"Marriage meaning… not *just* man and wife, correct?" Mason asked. Jamie looked at him and half smiled.

Bill glanced through the document for a full minute. "It doesn't say specifically, so I would assume that the distinction is irrelevant. Of course, I will check, because the law should be free from all *assumptions*—"

"Well!" Mrs. Bennet interrupted happily. Her eyes instantly flitted to Jamie. "I doubt there will be much fussing here, as Jamie is in a *very* serious relationship."

Jamie looked at his mother in mortification. But she was already radiant with smugness.

"I wouldn't be so sure, Aunt Nora," Bill countered. "Lawrence's grandson Kevin is very nearly engaged and I myself am interested in a particular girl...."

What a creep, Liam thought, bemused. *Interested in a particular girl.* Was this being done in spite? As if Bill Collins could set his sights on any girl and select her from a vending machine toy box, letting the claw descend on her to scoop her up as his prize.

"Gloria is the daughter of the senior partner at my firm; she is *delightful*," Bill was rattling on. "I'm sure that Grandpa Lawrence would have *more* than approved of her elegance and her class, as well as her fine breeding...."

"Oh, congratulations. None of us knew that you were dating a poodle," said Liam calmly.

Nate guffawed. Bill Collins smiled thinly in response and folded his hands across the parcel.

"*Liam*," Mr. Bennet warned, though his hand was concealing his mouth. "Be respectful to your cousin."

He didn't see why he should. Collins was a ridiculous little man, obnoxious about his wealth and always hungry for more.

"In all seriousness, this is silly. A rat race down the aisle?" Mr. Bennet chuckled. "I can see it now, Dad mapping this all out from his deathbed, planting GPS trackers in the lapels of your suits. He always did have a twisted sense of humor."

His wife sighed. "Anything else, Bill?"

Bill ducked his head and shuffled a few pages. The light reflected off his slicked black hair, greasy and unbecoming. "Oh yes," he said in surprise. "I almost forgot. He is leaving one of his cars to... Liam Bennet."

Liam looked up in surprise. "What?"

"His white 1998 Nissan Maxima." Collins removed a single key from his inside jacket pocket and slid it across the table. Liam caught it off the edge. "Lucky *you*. But I must warn you that the tailpipe needs to be repaired."

His mouth was ajar. He stared at the key in his hand. "'Kay...."

"That's great!" Jamie was grinning.

Liam's brow furrowed in some confusion. He only remembered talking to Grandpa Lawrence *once,* and he doubted that they had spoken of cars. He had been nine, for Pete's sake.

"Are you sure it doesn't say Ben Bennet?" Ben spoke up eagerly. He was itching to drive, though he still had two more years to go.

"No," Bill replied. He looked at his aunt and uncle. "And really? *Ben* Bennet?"

Nate shrugged. "There are five of us. You can't expect my parents to be that creative after the fifth crowning."

"Nathan, you shut your filthy mouth—!"

"Please be calm, Nora," her husband stressed.

Jamie snorted.

He and his brother had time to discuss things that night over the chorus of simulated gunfire of a video game. Liam won at least three games, and Jamie sighed, shoving away his controller in disgust. "I give up."

"Bow down to your king!"

"Don't be cocky now."

"Never. Only guy who's cocky is that little shit doling out Grandpa's will," Liam grumbled, switching to cable. He stretched out across his bed. "I'd like nothing better than to avoid seeing him for *another* ten years, thank you very much."

"Well...," Jamie said slowly. "Then don't go to Charlie's party next weekend."

"Excuse me? What?" Liam sat up. "Did you *invite* that little cretin?"

His older brother winced. "Yeah."

"*Jamie!* What the hell?"

"Look, I felt *bad*, okay? He cornered me after dinner and said how happy he was that I was dating Charles Bingley, *prominent CEO*," he said, and waited while Liam groaned. "Next thing I know, he's gushing about how much he admires him and how he's his lifelong idol and he would like nothing more than to meet the whole team behind Nerve because he's such a web geek himself and passes by the building every day on his way to the firm—"

"That's not *your* problem!" Liam continued groaning, throwing himself dramatically over the bed. "Jamie... you sweet, sweet wish-granting idiot."

Jamie sighed. "It's a gift and a curse."

"Don't kid yourself; it's a curse. People are going to walk all over you. You're too good for that." He looked upset now, and Liam felt sorry. "You excited to see your *beau*?" he baited him, half smiling.

Jamie shot him a look. "Don't be such an ass." He nudged the controller Liam's way. "Come on, tough guy—I want a rematch."

CHAPTER TWELVE

JAMIE TOOK matters into his own hands to ensure that his brother was properly attired for the ball at Netherfield. Liam woke to the crinkle of plastic at his feet and saw that his brother had a rented tuxedo waiting for him in a garment bag. Polished dress shoes rested at the dresser.

He stumbled into the kitchen. Charlotte and Jamie were having breakfast. Charlotte had her hair in red curlers; his brother was pouring coffee beans into the grinder. An omelet was sizzling in the frying pan on the stove, unattended.

"You know," mused Liam, "my job is enough to put me off coffee for the rest of my life. I think I'll have orange juice today."

"Somebody alert the press." Charlotte winked at Jamie. "Did you see the tux?"

"Yeah. I feel like Cinderella," Liam muttered, getting a spatula out of the top drawer. He separated the eggs and scrambled them.

"You're welcome," Jamie deadpanned.

His phone started buzzing on the counter, and Liam handed it to him. "Your husband is calling you."

"Brat." Jamie picked up and left the room to talk to his boyfriend in private. "Hey, Charlie...."

"Are you going to continue giving him such a hard time?" Charlotte asked. Liam divvied the eggs up and served some onto her plate. "Here's a more important question: do we have Parmesan cheese that I can top this off with?"

"Yes, and yes. Bottom shelf of the fridge," Liam replied.

"Third question," Charlotte said through a mouthful of eggs. "Please tame that tidal wave of hair you've got going on top of your head."

"That isn't a question, but *I* have one for you." He slid the plastic container of grated Parmesan cheese across the table. "Are you capable of chewing with your mouth closed or should I teach you how?"

She opened her mouth defiantly, giving him an eyeful. He scrunched his nose.

"We could make it work," Charlotte said after a while. "Put a little bit of product in your hair, make it all twisty and *tousled*—you're gonna look hot."

"No."

"Just *listen* to me! It'll look really good. Put yourself in mine and Jamie's hands tonight and we'll make a proper man out of you."

"Should I be offended at that?" Liam asked, pouring himself some coffee despite his earlier grumblings. "Sounds like that song from *Mulan.*"

"Don't be offended. You're a handsome kid, kid," Charlotte assured him. "We just want to upgrade you—"

"For all the yuppies and the socialites...," Liam finished dryly.

"Exactly."

"Thanks, *kid*," Liam said, amused. "Are you being upgraded, or are you going as your naturally cynical, artsy self?"

"Oh no, I'm going all-out tonight. Push-up bra and fake eyelashes." Charlotte's shoulders lifted breezily. "You know, the usual false advertisements."

"Well, you can still be tasteful about it."

"No promises, Mom," said Charlotte.

He was just about to bite back with a retort when Jamie came into the room, his phone pressed against his chest to block the mouthpiece. "There was a last-minute delay for the band tonight and Charlie's kind of freaking out—"

"*Charlie* is?"

"Caroline is," Jamie corrected himself.

"There you go," said Liam smoothly.

"Can you call your musician friend? They're desperate. No guarantees tonight that they will be there because their flight is delayed and the Bingleys need a backup act because they banked on *this* one and—"

"I'm on it," Liam murmured, scrolling through his phone's contacts. "Let you know in a minute." He excused himself into the living room and then slid the screen door open to the balcony.

George picked up on the third ring. "Hello?"

"Hey, George, it's Liam Bennet. We hung out at Militia—"

"Yes, yes, yes." The other man laughed. "You don't have to reintroduce yourself. I remember you and your friend perfectly. What can I do for you, Liam?"

He explained the situation and George paused thoughtfully for a moment or two.

"I see. Tell you what; I can't make it before six o'clock, but I definitely think I can swing by for a few numbers. Will it be a paid gig? My rent is due next week, y'see—"

"Yeah, I'm sure it will be paid. It's for Charles Bingley...."

"Oh right." He grew quiet. "That billionaire bloke. How do you know him?"

"My brother is dating him."

"I see. From what I understand, he's a friend of Darcy's too... is he going to be there as well?"

"Probably. Is that a problem?"

"No, no," George scoffed. "Of course not. It's not in my character to be scared off; if he's put off by my presence, he should be the one to leave, don't you agree?"

Liam hesitated for a moment. He ran his hand across the railing nervously. "George, can I ask you why you hate him so much? Don't get me wrong, it must require a great deal of effort to actually *like* Will

Darcy... but there seems to be a pretty strong animosity in this situation. You two have history, don't you?"

There was such a drawn-out silence on the other end that Liam wondered if George had hung up on him. But finally he sighed wearily and spoke up. "Perhaps it is a story for a different time."

"Short version, then," Liam encouraged.

"Well...."

"Yes?"

"We were mates, Darcy and I," explained George carefully. "We grew up together, as boys in Derbyshire—that's in England. You see, my mum was his housekeeper. I used to play with the Darcys whenever she worked. After some time, Darcy and I grew apart. We parted ways; it was the natural succession of becoming teenagers. We no longer had anything in common, to be perfectly honest... I stuck around because I got on so well with his dad. Lovely man—essentially the only father figure I had in my life at the time...."

"Go on...," Liam goaded curiously.

George drew in a heavy breath. "The bottom line is that Darcy eventually cheated me out of his father's will. Henry Darcy had promised a sizeable amount of money to me to pursue my passions and start my own record label... he always believed in my potential as an artist. But then Darcy had the paperwork revised in spite. He got his lawyers on it like hounds. They were hired to find a loophole and work me out of it... and they succeeded."

"Are you serious?" Liam clenched his fists reflexively. "Why would he do that?"

"Oh, dear William was always jealous of my relationship with his father. It was clear what his motive was from the very beginning—jealousy and hatred. Will Darcy does not have the purest of emotions, my friend. And this was his revenge. Can't say I can completely blame him... he was smart about it. Struck me at my weakest hour."

Liam scowled. "What an asshole... I had no idea—"

"What's more, he then forbid me from speaking to his family ever again, including his little sister whom I was very close to." George sounded somber now, lost in painful memories. "I loved her like my own sister."

"George, I'm so sorry," Liam began.

He thought of how arrogant Will Darcy was and added *manipulative* to his list of negative attributes. *Heartless*. How he could dupe an old childhood friend, especially one as grounded and kind as George, was completely beyond his comprehension.

"I don't even... I don't know what to say. I think it would be very admirable of you to come this evening and play in spite of what happened. You should rub it in that assbag's face—show him how successful you are now."

"It would make him squirm with rage, wouldn't it?" George said, no doubt grinning wickedly on the other end. "It's too tempting to refuse. Consider it done. I'll be there, Liam."

"I owe you one. Thanks a lot, George."

"Any time. See you tonight."

CHAPTER THIRTEEN

HE LOOKED *good*. He knew it before his arrival at Netherfield, before he had been hit on by men and women alike and had been treated with a lot more reverence than the last time around. Charlotte had called it first, ushering him to the narrow, floor-length mirror nailed to the inside of her walk-in closet. "Check *you* out."

He seemed taller to himself. Perhaps because the tux made his limbs look longer. Liam grimaced. "I feel like I don't fill this out enough—"

"No, you're fine." Charlotte shook her head, smoothing down his lapels. "Wearing all black makes the long and lean thing *work*. And I love your hair combed to the side like that."

"Thanks, Charlotte." He felt a little better and smiled at her.

"You're welcome. Can you dress like this every day?"

"No."

"Why?"

"Because I'm not 007," Liam retorted. "Is clean-shaven okay?"

"Yeah, it's perfect."

Despite Charlotte's own teasing self-deprecation, she actually looked very pretty for the occasion. She wore a navy strapless gown, its bodice embedded with crystals and its tulle skirt full and flowing. She had pinned her wispy blonde hair back in a loose chignon.

Liam grinned at her. "You look beautiful, my friend. We are pretty swanky tonight."

"Dressed to the nines." Charlotte winked and threaded her arm through his. "We have to take the umbrella, though. It's supposed to rain all night and I am *not* getting this gown wet. It's borrowed."

In the ballroom, Liam was surrounded by a swarm of suits and ritzy dresses. Bingley looked perhaps the most casual of the bunch; his hair was uncombed, and he was missing his tie—intentionally or not, nobody knew.

Photographers clustered in the main lobby, where there were two bouncers admitting guests and diligently crossing them off a list. Liam had never felt so out of place in his life.

"Except maybe when I tried out for the football team on a whim freshman year of high school," he told Charlotte.

They found Jamie quickly. He looked handsome in his suit, which came as no surprise. He and Bingley were inseparable from ten minutes into the party onward. Liam watched them for a while, noted the way Bingley smiled at Jamie perceptively, the way his hand lingered on the small of his back....

"Practically married." Charlotte singsonged his thoughts, and he smiled. "They need to have the talk, though, before Charlie skirts away from him."

"He won't," Liam assured her.

Charlotte snatched up an hors d'œuvre and cocktail napkin from a waiter's tray. "Nobody serves *real* food at expensive parties like this. I want a goddamn burger, you know?"

"You should have eaten before we left."

"I was too busy trying to fit into the dress."

"What do you mean about Jamie?" Liam asked, addressing her earlier comment. He turned toward her. "You think that Charlie's not in love with him?"

"Oh, it's clear that he's in love with him. Who wouldn't be?" Charlotte asked. She took a bite of her miniature bruschetta and chewed thoughtfully for a moment. "What I mean is that Jamie has to secure that love. He has to *encourage* Charlie or else that poor man is going to get the wrong idea and bail out."

"He *does* encourage him...."

"Look at them for a second."

Liam looked.

Bingley's focus was completely devoted to Jamie. He would lean toward him and whisper a funny anecdote, introduce him to a guest, brush his hand against him affectionately. And Jamie....

Well, Jamie was a little stiff. He would smile obligingly or reciprocate a gesture, but not before checking his surroundings first. He was reserved, cautious.

"He's just being shy," Liam explained. "You know that. It's how he is with someone he really likes."

"Yes, *we* know that," Charlotte agreed. "But others don't. They can misinterpret his behavior as cold. And *that*, my friend, is really discouraging to a partner."

"What are you, some sort of body-language wizard?"

"Witch, actually," she corrected, stoic.

Liam snorted. "Gryffindor?"

"As *if*. Ravenclaw."

They entered Bingley and Jamie's circle. Bingley had just ended a brief phone call and was looking out the window, where rain was pattering on the glass. He turned back and smiled at the pair, though not very convincingly. "You guys all right? Enjoying yourselves?"

"A little more than you are," Charlotte replied. "What's wrong?"

"This weather is throwing back a lot of my plans. I was supposed to have the car pick up Will at the train station, but I forgot to arrange it with my driver, Yuri, and now he's off duty. I can't reach him."

"Will can always call a cab," Jamie pointed out.

"Yeah," Bingley sighed, rubbing the back of his neck. "But I just feel like a shitty friend. I *promised* to pick him up, and now he has to pay for a ride. Maybe if I leave quickly, I'll have enough time to go and get him—"

"It's your party; it isn't appropriate to *leave*, Charles." Liam had been wondering where Caroline Bingley was. She joined them now, drawing a thin, pale arm across her brother's shoulders.

"I'll get him," offered Jamie.

"No, now I *feel* bad—" Bingley began.

"Enough," Liam interrupted them all impatiently. "*I'll* go pick him up from the train station. You can all stop whining about it for a hot second. It's really not that big of a deal."

Charlotte chuckled, and Caroline glanced over her, her lip curling.

Liam hated himself. He really did. Why did he have to do this? What stupid instinct had *possibly* possessed him? Liam grumbled to himself and jammed his key into the ignition, and the engine sputtered to life.

The Maxima was a wheezing, honking mess of parts that somehow ran fluidly together to get him from point *A* to *B*. It was a blessing and he was grateful for it, especially in weather like this. But the silence drove him crazy; Liam wasn't a fan of the broken stereo. *Be one with your thoughts....*

"Nope," he chirped. "*Can't.*"

He made it to the station without music, just as he made it everywhere without music.

Darcy was standing just under the streetlight, ocher rain beating off of his squared shoulders. Liam pulled the Maxima up slowly and rolled down the window.

"Where's Yuri?" Darcy shouted above the rain.

"I don't know!" Liam hollered back. "Get in the car."

He didn't have to be told twice. Darcy slid inside and Liam put the car in reverse and backed out of the parking lot. He waited patiently at the exit for a gap in the oncoming traffic. Then he got back onto the bypass.

Darcy was resolutely quiet, which was fine by Liam. The last thing he wanted to do was talk to him. But God almighty, this had to be the slowest lane in the county.

Darcy cleared his throat. "Thank you."

"You're welcome," Liam replied automatically.

Darcy went to turn on the stereo. It hummed its lone static song, and his mouth curled in disappointment. "Were you trying to lift the tension?" Liam asked disarmingly. "'Cause that ain't gonna work."

Darcy didn't humor him with an immediate response. There was a palpable silence, and then Darcy's dry chuckle. "*God*, your car is so shitty."

Liam felt a defiant sense of pride swell in his stomach. An idea suddenly hit him. He opened a radio app on his phone, and the car was flooded with static-y, muffled Dusty Springfield. Liam arched an eyebrow in the other man's direction, challenging him.

To his surprise, Darcy just smirked. They inched forward, wedged between cars. Darcy sighed and looked out the far side of the windshield. "Jesus," he muttered. "If I wanted to deal with traffic this bad, I would have just stayed in the city."

Liam turned, about to insist that he *should* have kept his sorry, arrogant, manipulative ass in the city. But then he caught himself simply watching Darcy, his mouth closing unconsciously.

The rain had matted down the other man's nearly black hair across his forehead; his jacket collar was raised. There was a refined handsomeness to him—something distinctly masculine in the sharp line of his jaw, the straight nose, and the dark smooth brow....

He didn't know if he was envious of it. He couldn't identify what he felt, nor did he want to examine it all that closely. Liam looked straight ahead again and gripped the steering wheel anxiously.

They did not speak for the rest of the car ride. Liam parked. Both men left the vehicle and walked up the stone pathway in silence; they branched off once they joined the party.

Charlotte was on the dance floor, shimmying with someone who looked *way* too ridiculous for her. His tuxedo jacket was powder blue, for God's sake, the light glinting off of his slicked hair—Liam's eyes widened. *Bill Collins.*

He confronted her about it after her fourth dance with the snot-nosed attorney. She batted her eyelashes mockingly at him and fished an olive out of a martini glass. "I'm sorry—" She chewed thoughtfully. "—but are you *prohibiting* me from dancing with this man?"

"Nobody could prohibit you from anything, Charlotte, but you have to realize that this man is a total skeeze," Liam explained. "He's my cousin; take my judgment to heart."

"He's *fun*. Just look at that blazer!" she cackled, swiveling on her feet. "And he's so cute in that awkward, nerdy, Michael Cera way."

Liam was revolted.

"Oh, come on. It's a party. Lighten up. Did you pick up Farcy yet?"

"Yeah. He's…." Liam turned his head, surveying the party. "Scratch that, I don't know where he's run off to. And I really don't care."

Charlotte glanced at him from the corner of her eye and drained the last of her glass. "Do you want to dance?"

"Not until Wickham gets here. This piano jazz gets a little old after a while. I want something *live*."

"Yeah, I agree," she said. "I'm going to go touch up my lipstick." And then she was gone.

Liam took a seat but couldn't stay there for long as restlessness started to seep into his bones. He had been on edge since the sporadic silence in the car with Darcy. He rubbed the nape of his neck and exhaled evenly.

At least George would be here soon to liven things up.

An hour passed. Then two. He felt full on miniquiches and bruschetta. And then Bingley found him wandering in the main lobby; now Liam's tie was off too, his jacket long abandoned and his sleeves pushed up, his hair sticking up from running his fingers through it.

"You are a tricky fellow to find." Bingley clapped him on the back. His friendliness had been heightened by alcohol. "Listen, I want to let you know that it's okay about your musician friend. Don't stress yourself out about him canceling."

"What?" Liam tilted his head, puzzled.

"Your friend—George, was it? He called the front desk and sent his deepest apologies that he couldn't make it," Bingley explained. "But fifteen minutes before that, I got a call from the original band's agent, and their transportation pulled through. They're setting up already…."

"Front desk?"

"Yeah, my assistant, Patty, operates the front desk. Didn't you see her?" Bingley had yet to stop smiling throughout this entire conversation. "I'm gonna go find Jamie. Because… I'm *crazy* about him and he owes me another dance."

Liam was too preoccupied to process his words. As Bingley turned on his heel and walked back to his party, Liam finally remembered to ask, "Did he give a reason? George, I mean."

Bingley shrugged. "Sick."

Coward.

The word popped into his head before he had time to analyze it. Then, composing himself, Liam turned and walked out of the lobby.

Most of the doors on the first floor of the Netherfield estate were locked. But he wanted to be alone, *somewhere.* The concept of socializing right now seemed exhausting; all he wanted to do was sit and think and work through his unease. And then he passed it….

A door left ajar. Liam poked his head in, felt his mouth open stupidly, and then shut the door behind him.

Bingley had mentioned the library briefly before, but Liam had been quick to tune him out. Suddenly, he heard a man and a woman chuckling, and froze. Charlotte emerged, then Collins, from behind a bookshelf three aisles back. Her hair was mussed and his bowtie was askew.

She paused when she saw him and grinned. "Liam! You've *found* us."

He exchanged a cold glance with Bill Collins and replied, "I wasn't looking. Trust me."

"Oh!" She touched Bill on the arm. "I forgot my handbag. Hold on."

"How are you tonight, Liam?" Collins asked when she was gone.

"Quite well, Bill, thank you," Liam said. "What happened? The senior partner's daughter dumped you that quickly?"

Collins sneered and opened his mouth to fire back when Charlotte returned, looking jovial as ever. "Bill, let's go dance some more."

"Darling, I'm tired."

Darling. Liam thought he was going to be sick.

"Oh, don't be such an old fart." She clasped his hand and led him toward the doors, before turning around to address her best friend. "Liam, why are you being such a loner tonight?"

"I just came to admire the library."

"It's beautiful, isn't it? Bill told me it was modeled after the one at Oxford."

"Yes." Collins straightened his lapels. "This one is a dim competitor to Queen's College Library, at Oxford University, in Oxford."

"Oxford University's in Oxford?" Liam asked.

Charlotte shot him a look and escorted her adopted date out of the library. When they had left, Liam shut the door behind them and relished the open silence before him.

For all of Collins's snobby knowledge, the library was actually breathtaking. There were two stories. Tall pillars flanked rows of books, canopied by white vaulted ceilings carved in intricate floral designs with gold plating. The floors were black-and-white checkered marble. In the center of the room was a giant, ancient globe, protected in a glass sphere.

Liam thought the library would be even more beautiful in daylight, with the sun filtering through the seven bay windows from the right side.

It was an effective distraction. He wandered upstairs and lost himself. Liam pulled out *Far from the Madding Crowd* and gingerly turned a page. His mouth fell open. "First edition? I don't believe it...."

"You should," Will Darcy said smoothly.

Liam nearly jumped out of his skin. The book toppled to the floor, but he was quick to pick it up. He was glowering now that Darcy stood before him, laughing. It was a warm laugh, pleasant in fact, but that it was at his expense was unacceptable.

"How long have you been standing here?"

"Only a minute or two," Darcy responded. He took the book from Liam and leaned against the bookcase, flipping through it. "I've been in the library for about an hour, total. I had the misfortune of having to listen to your friend and her date hooking up in the Biography section."

"He's *not* her date," snapped Liam. "But still, that's fairly creepy of you."

"I was going to make my presence known but they were at it so fast that I didn't know what to do," Darcy defended himself unhappily. "So I just sat down and waited for them to leave."

Liam began to laugh. Darcy relaxed, even smiled.

"Still a little creepy," the younger man muttered.

"Have you read this?" Darcy asked, lifting the Thomas Hardy novel.

"Yeah, for class."

"It's one of my favorites. Maybe we can have a discussion about it."

Liam stared at him warily. "What is this, Oprah's Book Club? I doubt we'd have the same feelings about books—and characters. You and I are two very, very different people, Darcy."

"Even better. We can compare our opposing opinions," Darcy suggested.

He didn't understand why Darcy was so keen on speaking to him all of a sudden. His entire behavior was strange. Well, it was usually strange, but perhaps stranger than normal.

"Listen," Liam began. "If you're trying to thank me for picking you up earlier, even if that means altering your en*tire* personality, you really shouldn't bother."

"I'm not," Darcy said curtly. "I'm just trying to be your friend."

This completely shocked him. Liam frowned. "Oh."

"And don't presume that you know so much about my personality."

He recovered. "You're right. I don't. Nobody does. Nobody's account of it is all that consistent," Liam muttered. "You might as well be three different people." He snatched the book and wedged it back into its row.

Darcy contemplated this for a moment. "What are you trying to say?"

"Nothing," Liam said coolly.

There was a long stretch of silence. Both men stared at each other wordlessly.

Darcy was the first to crack. He cleared his throat and adjusted his cuff link, though there was nothing to be adjusted. "I understand that you're friends with George Wickham."

Bingo. Liam let himself smirk. "Yeah, I am. It's a shame you couldn't join us the other day."

"I have to warn you," he continued, ignoring the quip. "It's not in my nature to control the actions of others, but—"

"It's not?" Liam feigned surprise.

Darcy's face darkened. "*But* you're better off choosing different company. He's a charming guy—the quirky, spiritual, impractical, poor musician. I get the appeal," he said dismissively. "It would make an excellent movie. But in real life, that man cannot be trusted. He is quick to burn bridges and he burns them very effectively."

Liam couldn't bridle his irritation. "I guess yours has been incinerated."

"Yes, it has."

"And you're sure that that is *his* fault?" Liam tested him.

Darcy clenched his jaw. "Why are you asking?"

"I'm trying to understand your character a little better. But I think I know it pretty well."

He didn't know exactly what he was after. But he wanted to see Will Darcy exposed, wanted to see all of his bravado fall away and reveal the manipulative bastard he knew him to be, not the faithful best friend or the shy multimillionaire enigma that the press portrayed him as. He was a bully, and he had made George Wickham suffer without a lick of remorse.

"You know nothing," Darcy retorted.

Liam curled his fists as the other man stared him down.

The doors swung open. Caroline Bingley, it seemed, was having an even worse night than the others. "William Darcy! You *promised* me a dance and we have been through *five* live numbers and I've had to fight off other men with a *stick*. What *are* you waiting for?"

Darcy looked down at her miniscule figure darkening the first-floor doorway. His shoulders rounded, and then he turned his gaze back to Liam's.

"Excuse me," Liam said, quiet but cold. He descended the staircase and moved past a stunned Caroline Bingley and into the hall.

Outside, the rain was coming down hard. His white dress shirt molded to his body, drenched through. His hands shook; he was enraged, and he cracked his knuckles. Nobody had ever gotten a rise out of him quite like Will Darcy did....

He couldn't account for it at all.

"Asshole," Liam spat. He drew his keys out of his pocket and walked briskly into the downpour.

CHAPTER FOURTEEN

IF CHARLOTTE was peeved at him for abandoning her, Liam never found out. She texted him not ten minutes after he arrived at the apartment to cryptically inform him that she would not be coming home that night, and that she was safe.

This stoked his rage all the more. Liam hurled his phone onto the couch and stalked off to bed, trying to stave off nightmarish fantasies about his best friend and Bill Collins procreating.

She was home just in time for breakfast the next morning, triumphant in her walk-of-shame dress. "Yoo-hoo!" Charlotte hollered, slipping off her silver heels.

Liam walked into the foyer in his plaid robe, holding a mug of coffee and looking sour.

"Hey, Grumpy. What's with the face?"

"I was born with it."

Charlotte chuckled and kissed his cheek. He scowled and took a sip.

"Charlotte," he began, following her into the kitchen. He watched her peruse the contents of the fridge, fumbling over bottles. "I'm not trying to go parental on your ass here, but that was just a one-night thing with Collins, right?"

Charlotte side-eyed him and chucked an empty carton of orange juice into the trash can. "If it's empty, why do you put it back in the fridge? Honestly Liam, your living habits are pretty disgusting…."

"Charlotte."

She shrugged. "What? I like him. He's taking me out on Thursday."

Liam raised his eyebrows. "Can I talk to you seriously about him?"

"Yeah, sure."

"He's looking for a quick relationship just so he can get his greedy little paws on my grandpa's—"

"Inheritance," they both chorused.

Liam was taken aback.

She took off her earrings, rolled her eyes, and walked past him and into the bedroom. He was quick to follow. "Liam, really, do you think I'm an idiot?"

"Did *he* tell you that?"

"Of course."

"And you're going through with it."

"I'd be stupid not to," she answered calmly. "Unzip me, please."

He obliged, and then stopped halfway. "Charlotte, he's going to take you all the way down the altar, provided you give him a lot of your time and willingness. This isn't a relationship, it's a business transaction."

Charlotte turned to face him, her gray eyes inspecting him blankly. "Sorry, I'm just waiting for you to give me information I *don't* know."

"He is ten years older than you," he argued.

"So what? I'm of age. Past it."

"You met him last night."

She shrugged. "I know enough about him."

"This is *wrong*," Liam insisted.

She sighed, irritated. "Who are you, my father?"

"You don't need the money."

"Actually," Charlotte protested, "I really do, Liam. I have to do this." Her voice lowered almost instinctively, as if there were always someone around to eavesdrop. "Mom is never going to pay off her debts; she can't even afford to retire in the next twenty years—"

"I know that," Liam said hastily. The Lucas's financial troubles had been a constant source of stress for Charlotte and her mother since long before Liam could remember. He knew how proud Mrs. Lucas had been when Charlotte got her scholarship, how she had sat teary-eyed through their entire dinner that night. "But it can't be so bad that you're considering—"

"Half a million in debt, Liam," Charlotte said smoothly.

He closed his mouth.

"She's been waiting for me to go off to college before she sells the house. Sells *everything*. All of those stupid investments… and the credit cards…."

Liam opened his mouth, still stunned. "Charlotte—"

"Hush." She drew her arms around him in a hug. "I'll still finish school. But this thing fell into my lap like a blessing. I can't *not* take this opportunity."

He pulled away. "You're gonna ruin your life."

"I'll get a really good prenup," she assured him.

"Okay," Liam bristled, "*that* is the kind of shit that ruins the sanctity of marriage."

Charlotte rolled her eyes. "Don't be so naïve, Liam. Nothing boils out of love, and if it does, it disappears quickly. You have to ensure that you're secure, that you are economically stable—"

"Yeah, maybe back in the olden days when a father would sell his daughter for *livestock*. Come on, Charlotte!"

"There is no other way right now, Liam—"

"Yes, there is," he insisted. "Let your mother file for bankruptcy. Go to school. Get a career, make your own living."

"We'll lose the house and everything she's worked toward before all of that even happens."

"She made bad choices and you should not have to throw away *your* future because of it," Liam fired back angrily. "You can barely afford your share of this apartment! God, does your mom even know that you're thinking of doing this?"

"No," she said quietly. She was still holding the half-zipped bodice of her gown to her torso. "Not yet."

"Think about this, Charlotte. You're making a big mistake. There are no promises with Collins."

Then she looked at him, her tawny eyes narrowing like a cat's. "Wait a minute. Is this about Jamie?"

"What?"

"Of course." Her eyes widened in apparent comprehension. "Jamie's entitled to the inheritance if he marries first.... You're doing this in Jamie's best interests! Why didn't I see this before?"

He scowled darkly. "Are you serious right now? You've known us since we were little kids, Charlotte, and now you're throwing around an accusation like that?"

"Charlie already *has* all the money he will ever need! Unless you think Jamie will never take it." She was thinking out loud now. "Who's to say they'll even marry? They could break up in a week!"

"Charlotte, it's not about that—"

"Come on, Liam, admit that you'd be thrilled if Jamie married Charlie and got the inheritance."

"Of course I would; Jamie's my brother. But I'm not discouraging you because of that, I'm discouraging you because you are doing something rash and stupid that could negatively affect your whole life—"

"Save it," Charlotte cut him off impatiently, her palm up. "I know where your loyalties lie."

With that, she shoved past him.

"What is this, *The Godfather*?" Liam whirled around.

"Don't follow me!" she hollered.

"Gladly!" he shouted back.

CHAPTER FIFTEEN

THEY NEVER fought, except for a brief falling-out during freshman year of high school. Also because of a boyfriend, Charlotte's first, to be exact. He had been right about him, and he *knew* he was right about Collins; the man was not to be trusted.

But still, Liam was fully prepared to sit down and discuss their argument—or he would have been if Charlotte had not gone to great lengths to avoid him entirely. For the next three weeks, their friendship coasted by on fragmented texts and glimpses of the other in the next room. Most nights, Charlotte didn't come home at all.

He'd catch her just leaving, a flurry of skirts and a blonde ponytail whipping past before the door slammed closed. If she did come home, she would come home late; he was always in bed already.

"It's like your marriage is crumbling," Ann told him cheerfully.

It was a chilly night in November, and she had taken him out to her favorite restaurant, Lotus, as a thank-you for getting her hired at the cafe. He sat across from her and watched balefully as she maneuvered chopsticks with a fair amount of precision, popping a spicy tuna roll into her mouth.

Liam sulked and adjusted his own chopsticks, though not very successfully. "She's my oldest friend and she's being an idiot."

"Live and learn."

"It's not so easy to watch people fall down and get their knees skinned, especially when you care about them," Liam explained.

Ann shrugged. She was growing her hair out, the longer layers of her pixie cut pinned back with bobby pins. Even so, she would pause to brush back flyaways. "I think the best thing you could do is—oh, wait a moment." Her phone was buzzing.

"Sure thing." Liam stole a roll off of her plate.

Ann answered, "Y'ello?" Her face relaxed into a smile. "Hey! I miss you too.... How's the Big A?" She chuckled then, poking at her rice. "Yes, I know that I missed his party. I even called to apologize. Well clearly I left town just to avoid you... I'm *joking*, don't get your knickers in a twist."

Liam chuckled and glanced out the window that adjoined their booth. Christmas lights were already strung up outside, decorating the trees that dotted the sidewalk. He suddenly yearned for home.

"It's not my fault that we never see each other," she said. "Stay in one place, why don't you...? Okay, okay. Love you too."

Ann sighed and set her phone down. "Sorry. My brother turns into a needy little girl around the holidays. Must have started a little early this year...."

"Younger brother?"

"Older, if you can imagine. We lost Mum a few days before Christmastime," Ann explained. "I was little but he was thirteen. He's usually very strong, but this time of year he gets into his annual mood."

"I'm sorry," Liam said genuinely.

Ann smiled. "Thank you."

It was good to see her again. He only saw her sporadically at work since they had nearly opposite shifts. Occasionally they would work a Saturday together. Even so, she would be heading back to England in December, after finals.

She took a roll of his, interrupting his reverie. "Thought I didn't notice your thievery?" Ann laughed.

"No, I thought I was stealthy." Liam grinned.

"You're so cute." She sighed and shook her head. "You know that, right? You're absolutely adorable. It's a damn shame."

"Thanks." Liam felt his face grow hot.

"You *have* to let me set you up with my friend Patrick," she chirped, thumbing through her phone's contacts. She eyed him again. "Unless... no, you're too sweet for my brother. But you and Patrick—I think you two could hit it off."

Liam looked up with a jolt. "What? Oh, Ann, that's not necessary. I'm not g—"

"Are you guys all set for dessert?" Their waiter had seemingly materialized out of thin air.

"Yes," Ann enthused. "Do you still have that delicious ginger ice cream, or is that a thing of the past?"

"We do." The waiter smiled.

"Excellent. Liam, you have to try it. It's homemade. I'd like a cappuccino as well. Two, for me and my friend."

Liam opened his mouth, uncomfortable, and then thought the better of it. "Thanks."

After the waiter left, Ann propped her chin up on steepled fingers. "What I was saying about Charlotte—you have to let her make her own mistakes or she's never going to take any of your input seriously. Maybe she expected support from you because that's what she's used to getting. The absence of it must have thrown her for a loop. Keep your distance and be cool."

Liam leaned forward, intrigued. "You think I should?"

"I absolutely think you should; quit trying so hard and she'll come to you," Ann insisted. "This is true of so many relationships and friendships. Less is more."

"Beacon of wisdom masquerading as a sixteen-year-old." Liam began to chuckle.

She stuck her tongue out. "Hey, I am twenty-one, all right?"

"Must be the haircut. And the fact that you stick your tongue out at people when they insult you—oww." He flinched when she stuck him with a chopstick.

Whether distancing himself helped or not, Liam could not really tell. But the next Saturday morning, he walked into the kitchen to find Charlotte standing in her coat, holding a suitcase and a backpack.

"Where are you going?" he asked calmly.

"London."

His brow furrowed. "So soon? I thought you said that the semester started January 17."

"Yes, but...." Charlotte sighed, tucking one of her blonde curls behind an ear. "I'm going to spend the holidays with Collins. His godmother is setting us up in some cottage in Hunsford—that's in the countryside."

"You're spending your winter break in the rollicking English countryside with a man you're on a last-name basis with," said Liam in a monotone.

"Yes," she answered, sounding agitated. "I'm studying in London for the spring semester after that. His godmother has an apartment in Westminster that she's renting out to me."

"Sounds like a pretty wealthy lady."

"Yeah, she's loaded," Charlotte chuckled, as if nervous. "She's some sort of dame or lady or something aristocratic."

"I guess you have it made now."

Charlotte met his eye. She sighed. "Can we not do this? I'm really going to miss you, Liam. I just wanted to say good-bye."

"I just—" He laughed and scratched the scruff on his chin. "I don't *understand*. We have two weeks left before finals. Where are you running off to?"

"I finished my exams early," Charlotte said. "I was going to tell you—"

"If you actually talked to me," Liam replied.

They were quiet for a few seconds. She cut off the distance between them and hugged him anyway. It was a very brief embrace. She broke it off and wheeled her suitcase to the door. "Bye."

"I'll help you with your luggage," he sighed.

Collins was waiting downstairs, his car parked at the shoulder; he rolled the window down. "Hi, darling." He flashed a shit-eating grin and lowered his sunglasses. "I'm going to pop the trunk for you, all right?"

"Yeah, don't bother getting up," Liam said gruffly. He lodged in two of her suitcases, took the backpack from her shoulder, and slid it in the trunk gingerly. Charlotte looked at him with apologetic eyes.

"Please keep in touch," she murmured, taking his hand.

"Be safe," Liam countered, squeezing back.

He watched the little Audi sports car rev up and take a right at the light, disappearing from view. Liam sighed and walked back into the building.

With Charlotte gone, the apartment seemed lonelier than ever. He wondered how he had failed to notice her slow, methodical packing over the last few weeks. Little by little, her belongings had disappeared, leaving behind an emptiness he couldn't shake now.

It plagued him for the rest of the day and long after he arrived at work. Ann wasn't working—neither were his usual favorite baristas, Megan and Joey. Rosemary Teflin was there; she was the surlier assistant manager who ran the shop when neither of the Brandons was in. They were vacationing in the Poconos for the week.

"Bennet," she barked, thirty seconds after he punched in.

Liam put on his visor. "Good evening, Rosemary."

"I have a new girl on register tonight. Cleanup is on you." She handed him a mop. "You can start with the ladies' bathroom. It stinks something awful."

His mouth settled into a grim smile. "Okay."

It didn't bother him more than usual. Keeping busy was a way to occupy the mind. But before he was even halfway done, Rosemary called him.

"The new girl punched out for her break. You're on register for the next twenty minutes." Rosemary took away his mop. "Be sure to push the St. Agnes Fund. We need $100 by tonight."

Liam sighed, washed up in the back, and tied his apron on. There was a full line of customers and two open registers. Of course, Rosemary wouldn't stoop so low as to ring.

"Excuse me, what's taking so long?" a middle-aged man asked him.

"I'm sorry, sir. We're a little understaffed tonight. What can I get you?" He took his order for a small decaf coffee and a blueberry scone. "Also, would you be interested in donating a dollar toward the St. Agnes Fund to help children fighting cancer—"

"No, thank you."

He really hated the holiday charity drives. It gave him the opportunity to see everyone's stinginess firsthand.

One order. Another. A group of five. Seven. Two girls. An elderly man. Nobody donated. His phone buzzed but he had to ignore it. Finally the line dwindled. He slid his phone out of his apron pocket—Jamie had left him a voice mail.

Looking around for a brief moment, Liam held it up to his ear and waited for the automated menu to pass. Then, Jamie's quiet voice: "Hey, Liam. Can you come over after work tonight? I'm not feeling so well. Charlie and I... well, Charlie broke up with me. I'll be fine, really. I'm okay. I'm just really confused and kind of depressed and—okay, I'll just stop talking. This is dumb. Bye."

"Bennet, are you talking on the phone?"

It dropped back into his apron. "Not at all."

Rosemary narrowed her slate eyes and disappeared into the back.

Liam stared down at the countertop, confused. What? *Why?* He shook his head and removed his visor to wipe the line of sweat it had left on his forehead.

I'm crazy about him and he owes me another dance.

He recalled Bingley's words clearly now. And it *was* clear, or else it had been. Bingley was undoubtedly in love with Jamie. And Jamie wasn't one to seek out a fight or a confrontation. He didn't hear any objections from him. He loved him. They had gone to the mountains together not two weekends ago.

There had to be an outside influence.

Liam clenched his jaw just as a gaggle of customers came in.

A tall, slender blonde woman in a cinched fur coat took about a century to figure out what to order. When he finally keyed it in, she changed her mind another couple of times. "Soy," she trilled. "Or nonfat milk. Which one has less calories?"

"Nonfat."

"But that's still dairy."

"Yes," he said, clipped.

"I'll take soy."

"Two eighty-nine. And would you like to donate a dollar toward the St. Agnes Fund to help children fighting—"

"Oh." She waved her hand. "I already donated."

"Really?" Liam asked in a deadpan. "Well, they still have cancer."

CHAPTER SIXTEEN

"WISEASS," JAMIE chuckled.

It was a frigid night, and his breath came out in silvery tufts. The brothers were walking in silence along the icy routes that crisscrossed the Oakham campus. Liam grinned and dipped his head low.

"Was your boss pissed?"

"*So* pissed," Liam laughed. "Told me she'd tell Callum and Mindy Brandon all about my *indiscretion* first thing in the morning."

"Sucks, kid."

"Whatever. It was just that kind of shift," he said with a sigh. "I really hate people—especially customers. People think that they have a little bit of money to spend and they're suddenly entitled to everything."

"Not everybody thinks that way," Jamie said reasonably. "Charlie has a ton of money. But he's very nice to everyone, always polite and understanding. He never tipped a waitress below 20 percent."

"Even that time that his throat closed up?"

"Yeah." Jamie laughed. "He still tipped her. Poor girl was mortified. They cooked his pad thai in peanut oil. Five minutes later, he broke out in hives and started breathing funny—it was awful."

"Worst date ever," Liam mumbled. He cocked his head and led them up a back trail. "It was good that you found his EpiPen."

"I got so scared for him," Jamie sighed. He ran his fingers through his hair, and Liam knew he was reliving his agitation. "He's asthmatic too; I didn't know. I just wanted to take care of him."

"Do you still want to?" Liam asked gently.

"Yes," Jamie responded. "Just because he doesn't want to be with me anymore doesn't mean that I've stopped caring about him."

Liam was shaking his head. "I don't understand what his problem is."

"Me neither," Jamie murmured. He shoved his hands into his jacket pockets, collar raised against the wind.

"Can I listen to that voice mail again?" Liam asked.

"Sure."

Jamie handed him his cell phone. The way Liam understood it, Bingley had been a flaky conversationalist since the Netherfield ball. He wouldn't call anymore, and when Jamie had finally secured some alone time with him, he seemed chilly and distant. *Darcyish behavior*, Liam thought skeptically.

Jamie knew that his boyfriend would be returning to the city. Bingley had promised to be gone for a few weeks at most, until his sister left Jamie a saccharine voice mail that casually hinted otherwise. Liam listened again:

"Jamie darling, it's Caroline Bingley. I just wanted to tell you how wonderful it was to meet you and to spend so much time with you these last few months. You are such a sweet, hard-working young man and you've been an excellent companion for Charlie—"

"Companion," Liam scoffed.

"Right?" Jamie balked, laughing. "Ignore the existence of an entire relationship, why don't you?"

"—Charlie is spending the holidays in Palo Alto this year, and then we're off to Aspen. Daddy owns a few cabins down there and we're due for our annual ski trip. No telling when we'll be back; Nerve is gaining a lot of popularity so Charlie and Will have scheduled many publicity events."

"I don't understand this at all," he sighed.

"Don't worry, though! Charlie will write you a lot. I'm sure you boys exchanged e-mail addresses a long time ago. Have a wonderful holiday. Ciao."

Liam tossed the phone back to his brother, disgusted.

"It's like he's petering out of this relationship," Jamie said gloomily, "through his sister."

"No, no. All these bullshit trips are recently planned, I guarantee you. And the fact that *Caroline* called you? Charlie's not thinking for himself; he's given the steering wheel to others."

"Well, that's pathetic," Jamie snapped. "The man is nearly thirty years old. It's easier to believe that he lost interest in me and is too much of a coward to break up with me in person."

Liam turned, surprised at his temper. He couldn't blame him in the slightest, though. "That's what it looks like, doesn't it? And I would think the same exact thing if I didn't know that the man *loves* you."

"He obviously does not." Jamie rounded his shoulders.

"Yes, he does. He was smitten at Netherfield."

"You know how these things work, Liam. People change their feelings overnight. Things break," his brother said unhappily. "It's a part of life."

"Okay, stop being so cool about this!" Liam laughed. "Wait your turn to impart wisdom. At least reach your bitterness stage. I think that's a-comin'."

Jamie smiled, but it was short-lived.

There was a lengthy silence between the brothers. Then, "I like how she says *we're due for our annual ski trip*," Liam snorted, "like it's a goddamn dentist appointment. I'm so sorry that you have real estate in Aspen."

Jamie began to laugh, genuinely this time. "Oh, she's so full of shit, isn't she?"

"There you go," Liam said, laughing.

His brother shook his head. "I really thought Charlie and I... I don't know. I was really starting to fall for him. We didn't have that conversation; I didn't know where we stood but I *felt* it and I thought he did too. I loved him—I still do."

Liam looked at him sympathetically. "He loves you too. I'm sure of it. This is her influence."

"But why would she do this?"

He shrugged. "Maybe she has a richer prospect in mind. These people are all about mergers and money."

They had reached the baseball field. Jamie stood sulking at the ground. Liam climbed the fence up to its midpoint and waited, peering out across the rungs at the vast empty blackness of the pit. He craned his neck, and his hood fell to his shoulders.

"Hey!" The flashlight's glare hit his back. Jamie tugged him down urgently. They saw the security guard sprint toward them. "This is private property!"

"My brother goes here," Liam insisted.

"I don't care. It's after hours and you're trespassing."

"He has a student ID," he argued, annoyed. "Jamie, show him your—"

"Keep your hands where I can see them, please," the guard barked.

"Jesus Christ, did you fail the police academy test? Is this your misplaced aggression—?"

Jamie cut him off and told the guard, "Don't worry. We're leaving." He shoved Liam back on the sidewalk. "Sorry about the trouble, sir."

The guard grunted and watched them for a while. They rounded the block, and his light finally faded. Liam sighed, irritated.

"You're such a little shit." Jamie shoved him, snorting. "See, I would have booked it as soon as he saw us."

"That's the difference between you and me."

"Yeah, you challenge everybody. Unnecessarily."

Liam shrugged. "It didn't state hours of operation on any of the signs we passed."

"He probably thought we were breaking into the baseball field."

"Well, that's his own ignorance. I can't be held accountable for that," Liam said. Jamie rolled his eyes, and they walked out beyond the campus and toward his neighborhood.

In the days that followed, Jamie and Liam saw very little of each other. Final exams made hermits of everyone. Liam took to the library for a good week and a half, his desktop constantly littered with textbooks and highlighters.

It was flurrying outside the night that Ann tapped him on the shoulder. Liam looked up with a start and unhooked his headphones. "Hi Ann." He smiled.

"Hello." Ann beamed. She wore a hat with fuzzy earflaps, and snow still clung to her peacoat, though it was starting to melt. "I had a hunch you'd be among the miserable souls cooped up in here."

"*That* and I texted you that I was in here," Liam replied.

She nodded. "Valid point. I'm actually off to the airport. The car's loaded with all my luggage, and Roger is probably asleep at the wheel waiting for me."

"Oh, the elusive Roger."

"That's right—you have yet to meet."

"I'm not so sure that he exists," he laughed.

"He does, unfortunately," Ann muttered. "We broke up," she added in a hushed whisper. "Don't make that face; it was my idea. I am fine. A little sour but mostly fine."

Liam still made his grimacing face. "I'm sorry."

"*Don't* be." Ann ran a hand through her hair impatiently. "He's giving me a lift to the airport. This does throw my holiday plans into a tizzy. And I thought I would be celebrating Christmas with my brother, but he's off to the West Coast like the loser that he is."

"You're free to celebrate the holidays with me," Liam offered. He closed his notebook. "Granted, you'd be stuck with my family too, which does really cheapen the deal."

"No, that's okay, Liam. You are far too sweet. But I'll just go back home—I miss it."

Liam nodded.

She knelt down to kiss him on the cheek. "Bye! Oh, but *please* let me know when you're done with school. I'd love to see you. I'll pay for your airfare."

"No, I wouldn't let you do that," he insisted. "But yeah, I'll let you know when I get sick of being here. It's gonna happen pretty quickly."

"Okay," she chuckled. "Bye, Liam!"

When she left, it seemed the entire library itself had grown drearier. What little motivation Liam had to study bled out. He closed his textbook and shoved it to the side. He couldn't pin it all on Ann. Three finals had drained him, and he was now functioning on four hours of sleep.

Light snoring distracted him and he looked over to the next table. A guy from his Economics class had his baseball cap brim lowered snugly over his eyes and his head cushioned by a closed notepad. The spiral had already left an indentation on his cheek.

Liam sighed and gathered his supplies. He slung his schoolbag over his shoulder and headed out. The snow was picking up a little. It wasn't sticking to the grass though; he knew he shouldn't bank on any exam cancellations.

He walked to the Oak Café thinking that a nice cup of coffee would warm him up, but he stopped cold in his tracks just at the entrance. George Wickham got up from the front step and smiled broadly at him, extending his hand.

Liam rebuffed it and George's smile waned. "Listen mate, I'm very sorry about the party. I had family affairs to sort out."

He arched an eyebrow skeptically.

"Okay, maybe not family. But my flatmate, Tony, was having a get-together and we got a little messy and—"

"Forget it, George. The original band pulled through."

George gritted his teeth. "You're upset."

"I don't care anymore. I hardly know you. Flakiness isn't always detectable during a first impression," he mumbled, shoving his hands into his pockets.

"Don't be like that, Liam," George chuckled. "There are loads of other gigs out there. This wasn't anything personal to you, mate."

Liam clenched his jaw, pissed. "I was trying to be a good friend. *You* bailed because you were too much of a coward to risk a confrontation with Will Darcy."

George didn't deny it. His shoulders slumped. "I'm sorry…. How was the bastard?"

"Miserable, but that's always the case."

He chortled, "Too true."

Liam didn't smile. "I'll see you around." He extended his hand and George shook it. "Have a good holiday."

"You too, mate," George murmured. "I do apologize. I didn't realize it meant that much to you. You're a better man than I am, and I was too thick to realize it. And a coward," he sighed. "Let bygones be bygones and all the rest?"

Liam hesitated. "Okay."

"If you're around for New Year's, give me a ring." George smiled, his relaxed friendliness back again. "I'm going to Times Square with a few people, and you would round out the group nicely."

"Yeah, I'll let you know."

It was a loose engagement that they both knew wouldn't happen. They smiled at each other and went in opposite directions.

CHAPTER SEVENTEEN

THE BENNET residence was a madhouse that Christmas. With finals over, Liam had little excuse to tear away from family squabbles, chores, and his mother. He fell victim to her constant list of errands.

"This is the third time you're sending me to the grocery store today, Mom," he told her. "Please can you just take a second and compact this all into a single list?"

"Liam, I've told you this before—I don't know what I need to cook until *after* I've started cooking. Unless you want to take the reins on Christmas dinner, I suggest you don't start with me!"

It was difficult to argue with her, especially when she had a flour handprint pressed to her cheek. His father snuck behind her and stole a cookie from the tray, still warm from the oven. She smacked him with her spoon, and he grinned and hugged her from behind, which practically lifted her off her feet.

"Nora, Nora, my beautiful Nora. Don't be so tense, my love."

"Dad made eggnog a little too early," Jamie briefed them all from the dining room. He wore a Santa hat as he set the table, and Nate followed each plate that he set with a fork and knife. "No, no, Nathan. *Fork* is left, butter knife right. Tuck the napkin under the fork."

Nathan nodded but said nothing. Every few moments, he would glance into the kitchen at his older brother and his face would darken. Mason was sitting at the table looking polite and dapper with his hair combed and his shirt tucked in. To his right sat a girl his age with long blonde hair. He leaned forward to explain his family's quirks to her in hushed, urgent whispers.

Liam half smiled. Mason had been pining after Becca Huntington since the third grade but never had the chance to speak with her apart from sharing animal crackers at recess. He didn't get the chance until the year of high school when they shared a stand for orchestra—they both played clarinet. She was a sweet girl. It was the happiest he had ever seen Mason.

The Gardiners came for dinner.

Frank Gardiner was Mrs. Bennet's older brother. He and his wife Maureen ran an independent travel journal and, as a result, were constantly on the move. They were Liam's favorite aunt and uncle, and it was always a treat to have them in one place long enough to celebrate a holiday.

"We're going to Ashford, Washington in January," Frank shared happily. "Mount Rainier. We're doing a feature on the nation's best national parks."

"I can't wait to develop my film from Acadia." Maureen grinned. "*That* was breathtaking."

"Maine, right?" Mr. Bennet guessed.

"Yes. It had the most beautiful shoreline."

Mrs. Bennet watched her brother and his wife with a terse little smile, and then disappeared into the kitchen to check on the roasted potatoes in the oven. She wasn't Maureen's biggest fan, having been put off from the very beginning by her black dreads and the nose stud she wore.

Across the table, Liam watched Mason and Becca accidentally brush shoulders—Mason blushed and apologized, which just made her giggle. Liam smiled and looked into his plate.

"And where to after that, Uncle Frank?" asked Ben eagerly.

"England," Frank told him. "Maureen has been trying to drag me back there since our honeymoon. Nothing urban, though—mainly stately homes and mansions and castles. The trouble is, our staff photographer can't make the trip, so we're looking for a replacement."

"You should take Jamie with you," Liam said.

Jamie turned, shocked.

"Oh?" Maureen smiled. "Jamie, are you good with a camera?"

"He's good," Liam answered for him. "He was always the more artistic one in the family. He just interned with an art director in Manhattan. *And* he just started a full-time position with a graphic design company."

Jamie shot him a look. He had only started a week ago. "Liam, I don't know much about photography besides basic—"

"Basic is good," Liam cut him off. "*Clean*, you know?"

Mr. Bennet started to smile.

"We would love to have you," Maureen encouraged. "But we don't go to England until March."

"Take him with you to Washington, then."

"Liam—"

"Shush."

Liam needled his brother until he couldn't *not* go. After all, a getaway across the country was what he needed after his stressful semester.

After dinner, they all took to the living room. Liam sat with his father, both in identical positions, with their ankles crossed atop the coffee table. A fire was crackling in the hearth, tended to a little too diligently by Ben, who kept jabbing at the firewood with a poker.

"Ben," Liam warned, yawning. "Don't sit too close."

"You know," Mr. Bennet murmured, "you are fiercely protective of your brothers. Makes me a little proud."

"Oh, don't get sentimental, Dad," Liam joked. "It ages you."

Mrs. Bennet was asleep on the loveseat. Nate had his head on her lap, a plaid blanket drawn up around his shoulders. Mason and Becca were gone and most likely in his bedroom.

"I believe a rite of passage is happening upstairs." Liam mimed a silent trumpet fanfare.

"Don't be crass," his father warned. "I told him there's a box of condoms in the medicine cabinet—God knows how long they've been expired."

"I'm crass, huh?"

"I am just being *helpful*."

Liam snorted.

Mr. Bennet folded his hands across his belly. "Your mother tells me that Charlotte is dating my nephew."

"She is correct."

"God help her," he sighed.

"She's been asking me nonstop to fly up there," said Liam. "The godmother is offering to pay for airfare."

"And you're turning that down?"

"I just know that she's asking me to attend an engagement party or something." He scowled, crossing his arms. "They're after that inheritance, and if I attend all these bullshit celebrations, doesn't that mean that I condone her behavior? That I'm supporting a sham marriage?"

Mr. Bennet was quiet for a while. Then he said, "It could just mean that you're supporting your best friend—unconditionally."

"Maybe," he said quietly.

"Plus, free airfare."

"Economy class too."

"Son. *Go.*"

Liam laughed.

"I'm serious," Mr. Bennet said. "You've also had a stressful semester. You will be cooped up in this house for a good few weeks before school starts, I assure you—so what's a week to yourself and some friends across the pond?"

Liam knew he was right. He checked his phone. Two missed calls from Charlotte. He had been staring at the notification all night. He sighed, considering it.

He turned. "Bring you back a Paddington?"

"No. You bring me back a sonic screwdriver—get your *mother* a Paddington Bear."

CHAPTER EIGHTEEN

CHARLOTTE WAS overjoyed to see him three days later at Heathrow Airport. They had an emotional embrace outside the terminal, punctuated only by Bill Collins' time-conscious sighs. Liam strapped his messenger bag across his chest and hoisted his duffel bag overhead.

"I heard it's raining. *Sucks*. Come back home." He smiled at Charlotte.

"It's only drizzling a bit," said Charlotte. "How was your flight?" They began to walk toward the baggage carousel, for Liam's lone suitcase.

"I slept through most of it," he answered. "But then I woke up six hours through with the worst leg cramp, so I did my fair share of laps around the plane. Got yelled at by like three flight attendants."

Charlotte snorted. As they waited, Liam had time to properly examine his friend. She looked a lot prettier. A lot classier—in a black dress, a trench coat, and nude pumps. She had worn very minimal makeup before, but now her eyes were rimmed with brown kohl, her lashes long and black. "Are you wearing blush?" he asked her.

She blushed, ironically. "Maybe."

"My godmother," Bill said, and cleared his throat self-importantly, "has been shopping the *whole* week with Charlotte to buy her a new wedding and honeymoon wardrobe. She also has a professional makeup artist on call."

"For all your cosmetic emergencies," Liam quipped. "Is this your way of telling me that you're officially engaged?"

"I guess it is," she said. She wasn't looking at him, but pretended to watch for his luggage.

"Congratulations," Liam said softly.

Charlotte turned and gave him a thin smile.

The drive to the Rosings estate took two and a half hours from Heathrow. Liam had a feeling that Collins didn't know where he was going. When they were finally en route to Kent, Liam could only tolerate ten minutes of Collins' yammering before he hooked in his headphones and fell asleep to his music.

His joints ached even more when he woke up because he had slept with his neck craned against the window. When they parked in the long, winding driveway, Liam jumped out and stretched. To his surprise, two doormen deftly took all the luggage from him and carried it to the foyer.

Rosings itself was a building in the middle of a facelift. It was ancient, undoubtedly. But scaffolding was set up along the outside of the house, propped against the stucco, and plastic film was wrapped over the railings and walls.

It gave the whole place an unfinished vibe, as if it would never be completed in this century.

When they reached the main staircase, Collins gave Liam his instructions in a very urgent whisper. "Dinner is in an hour. Please go wash up and dress accordingly. I know this may be asking you too much, given what you're wearing *now*—"

"Just wear whatever you brought that's best." Charlotte smiled at him.

Collins gave his fiancée a pained look.

Liam pursed his lips, nodded, and headed upstairs.

He showered quickly, propped open his suitcase, and took a gander inside. It didn't look very promising. "Charlotte's instructions it is." He pulled on a black T-shirt and blue jeans, and ran a hand through his still-damp hair.

When he went downstairs, he made the mistake of turning into the empty dining room before he realized that the chatter was coming from the parlor. Cautiously, Liam walked down the hall and made a right.

The parlor seemed to be the only room not marred by construction, but it was sickeningly opulent. There were many dead animals mounted to the wall, and crystal candelabras. The entire room was dim, and the only high point seemed to be the gleaming, black, baby grand piano in the corner by the stone fireplace.

An older woman sat in the loveseat with her white hands folded delicately over her skirt. Her lips twisted into a smile. "Ah, this must be your friend."

Charlotte and Collins nodded eagerly before her, so Liam introduced himself, extending his hand. "Hello. I'm Liam Bennet."

"This is Lady Catherine de Bourgh," Collins informed him. "She is my godmother, and the reason why we can all stay in such lavish accommodations."

"Indeed." Catherine gave a lyrical little laugh. "Collins, you try a little too hard. His father and my husband were best friends, you see. They went to Cambridge together. Why he moved to America afterwards, I will never understand."

Liam pressed his lips together and shrugged.

"This is my stepdaughter, Violet."

His eyes shifted and his mouth opened. To Catherine's right sat a pale wisp of a girl, her honey-blonde hair pulled back into a severe bun. Her eyes were the color of water, and her cheekbones were as prominent as her mother's, despite the lack of biological relation. All Liam wanted to do was plant her in the sunlight and feed her turkey sandwiches.

Violet de Bourgh.

With a jolt, he remembered her from the tabloids—Darcy leading her intimately away from the cameras. So this was his girl….

"Pleasure to meet you." Liam shook her cool hand. She just smiled. For an heiress, she seemed terminally shy.

"Where is my nephew?" Catherine asked one of her maids. "Is he still out by the pool?"

"Yes, ma'am."

"Pool?" Liam whispered to Charlotte.

She nodded. "They have an indoor pool. Left wing of the estate."

A young man with a crest of red hair suddenly entered the room, talking with his mouth full and carrying a handful of mini chocolate éclairs. "Rosie," he told the maid, "I don't know where you bought these from, but they are *phenomenal*."

"Richard," Catherine sighed. "*Manners*."

"Oh." He turned, suddenly aware of his audience. He found the only unfamiliar face in the room, wiped his hand clean of crumbs, and shook Liam's hand. "You must be Liam."

"Nice to meet you." He smiled.

"I've heard a lot about you." Richard smiled cryptically. "I'm the dreaded nephew."

"Dread*ful*," Collins corrected.

"Pipe down, Collins," he shot back.

Liam was delighted.

"Richard." His aunt cleared her throat. "Make yourself useful and show Liam the rest of the grounds. And get your cousin out of the pool. Dinner will be served soon."

"Aye." Richard mock-saluted. He cocked his head toward the doorway, and Liam followed him out. "Onward march to the pool. It's massive. Did you bring some trunks?"

"Nope," Liam said.

He tsked. "So, you're Charlotte's best friend?"

"Since we were kids."

"She's adorable. It's a damn shame that Collins snatched her up first."

"Oh, it's not too late," Liam assured him. "I can give you some pointers."

"You don't like him either?" He raised his eyebrows.

"Collins?" Liam snorted. "I'd be surprised if his own mother liked him."

Richard grinned. "Catherine tolerates him. But then again, he's only kissing her ass so that she eventually hires him as her personal counsel. Collins thought he would be her instant hire after he finished law school, but Catherine's making him work for it."

Liam nodded, impressed. "Good for her."

The long corridor winded down to a set of double french doors. Richard propped one open and allowed his guest to pass. Once inside, Liam marveled. The poolroom was massive. Large bay windows allowed the last of the dying sunlight to filter through.

The other nephew was doing laps, bobbing to the surface to take a gaping breath before he disappeared under the water again. He was quick and concentrated, a properly trained swimmer.

"Hey!" Richard aimed a pair of goggles at him like a slingshot. He released them, and they pegged his cousin on the head.

He wasn't fazed. Instead, he finished the lap and pulled himself out of the water. Liam felt his entire face flood with color. Will Darcy propped himself by the pool's edge and smoothed his wet hair out of his eyes.

"Hello," he said.

"Hey…." Liam opened his mouth stupidly.

Darcy got up and moved past him to fetch a towel. Liam caught a quick glance of broad shoulders and long defined torso and looked away.

"Will, Aunt Catherine wants you at the dinner table in about thirty seconds," Richard told him.

"I bet she does," Darcy sighed, slinging the blue towel around his neck.

"*You* two are cousins," Liam said, feeling dumb.

"'Fraid so," Richard sighed. "His mother and mine were sisters."

"Catherine's the third sister?"

"Correct-o."

Liam scratched his head, still puzzled.

"You'll have to give me two minutes to change," Darcy told his cousin gruffly. "Catherine sets extremely unrealistic expectations." He disappeared into the changing rooms.

Liam crouched down by the pool and dipped his fingers in. The water was warm. "Heated pool, huh?"

"Yep."

He drew his hand back and watched the ripples expand.

At dinner, all the guests had to wait for Catherine to sit before they could be seated themselves. Liam found it to be an odd, old-fashioned sort of quirk. He sat beside Charlotte, with Darcy and Richard directly across from him. To Charlotte's left sat her fiancé, and at the head of the table, Catherine, with Violet at her left next to Darcy.

Violet and Darcy barely interacted, strangely enough. Liam wondered if they were keeping it to a minimum because of her stepmother.

His mind did the math quickly. *Catherine's stepdaughter and her nephew dating....* His lip curled. *How very Brady Bunch.*

"How are your brothers?" Darcy suddenly asked him. Liam started.

"They're fine, thank you."

"You know my nephew?" Catherine asked Liam pointedly.

"Yes, ma'am," he said. "We met around Hartford and Oakham this past summer."

"Liam's brother interned for our company this year," Darcy told his aunt. "He's quite skilled at art direction."

Lady Catherine made a noncommittal noise in the back of her throat, and then turned to Rosie to ask her to serve the soup.

Liam watched Darcy with surprise. Darcy's blue eyes flickered to his, and Liam looked back to his empty plate.

Lady Catherine began a discussion about the engagement. They were to go wedding-dress shopping in the morning; she had already made an appointment at the boutique. Herb-crusted salmon was to be served at the bridal shower, along with a warm brioche....

"I am probably going to stab myself in the eye, with this fork," Richard informed his cousin.

"Do as you please, but I think that will just increase her volume," Darcy said in a hushed whisper.

"If anything, she'll just be upset that you got blood on the tablecloth," Liam agreed, shrugging as he popped a piece of bread into his mouth.

"It is a divine tablecloth," Richard said dryly.

"Liam," Catherine interrupted again. "What are you studying at university?"

"English, ma'am."

Her blue eyes narrowed, and suddenly Liam saw the family resemblance quite clearly. "What do you plan to do with that?"

"Burger flipping," he answered happily. He took in a spoonful of soup and smiled.

Darcy coughed and Richard hit him on the back. "Down the wrong tube, eh, Willis?"

Darcy motioned at his throat and nodded at his aunt, still coughing. Liam raised his eyebrows, amused.

"Do drink some water, William," Catherine told him.

Charlotte spoke up then. "Liam has his heart set on teaching. He's also a very talented writer—I've read his stuff."

"Oh?" said Catherine. "That hardly sounds practical. There is quite the teaching shortage these days. I know your country is even worse off with its budget cuts. It's so *difficult* to find a proper education these days. Good luck to you."

"Thank you," said Liam tersely.

"You have an ice cube's shot in hell," Richard whispered, "but every happiness to you."

Liam chuckled and had to set his spoon down.

Darcy was watching Liam again. "I've never read your writing."

He pressed his lips together. "Neither have a lot of people. Are you asking to?"

"I might be. What do you write?"

"Uh…." Liam shrugged, playing with the edge of the tablecloth. "Just some short stories. Nothing very groundbreaking."

"You don't have to discredit yourself," Darcy replied. "Let somebody else decide that."

Liam opened his mouth.

"So, I was telling Charlotte this yesterday." Richard scratched his ginger beard thoughtfully. "Or two days ago. *Anyway*. New Year's Eve,

I am taking us all to Webster. Dress accordingly. We're going to get silly."

"What's Webster?" Darcy asked.

"A club down in Hammersmith."

"And *you're* driving us all the way to London?" he asked doubtfully.

"No, I'm asking Clarence. Aunt Cathy's chauffeur," he explained to Liam. "I wish I could take him home with me. He is the sweetest old man I have ever met."

"Where is home for you?" Liam asked.

"Santa Barbara," Richard replied. "I'm still rusty on the plans for tomorrow. I don't know what there is to do around here besides marinate in the pool."

"It's an excellent pool," Darcy assured him.

After dinner, they all adjourned to the parlor again for tea. "How quaint," Liam murmured, lifting the delicate porcelain cup out of its saucer.

Richard took his seat at the baby grand before him and, to Liam's surprise, plucked out some very pretty notes. He recognized Beethoven. "What symphony is that?"

"Seven," Richard answered. "It's the second movement."

"You're a musician."

"The guitar is more my instrument," he said. "But I had to suffer through piano lessons throughout my childhood and adolescence. Many piano recitals. Mom wanted me to be proficient." On cue, he hit the ugliest keys. They both winced.

"Richard!" Catherine shouted. "*Decorum.*"

He mimed her expression but slid the cover down. He got up. "You should have a go."

"All right." Liam smiled and took a seat. "Hope you like scales and 'Ode to Joy.'"

"I *love* it. Have you heard Kanye's cover?"

Darcy joined them. He had been running his fingers through his hair as it dried, and now it stuck up on end in messy tufts. Liam fought a smile. It was nice seeing him like that, though—it somehow humanized him.

"You play very well," Darcy deadpanned.

Liam smirked and finished his scales. "Then by all means, Mr. Darcy, kindly place your tips in that teacup over there."

Darcy rubbed his mouth.

"Tell me, Liam." Richard leaned his elbows against the baby grand. "Was my cousin friendly to you in Philadelphia?"

"University District is about fifteen minutes outside of the city," Liam clarified. "And no."

Darcy crossed his arms over his chest. "I was polite."

"He was rude and antisocial," he countered casually. "I first met him at a party and he spoke to nobody beyond the people that he came there with."

"I didn't *know* anybody—"

"Hi," Liam cut him off, "is a really good place to start."

Lady Catherine summoned Richard, and he left with a sigh, leaving his companions alone. Liam hesitated, and then continued to play a choppy rendition of "Moonlight Sonata."

"It's difficult for me to fake it," Darcy said urgently. Liam looked up with a start and he continued. "I'm not good at small talk and I have difficulty looking like I care about other people's concerns when I really don't. I don't pick up on tones. I'm just not good at it. I find it easier to be silent when there is nothing important to be said."

"Well—" Liam cocked his head thoughtfully. "—I'm not good at playing the piano. But I'm sure if I *practiced*, I might be able to get something beautiful out of it someday." He looked up at him. "See how that works?"

Darcy stared at him pensively for a while. Then Lady Catherine interrupted their shared silence. "William, come *here*. Tell me how Georgiana is doing."

He pursed his lips and turned, leaving Liam alone.

CHAPTER NINETEEN

LIAM SPENT upward of three hours in the bridal boutique. He heartily gave his opinion on each dress for the first hour and a half, before he resigned himself to the cushiony floral armchair and tried to beat his highest score of Tetris on his cell phone.

Well, that was the plan before his phone hit 10 percent battery level. "Shit," he muttered, tossing it onto the end table.

Charlotte marched out with the skirts of her newest gown bunched up in her hands, exposing the brown suede riding boots she wore underneath. Liam beamed.

"What's cooking, good looking?"

"You bailed." Charlotte pouted. "Are we boring you? Does this not look pretty?"

"It looks very pretty—" He hesitated. "To be honest, I'm pretty partial to the second one you tried on. But Charlotte—"

"Really?" she mumbled distractedly, fixing her cap sleeves. "But this one is A-line, which is super flattering."

"*Charlotte.*"

"What?"

"Shouldn't your mother be here?" he asked her.

Charlotte let out a heavy sigh. She pivoted her hands on her hips. "I told her two weeks ago and she was furious. She refuses to come out here."

Liam chewed the inside of his cheek.

"Don't say it." She pointed a finger at him. "I'm still going to go through with it."

"Are you sure?" he asked softly.

"Yes."

"Okay."

"Charlotte!" They both jumped at Catherine's voice. "Come look at this fabric."

"Coming!" Charlotte blinked and cleared her throat, smoothing her hair fretfully. "Now your honest opinion—what do you think of this dress?"

He hesitated. "Looks like Lindsay Lohan's zombie-bride Halloween costume from *Mean Girls*."

"See? That's all I need you to do. Thank you." Charlotte beamed, bustling back into the dressing room.

Liam half smiled. His phone began to ring.

"Hello?"

Jamie's voice greeted him. "Hey, brother. How's Jolly Old England?"

"It was better before you called it that," Liam said. He got up and walked to the front of the boutique, pacing. "Are you enjoying your trip?"

"Yeah, very much so," he said. "Frank and Maureen are such well-seasoned travelers. I feel like they know of every hole-in-the-wall place to ever exist."

"How's the park?"

"Breathtaking. I think I might actually take up photography as a serious hobby now. Who knew?"

Liam smiled. "I'm glad. Is that volcano active?"

"Yes, but the chances of it erupting are very low." Jamie paused. "I hope. We're exploring Seattle tomorrow. What are you up to?"

"Offering what little moral support I have while Charlotte tries on wedding dresses."

"Ooh." Jamie was probably making a face. "Poor girl. Do you really think she'll go through with this?"

"I don't know," Liam muttered. He rearranged a centerpiece, a vase full of fake plastic lemons, before a sales associate glowered at him. "I hope not, but it's not my decision to make."

"At least you get to see her, though. How's the rest of the company?"

Liam bit his lip. He considered telling him that Will Darcy was here. But he knew that his brother would automatically think of Bingley. He thought better of reopening a wound that was just starting to heal.

"Good," he muttered. "Not much to write home about."

Jamie had to go soon after, and Liam ended the conversation with a strange mixture of guilt and reassurance.

Catherine de Bourgh left the boutique a few minutes later for a hair appointment. This left the rest of the afternoon to Charlotte and Liam. They walked along the cramped but pleasing streets of Rosings in Kent, window-shopping, before they stopped at a bistro to get something to eat.

Liam took a bite out of his turkey sandwich and stared past their booth, thinking of his brother. Charlotte stirred her chai absently and tried not to look her best friend in the eye.

"So…," she began. "You all set for New Year's Eve tomorrow, or do I have to go shopping with you?"

Liam fixed her with a stern look. "You *don't* have to go shopping with me. I have a nice button-down I'll just wear with jeans. I won't embarrass you in a Hartford crewneck or anything."

"Good," Charlotte chirped. She popped a french fry into her mouth. "So how did you finish the semester?"

He shrugged. "I don't know my exam scores yet, but I feel pretty confident about them. Otherwise, I just spent all my time in the library or at work, drinking coffee at both. Nursed Jamie's broken heart. Met with Ann a couple times."

"My replacement," she said without missing a beat.

"She is *not* your replacement." Liam rolled his eyes. "I can be friends with other people."

"Not adorable British pixie girls who give me a best-friend complex," Charlotte clarified, pointing her fork at him. Her shoulders slumped. "No, I'm lying. I met her doing laundry a few times and she's the nicest thing to ever grace this earth. I'm bluffing. How is Jamie?"

Liam chuckled and shook his head. "Jamie's fine—traveling. I decided not to mention seeing Darcy here. Not when he finally seems stable."

"Probably for the best." Charlotte looked up. "Sorry I didn't mention that he would be here. I was preoccupied with engagement stuff. I know you dislike him, but I didn't think it would be such a big deal."

"No, it's all right." Liam took a long sip of his coffee.

"I'm sure you two can find creative ways to avoid each other," Charlotte teased.

"Challenge accepted," he declared.

"You know…," she began. "He's really not that bad. I had a chance to hang out with him for a couple of days before you arrived, and he's actually pretty *nice* once you get to know him."

"Yeah," Liam agreed. "He's nice once you've touched into his inner circle. He's very elitist, Charlotte. Very snobby."

"I didn't get that vibe, though," she said carefully.

Liam shrugged again. "His cousin is practically his opposite."

Charlotte's face lit up with her massive grin. "Oh, Richard is hysterical. That man puts me in stitches."

"He asked about you" Liam smiled.

"What?" Charlotte instantly straightened.

"Said it was a shame that Collins snatched you up first."

She looked confused for a moment, and was quick to shake her head. "He was joking."

"Maybe he was." Liam wiped his mouth with his napkin and set it down. "Maybe he wasn't."

She twirled a strand of her blonde hair and stared into her empty cup. "Shall we get going?"

When they returned to the estate, it was already dark. The mansion looked even more sinister at nighttime. Liam turned in early and fell asleep with his television on, comforted by the light and the background noise. But he slept restlessly that night, his mind uneasy with Jamie and Bingley, with Charlotte's wedding lurking ahead like some great, big, ominous cloud.

He woke around noon the next day.

It was eerily quiet at Rosings. Liam found out from one of the maids that Lady Catherine, Violet, Charlotte, and Collins had gone to church for morning services. It took him quite some time to process this, due to his haze of sleepiness and also due to the fact that Charlotte had always been nonreligious. He pictured her wearing a skirt suit and a big floppy hat with feathers sticking out of it, identical to Lady Catherine's.

He decided to get fresh air. He got his coat from the closet, pulled on his beanie, and headed to the back of the property, where a trail ended at the veranda and another began toward the woods.

The air was cold and crisp; it woke him in a matter of moments. Liam hooked in his headphones and blasted his music. He took a deep breath and began jogging steadily, building up momentum after the first ten minutes.

Don't think. Don't think. Thinking is bad.

He hated that he had lost an entire night's sleep to these stresses that were outside of his control. What was he supposed to do about his best friend? About Jamie? No, the burning in his muscles was a lot more manageable.

Once inside, Rosie fixed him a hot cup of tea. He finished it, thanked her graciously, and disappeared upstairs, where he peeled off his wet, cold clothes and hopped into the shower. He relished its warmth. Then he crawled under the covers and napped for hours.

Richard woke him up around dinnertime. "Dude," he laughed. "You're sleeping New Year's Eve away."

"So?" Liam slurred, switching sides. Pillow creases had left lines on his cheek, and he wiped the drool from his mouth haphazardly. "I'll make a resolution to get up tomorrow."

"Nope, we have plans. We're having dinner and then we're going out to Webster."

Liam couldn't bear the thought of another atrocious dinner with Lady Catherine de Bourgh and her sickly, sort-of-Will's-girlfriend daughter. He screwed his eyes shut and groaned. "*No*.... No more dinners."

"Not even Chinese takeout?" Richard asked innocently.

He couldn't say no to that.

After dinner, the group dressed properly before heading out. Liam shaved, combed his hair, pulled on a gray button-down, and folded the sleeves neatly to his elbows. He pulled on his worn, dark blue jeans, double-knotted his sneakers, and made sure that he smelled reasonably nice.

Charlotte had her hair down and wore a short, tight metallic dress. Liam helped her into her coat. "And gloves, take gloves. It's freezing out."

It had just started to drizzle when they stepped into the driveway. Clarence was waiting with his town car heated and running. Richard handed Liam a hotel keycard. When Liam looked up for an explanation, he told him, "We are *not* driving all the way back to Kent on New Year's Day. I am doing the safe, practical thing here. You're welcome."

Liam slid it into his pocket. He helped Charlotte in while Collins plucked dust particles from the lapel of his suit jacket. Then Collins took the passenger seat beside the driver.

It was a tight squeeze in the back and Liam had unthinkingly placed himself right in the middle of Charlotte and Darcy. Whenever the car turned right, he held his body very rigidly to avoid being thrown into the other man. But on occasion, their knees would brush and neither would look at the other to acknowledge that they had done so.

Webster had three floors to it. The first was designated specifically for dubstep. The other two were indiscernible, but the second seemed to have the best music, as well as the bar.

"You know what New Year's Eve in London means?" Charlotte asked Liam with a sly smile. "We are of drinking age."

"That alone warrants a round of shots." Richard slapped his credit card on the bar top. "On me! Enjoy it while it lasts."

The group toasted to an amazing evening—and then quickly disbanded.

Charlotte dragged her best friend to dance, leaving Collins to awkwardly explore on his own. Darcy stuck to the bar, while Richard hit on as many women as luck would allow him.

Liam felt himself relax for the first time in days. The alcohol loosened his limbs, and he felt the bass of the music reverberate through his chest. They must have danced for at least thirty minutes before Charlotte took off her heels and sat on one of the lounge benches to rest her feet.

"Water!" she shouted in his ear above the music. He nodded and set out toward the bar.

The cluster of people rimming the bar was so thick he could barely get through. Richard yanked him aside, smiling. "You said three shots! You only did two!"

"No, I didn't!" Liam laughed.

"Yes, you did!"

The music died down, replaced with a slow, lover's ballad.

"I have to get Charlotte water—"

"She's a big girl, she can do it herself. *Three* shots." Richard slid the shot glass to him and raised his own. "I know you can do it. Cheers!"

Liam tossed it back and grimaced.

"Attaboy." Richard clapped him on the back. "I have to go find my cousin. I lost him like an hour ago."

"Leave him." Liam waved his hand.

"No," Richard chortled. "I would never!"

"He's an asshole." He shook his head, adamant.

"He is the best friend a man can have," Richard assured Liam. "Rough around the edges, our boy is. But you will never find somebody more loyal."

Liam raised both eyebrows in disbelief.

"Check it out." Richard motioned him forward with two fingers. "I got into a really bad car accident last April. I was living in Jersey at the time. Do you know who drove me to physical therapy three times a week?"

"Will?" Liam ventured to guess.

"If he loves you, he will take a bullet for you. He is the most protective, trustworthy son of a bitch I know. And he is an *excellent* judge of character. You know how many girlfriends of mine he's vetoed?" Richard shook his head. "And he was completely right about them too. Because 99 percent of them were after my family's money."

Liam stared down into his empty shot glass. "How would he know?"

"He doesn't trust people very easily—and for good reason too. He did the same thing for his friend, Charlie. Granted, the man is gay, but that doesn't matter. Money hungry is money hungry."

Liam looked up with a start. "Charlie?"

"Yeah, Charlie Bingley. He's his business partner. Sweet, sweet guy. As I understand it, his ex, Miles, tried to swindle him out of a lot of money. So Will was quick to analyze the new boyfriend, realized he was taking advantage of him too, and cut him loose."

"When was this?" he asked coolly.

"I don't know; a couple of months back."

Richard ordered two bottles of water then. He left a couple of bills on the table and tossed Liam a bottle. "Stay hydrated. I'm serious. I have to go find a pretty girl to kiss—it's five till midnight." He clapped him on the back again and left him there.

Liam barely processed his words. He clenched his jaw and shut his eyes. *Darcy separated them.*

He looked toward the dance floor. Charlotte had found Collins; they were dancing front and center, Charlotte barefoot with her heels raised high above her head, a smile on her face as she rocked her hips back and forth. Her fiancé tried awkwardly to keep up.

Shaking, Liam moved to the back of the club, to the narrow corridor that housed the restrooms. It was cool and dark back here, and the music was less penetrating. He leaned against the wall; he felt light-headed.

The music screeched to a halt and the countdown from sixty began. Liam unbuttoned his top button and raked a hand through his hair. He felt unbearably hot.

Thirty-five... thirty-four....

He wondered where he had left his coat.

Twenty... nineteen....

That bastard....

Ten...nine....

Somebody was walking toward him, but his body felt too lethargic to stand properly and assert itself. Will Darcy's face came looming into view then; he looked concerned. "Are you all right?"

"Piss off," Liam muttered, leaning his hands on his thighs. "Oh, look at that, I'm learning the slang."

"Come on." Darcy took his hand and led him toward the back exit. "Let's get you out of here."

"I feel *fine.*"

"You look like shit."

One....

"Fuck you." The club erupted in noise and celebrations. "Happy New Year."

CHAPTER TWENTY

THE HUNSFORD Inn, despite its rustic connotation, was a surprisingly upscale establishment. Liam couldn't tell if it was his buzzed state that made him fascinated by the marble pillars in the lobby, or if he had a genuine appreciation for interior design now. He wandered while Darcy spoke to the concierge; then Darcy pulled him along to the elevators.

An image of a lion toting its cub by the scruff of its neck came quickly to mind, but Liam shook his head and cleared it away, as if dusting off cobwebs.

Once in the room, Darcy turned the heat on and supplied Liam with lots of water. Why he seemed so troubled was beyond Liam's comprehension. But he knew that he could properly call him out on his despicable behavior once the room stopped spinning….

Twenty minutes later, his head was starting to clear. Darcy smiled. "You're a lightweight. How adorable."

"I hate your guts," Liam said miserably.

He was still chuckling. "Come on. I have aspirin in my room. Take two and you'll sleep the rest of the night."

Liam got up with him, but they barely made it to the door. Darcy turned to look at him, smiling his stupid, confident, shit-eating grin, and suddenly Liam couldn't bridle his irritation—he dealt him a swift uppercut to the jaw.

The force of the blow sent Darcy hurtling to the wall, and he stopped Liam just as he was about to hit him again. "What the hell is *wrong* with you?"

"What's wrong with me?" Liam thrashed against him, catching him in the ribs. "What's wrong with *me*?"

"Yes, what's wrong with *you*," Darcy spat out. He shoved the other man back two feet. "Goddammit, Liam, control yourself!"

"You got a *lot* of fucking nerve," Liam yelled, swinging at him again.

Darcy was prepared this time; he landed a punch on his left cheekbone before he slammed Liam against the door, struggling to pin him. "Calm down. Calm *down*. I'm sorry I did that. I'm sorry. I don't want to hurt you. Believe me, I don't."

Liam struggled against him for a good two minutes before he slumped and began to laugh helplessly. "*Wiry*, Mom said. She was right."

Darcy stared at him, breathless. "Why did you hit me?"

"I've been itching to hit you since Netherfield. I really have. I really, *really* have. I just forgot to become a bodybuilder beforehand."

"If this is about your brother—" Darcy began.

"*It is*. Can you let go of me now? I need to chew you out."

"Yeah." Darcy nodded. He looked puzzled, as if struggling to regain his composure. He didn't let go. He remained pressed up against him, fistfuls of Liam's shirt in both hands.

Liam stared at him with his brow furrowed, his mouth slightly open.

Darcy's hands were gripping his collar tightly. His blue eyes met his. There was a mark of desperation on his face, and something else... something Liam didn't necessarily want to read into. Like the spike of anxiety he had felt in the car with him.

The same anxiety he felt now.

"Listen—" Liam started.

Without another word, Darcy took a step forward and fit his lips against Liam's. Liam felt his body grow numb in a vague sort of paralysis—felt his thoughts scatter like marbles.

What the hell is he doing?

What's going on?

What...?

Liam thought for a flash of a moment to shove him off roughly. Hurl him into the mirror, shattering it to pieces. Had he lost his *mind*?

But then Darcy pushed him against the wall, determined in his conviction, and unsnapped the button of his trousers.

It knocked the wind out of his body. Liam sucked in a breath. "Wait."

Darcy kissed him again. Liam felt a slow heat creep into his limbs. His tongue grazed his bottom lip, tentative. And then Darcy kissed him with more certainty, his fingertips slipping below the waistband of Liam's jeans, curling around him....

Liam shuddered.

Darcy pressed hot, open-mouthed kisses down his neck. Liam's hands slid down Darcy's chest, curling of their own volition, grasping the fabric of his shirt—he leaned into the kiss now, lips fumbling. His fingers trailed down to Darcy's narrow waist, his fingertips skimming the hot skin beneath the hem of Darcy's shirt.

Darcy rested his forehead against his. His eyes fell shut, his lips parted, and he breathed, "You don't know how long I've been fighting myself on this."

Liam's heart thudded in his chest, so frantically that he thought for a moment it might burst and this might all be over. He pushed Darcy back and put distance between the two of them. Then he slid down the wall until he was sitting with his knees bent. Liam shut his eyes.

"I'm sorry," Darcy said softly.

Liam was shaking his head; his eyes were still pressed shut. The other man knelt down before him. He touched the cut on his cheek, and Liam pulled back reflexively, wincing.

"Liam, I can't seem to stay away from you. I've been trying very hard," Darcy said urgently. "Every fiber of my being is screaming at me to abandon this. Your age, your family, your circumstances. This is all wrong. It's been the thorn in my side for *months*."

Liam opened his eyes. He was struggling to dissect his thoughts, but he couldn't neglect the irony of the situation. "That's very flattering of you, Darcy," he said in a deadpan. "Allow me to save you a lot of grief and pluck out the thorn: I hate you."

Darcy rubbed his cheek. "You kissed me back."

Liam looked at him. He noted his state of undress, the buttons undone, the hair mussed, the beginnings of bruising near his strong, handsome jaw... he had done all of that.

And he had wanted him too. More than anything. That delicious thrumming in his body, the want for more.... God, that hadn't happened with anybody. His hands were still shaking. He couldn't deny his attraction to Darcy any longer. After all, what had been building between them all these weeks?

How could I be so stupid?

How could I have not known?

"Jamie," he said, feeling helpless.

"If your objection is because of your brother," Darcy began, "then I apologize. I was looking out for Charlie's best interests. I know your brother is important to you. But Charlie is the brother I never had."

Liam looked up, alert now. "My brother is one of many reasons to this objection. *Jamie* would have been Charlie's best interests," he told him. "He was in love with him."

"He never told him that—"

"Because that's so easy to do, right?" Liam scowled.

A heavy silence passed.

"He seemed unattached." Darcy rose to his feet. Liam followed suit. "Every time I saw them together, it was obvious to me that Charlie felt more strongly of the two."

"That's because Jamie is *quiet*, you idiot. He doesn't advertise his feelings to the world," Liam explained, sighing in frustration. He leaned back against the wall. "Did that slip under your professional relationship expertise, Will? Charlie *broke* his heart."

Darcy clenched his jaw and stared to the side. Liam could tell— he despised being wrong. It looked like it physically hurt him. *Good.*

He wanted him to hurt.

He also wanted to kiss him again.

He mostly wanted to sedate himself with aspirin and fall into a deep, sated sleep.

"Any other qualms?" Darcy asked, spreading his hands out before him. He was staring at Liam now, his expression a muddled combination of hurt and frustration.

"Yes. I want to hear your excuse for cheating George Wickham out of your father's will."

"*I* cheated George Wickham out of my father's will?" Darcy looked genuinely amused. He folded his arms across his chest. "This is an interesting development. Tell me more."

"Oh, fuck you," Liam snapped. "Don't patronize me."

"*This* is what you're basing your opinion of me on?" Darcy demanded. "I suggest you get your facts straight before you make allegations like that."

"I do have my facts straight."

"Clearly you don't." Darcy laughed mirthlessly. "You think that I'm some meddlesome, lying, manipulative bastard, Liam. You really do. Thank you for bringing this all to light. I can understand your choice perfectly now."

Liam started, "You have given me no reason to think otherwise—"

"I think you're afraid," Darcy cut him off, taking a step toward him. "I think you're scared *shitless* of what this is, and you're hiding behind these fallacies like they're made of concrete—"

"Do you *really* think that your personality lends itself to any other explanation?" Liam demanded furiously. "Do you think I can believe *you*? These opinions haven't been gathered overnight, Darcy. Since day one, you've been the most unbearable, arrogant, *unlikeable* asshole—I had zero desire to make you a part of my life."

Darcy fell silent. Liam swallowed the big lump that had been forming in his throat.

"I'm sorry for ruining your evening," Darcy said quietly. "And I hope you have a good night."

Darcy collected his things and closed the door behind him.

Liam gaped at the emptiness of the room, feeling wretched. He closed his eyes again.

CHAPTER TWENTY-ONE

THE GROUP that met outside the hotel entrance at ten in the morning was washed out and sleep-deprived, a dim shadow of their vibrant, champagne-swilling selves.

Charlotte's eyeliner was smudged and her stockings had a long tear along her right thigh. She squinted at Richard's hair, and Liam imagined that the shock of red against the backdrop of gray, sleepy London had to be overpowering her hangover. Richard and Charlotte shared a cigarette and Bill Collins glowered his disapproval.

It was only four of them who waited by the curb for the driver to pull the car around. Darcy was returning room keys in the lobby. Each had, as of yet, successfully ignored the other's existence. Liam buried his hands in his pockets. Richard blew a plume of smoke in his face.

It was a painfully long car ride, especially when the clouds knit together and rain began to tap against the windshield. Liam felt stiff. Charlotte sat next to him. She was resting her head against his shoulder, and he tried to ignore the wisps of blonde hair that tickled his neck.

Liam had his headphones in, and he had put on some track that was melancholy and introspective, just to match the weather. He couldn't help but glance at Darcy in the passenger seat. The other man stared straight ahead, never looking around, his shoulders squared.

Liam swallowed and looked away.

"Your shoulder is bony," Charlotte said quietly. She pivoted her face up to his, gray eyes regarding him through heavy lids. He smiled at her, and she smiled back. "You are a beautiful boy."

"Are you still drunk?" he murmured. He fixed the edge of her coat, which was now being used as a blanket.

She burrowed her face into the crook of his neck and dozed off again. Liam was aware of Richard's eyes on them, cool and perceptive.

HE WAS to spend one night in Kent before his flight the next day. Liam busied himself packing, slowly, to avoid Rosings' inhabitants. But he couldn't escape Charlotte. She had showered and napped and eaten brunch, and entered his room bright-eyed.

Charlotte rested a mug of coffee on the dresser, and Liam glanced over his shoulder. "It's a little late for coffee."

"Sweetheart, have you *seen* you?" she chuckled. "You clearly never went to bed last night."

"Did you?"

"Nope." Charlotte popped the word off her lips. She was sitting on the edge of his bed now, tracing patterns onto the duvet. "*Collins* did. But uh… Richard and I had other plans."

Liam stood up. "You didn't."

She was smiling secretively, but then her shoulders slumped and she laughed. "*No.* I snuck out and met him in his room. Let's just say there were a couple late-night sojourns into the Jacuzzi."

"Sojourns? How far did that go?"

"I don't kiss and tell."

"Please," he said dryly, tossing his T-shirt into his duffel bag. "You do it *all* and tell. I've been hearing intimate details since Danny Kesselman grazed your boob in eighth-grade gym class."

"That was intentional." Charlotte pointed at him. "And I really like him—it's a problem."

"Danny?" Liam teased.

Charlotte hurled a pillow at him. "Shut up." She grinned. "We didn't do anything. But it was tense and we were both being good and I'm… confused."

"Well, of course you didn't do anything. Richard was sharing a room with his cousin."

"Didn't matter. I didn't see Will at all until the morning." A beat. "Which is a little suspicious. Secret party animal?"

Liam made a noise of agreement in the back of his throat and folded his T-shirts with an unparalleled concentration.

"I didn't see you either," Charlotte said softly, drumming her fingers against her mouth. Her eyes narrowed. "You jerk. Did you two *bond*?"

"No. I didn't see him."

"Well, you didn't *sleep*," she argued. "What did you do?"

"Wandered drunkenly down the hall and robbed other guests."

She got up. "You're sharp, Bennet, but not that sharp. I'll find out sooner or later."

"*Pfft.*" Liam threw her a look.

When the door closed, he felt the muscles of his shoulders loosen and relax. He shut his eyes and dropped the T-shirt he had been trying to fold three times. "Jesus," he muttered, and pinched the bridge of his nose.

Around dinnertime, Richard caught him in the kitchen, staring at his laptop. "You hungry?" he asked, and Liam started. "I'm making pasta."

"Yeah. Sounds good."

"You know," said Richard whimsically after a while, as he brought the pot to boil, "I was the sous-chef at Il Tratorio in Santa Barbara."

"Were you really?"

"No. But I dated her, and I learned how to make a really mean plate of penne alla vodka."

Liam snorted and turned back to his laptop. His final grades had just been posted.

Richard was surprisingly skilled at cooking. He filled a bowl with penne, topped it with grated Parmesan cheese, and passed it across the counter to Liam.

"Shit." Liam set his spoon down. "Rich, this is *good*."

"Way to suppress your shock," he muttered, wiping down the sink. He took off his apron and threw it over a barstool. "So... you and Charlotte. You're friends, right?"

"Oh, don't worry, I'm no threat to you." He smirked. "Her *fiancé*, on the other hand—"

"Yeah," he sighed, spreading his arms wide on the countertop. "I'm not even the type of guy to do this—*stop laughing*—I mean it! I don't steal women! But she's just... I like her."

"She's okay," Liam deadpanned, taking another bite. After a moment, he said, "Your time together is limited. I mean, if Collins wasn't in the picture, you would still have to deal with living on opposite coasts."

"If Collins wasn't in the picture, we never would have met."

"That's right. Oh Fate," Liam said, "what an ironic bitch."

Richard watched him, and a slow smile spread out across his face. "I can see why Will likes you."

Liam colored. He looked back down into his bowl. Richard was being too perceptive now, staring at him intently.

"So," Liam said lightly, hopping off the barstool. "Any plans to visit the East Coast anytime soon?"

"Well, I'm in England for the next two weeks on holiday," Richard told him. He kindly took his bowl from him and washed it in the sink. "Then I'm headed back to California for work, but who knows? I visit the UK more than the East Coast."

"It must be nice to have family live here."

"Oh, this is nothing." Richard dried his hands. "Have you seen where my cousins live? Pemberley. It's fucking amazing. I think it's been featured on the Travel Channel at least three times."

"No, I haven't," said Liam.

"It's hours from here, but maybe you should see it before you leave." Richard smiled. "My little cousin should be home— Georgiana."

"My flight is in the morning." Liam smiled, unapologetic. The last thing he wanted was a trip to Darcy Manor, walking the spooky, hallowed halls and suffering through insipid conversations with the frigid female version of William Darcy.

Richard shrugged.

Liam retreated into his room after dinner. He felt beat-up, weary and exhausted physically and from the constant struggle to stifle his own thoughts. He didn't want to think, or *examine*, or reflect.

Liam fell asleep early and woke up early. A quick jog outside cleared his mind, and the cold air reenergized him. Once inside, he closed the door behind him and sank onto the last step of the main staircase. He slid off his hood and ran his hands through his hair. Then he covered his eyes. His heart was racing.

He heard footsteps down the hall and knew better than to flinch when Will Darcy said, "Hey."

Liam turned.

Darcy was on his way out, but didn't have any luggage with him. He had his coat on and car keys in his hand. Liam stood up.

Wordlessly, Darcy handed him a white envelope. "I guess you can trash this, if you really want to. At least wait until I leave. But I would really appreciate it if you read it. I wanted to address some of the things that were said against me the other night."

He was still holding out the envelope. Liam's gaze lowered, and he saw his hand mechanically take it.

"Okay," he said.

Darcy nodded once, very slightly. His blue eyes looked nearly gray in the wan morning light.

And then he was gone, and the door clicked shut behind him. Liam looked at the white envelope, the elegant penmanship that spelled out his first name.

When he turned around, Charlotte was watching him in silence from the kitchen doorway. Her hair was gathered into a scrappy ponytail, and she took a long, loaded sip from her coffee mug.

"Morning," Liam said. He shrugged out of his jacket and walked past her into the kitchen.

Charlotte's gaze followed him while he helped himself to the pot of coffee. "Something happen between you and Will?" she asked abruptly.

"No."

"*Liam.*"

"What?" He looked up from stirring his coffee.

She pivoted her hands on her hips, and then gestured out to the foyer. "What was that?"

He shrugged. "Just a misunderstanding."

"Why are you shaking?" she asked softly.

Liam set his spoon down and took a deep breath. He ran his fingers through his hair again. "I'm just not dealing with things well lately, Charlotte, that's all."

"Why can't you talk to me?"

"Because I don't want to!" Liam erupted. "Not here."

When she made him put his coat back on, she was in full, authoritative, mother-hen mode. Charlotte tugged on her fiancé's beanie and his parka and patiently led her best friend outside. They walked until they had left the property, and were at the cusp of the woods. Liam stared at the barren trees before him.

They walked farther in, and stopped at a clearing where a row of trees had been chopped down. Charlotte sat down on a log and patted the space beside her. She waited patiently for him to open up. But when he said nothing, she nudged him.

"What happened two nights ago?"

Liam was scowling at the ground, moving a clod of dirt with the sole of his boot.

"Did he kiss you?" Charlotte asked. Liam jolted, staring up at her. She smiled. "It took me a little while to figure out that he was gay. But between his *rugged beauty* and the way that he *constantly* stares at you… I caught on eventually."

"I—oh."

"It's okay." Charlotte squeezed his wrist. "Take it as a compliment. Hell, I certainly would. But I assume you threw a fit, like most straight boys do."

"I kissed him back."

"I—excuse *me?*" Charlotte's eyes widened.

Liam was staring down at the clod. "I kissed him back. I'm attracted to him."

Her mouth remained open.

He turned to gauge her reaction. It was an agonizingly slow process. Her gray eyes searched his face for what had to be a full minute. And then, without another word, Charlotte wrapped her arms around him and pressed him close in a tight embrace.

"I'm not dying, Charlotte," Liam croaked.

When she pulled back, she was smiling. "I *knew* it!"

"No, you didn't."

"Okay, but it makes a *lot* of sense in hindsight!"

"That's just hindsight bias."

"Shut *up*." Charlotte shoved him and Liam laughed, genuinely laughed, for the first time in two days. "Liam! You *like* somebody! And he is a beautiful specimen of a human being!"

"I don't like him," Liam insisted. "He's an asshole."

"Ooh, was it a *hateful* hookup?" Charlotte crossed her legs and leaned in close, earnest. "Tell me more."

"Charlotte, I am having an identity crisis here and a massive conflict of emotions. Do I really have to give you a play-by-play right now?"

"Yes."

Liam sighed, exasperated.

"Is he a good kisser?"

"Phenomenal, unfortunately," Liam muttered, rubbing the back of his neck. Charlotte made a squeak of a response, and he snorted. "But he... I *don't know*. It's so strange, Charlotte—and not strange. Being inside my head is so exhausting right now. I don't know if this was just circumstantial, if this was about *him*, or if this is just a part of me I never acknowledged before.... I *don't fucking know*."

"I've never seen you like this," Charlotte murmured. Liam was worked up to the point of frustrated tears.

He took in a breath, held it, and exhaled evenly.

"Liam," she said. "You have to realize that you have nothing but time to break everything down and figure it out. I think you're giving yourself a migraine just trying to *categorize* everything and put it into its proper box, but it's not that simple."

"I wish it was."

Charlotte chewed on her lower lip. "Do you want to stay here with me an extra week?"

"No. No, I have to go home."

"I'm a phone call away," she reminded him. "Don't get overwhelmed, and don't do anything stupid."

Liam turned to her gratefully, and Charlotte reached around to hug him tightly again. He pressed his nose against her shoulder.

CHAPTER TWENTY-TWO

THE LETTER remained unopened throughout the entire duration of his ride to the airport, and during the flight itself. It wasn't opened when he tossed it onto his end table, took a long, hot shower, and settled under the covers for a nap.

It stared at him during dinnertime, mocking and impolite in its stark, pristine-white glory. The handwriting looked irritatingly perfect. As if Darcy had written it with a quill, stopping every few moments to dip it in an inkpot and straighten his cravat.

He tore it open.

Dear Liam,

Your first impulse is probably to rip this letter in pieces. You can take a deep breath; I'm not going to humiliate myself anymore by repeating how I feel. I think I'm mortified enough, and you've made me acutely aware of how you feel on the subject.

Liam set down the letter, took a sip from his cup of tea, and scowled. *What a victim*, he thought. Then he continued reading.

The purpose of this letter is to defend myself. I think it's only fair that I address all that you accused me of; I'd appreciate it if you read through. First off, I know we argued about your brother. And I'll repeat myself. I helped encourage Charlie to end the relationship, but with no malicious intent on my part, whatsoever.

He's had rocky relationships in the past and I've seen him devote so much to those he has loved, only to walk away absolutely devastated in return. Maybe my judgment was flawed in thinking that Jamie was apathetic, but please understand that I only wanted what was best for my friend.

When Caroline told me about the nature of the relationship, my priority was to look out for Charlie. He might as well be my brother. Surely you can relate to that. I didn't think about the ramifications, or the suffering that would come at your brother's end. Or yours, for that matter. I regret that this has caused you so much pain too.

I also wanted to discuss George Wickham, simply for the sake of clearing my family's name. I don't know what this man has told you, but obviously, he has lied. You might not want to, but I think it's wise to take my word for it.

George and I grew up together. He was, for a very long time, one of my oldest friends. His mother helped run my family estate in Derbyshire, England—he was my childhood playmate for years.

My parents divorced just before my eleventh birthday. As a consequence, I was very often between Pemberley and New York, where my mother is from. My friendships naturally unraveled from the strain of constant travel. My relationship with my little sister was difficult to maintain at the time; she stayed in England with my father. I visited often, but for the most part, I lived with my mother in the states.

My father became ill a few years ago and this drew me back to England for a while. George Wickham had been in college at the time. When my father's condition was stable for a few weeks, I returned to New York for work.

He had a heart attack while I was gone, and everybody had scrambled to keep this from me. When I got back to Pemberley, my father was dying. And who was at his bedside but George Wickham, fervently discussing his will. The same George Wickham that we hadn't seen or spoken to for years, conveniently resurfacing.

My father passed away a month later. By then, I learned that George had been living in our house since I was gone, taking advantage of my father's hospitality while he was ill. The week of my father's funeral, he and Georgiana approached me and told me that they had gotten very close through this entire ordeal with Dad—they were apparently in love.

I had a huge fight with Wickham and we said terrible things to each other. I accused him of interfering with my family's affairs at the last minute, just to work himself into my father's will. I called him a leech because I believed that he was after my sister's inheritance and my father's money. And he accused me of being jealous because he had been there for Dad when I hadn't been.

To make things short, I told him that I would pay him as much as he wanted if he left town and didn't return. He accepted immediately. Georgiana was devastated. She went through a succession of heartbreaks that year.

That's the truth, and that's all I really wanted you to know. I'm not going to address what happened between us. It isn't difficult to understand that you probably want to forget about it. I made an ass out of myself and I was presumptuous and for that, I'm sorry. But what's done is done, and I won't be bothering you in the future.

Take care,

Will

Liam folded all three sheets of paper neatly along their already established creases. He finished his tea, threw away the tea bag, and rinsed out the mug. Then he sat down at the kitchen table.

"*Shit,*" he swore.

He reread the letter three times that night.

CHAPTER TWENTY-THREE

"You okay?"

Jamie's question was abrupt. Liam stared at him, somewhat vacantly. He smiled mechanically. "Yeah."

His brother was leaning against the espresso bar in the coffee shop. Behind him, a teenage boy was scribbling in his notebook and peering at the text before him. Jamie glanced at him from over his shoulder. "You finished, Matthew?"

The boy looked up. "I'm on the last set of problems."

"Awesome—holler when you're done and I'll check it out."

He nodded and turned back to his studies.

"Work must be slow if you're tutoring high school kids," said Liam. He took off his visor and smoothed his hair back.

"Matt's my boss's kid. He needed SAT prep," Jamie explained. "What about you? This place is a ghost town."

Liam looked around. Oak was depressingly empty, as it would be until the start of the semester. He thought about going home, but he was uncomfortable with the idea of spending the rest of his winter break with his prying family. People in general, to be perfectly honest.

"I like it this way. I don't feel like dealing with anybody," Liam replied. He had worked his entire shift in just a T-shirt and jeans, not even bothering to find his apron. It was a welcome change.

Jamie tilted his head. "When did you get so salty?"

Liam grimaced, showing his turtle face. "I hate kids. All of them. Get off my stoop."

"Okay, Clint Eastwood," Jamie said. He finished his latte and dunked it over the counter and into the trashcan. He made it, of course. Because he was flawless. "You still haven't told me about England."

"Yes, I did."

"*Barely.*"

Liam looked up and gave his usual answer. "There wasn't much to tell, Jamie. I helped Charlotte pick out a dress. Met Collins's godmother and her nephew. Went to a club with them for New Year's Eve. *Boom.*"

"Well then. You had an exceptionally boring international travel experience," Jamie scoffed.

"That's all I've been sayin'," he muttered, slinging a rag over his shoulder.

Jamie returned to his seat and helped Matt Forrester correct his second set of geometry problems.

They left twenty minutes later, leaving Liam to the empty chairs and empty tables and an endless loop of overdue Christmas music. Mindy Brandon was in the office, handling payroll. Nobody else was scheduled to work for the night. He spread his hands wide against the countertop and sighed.

He hated lying to Jamie. He *hated* it. But the thought of admitting what had happened made his stomach lurch. Often, he pictured himself beginning to explain, saw his mouth making shapes with no words coming out and his hands gesturing uselessly.

He didn't know what to say, where to begin, how to say it.

He just knew that he hadn't slept the entire four days since he had returned from England. It was too empty in the apartment and too cold—the heater hadn't run properly for months. Most nights he burrowed under the covers in his sweatshirt, with the hood drawn up over his head. And then, when he closed his eyes and began to drift off....

Liam would recall lips lingering just beneath his jaw, fingertips mapping out skin, and *heat*, warm, thrumming heat, settling at his lower abdomen.

And then he'd jolt upright in bed. The back of his neck would be damp, and he would try to ignore the dull ache in his chest that was partly guilt and mostly something else.

"Well," said Liam cheerfully to the emptiness, staring out past the tables. "I guess I like men."

A snort from over his shoulder. He whirled around, and Mindy was smiling at him from her office doorway. "Good for you, kid. Can you make me a vanilla latte? Skim milk."

CHAPTER TWENTY-FOUR

IT WAS mid-February when Liam met Jamie's new boyfriend. It had been a feat on Jamie's part to unearth his brother from his wreckage of textbooks, novels, and papers. It concerned Jamie, the willingness that Liam had applied to excel in school. Granted, he had been an excellent student before, but had only just pulled it off—kicking and screaming and ignoring his academic responsibilities until the very last minute.

Now it was common for Liam to duck out of any plans because he had to study or had an urgent paper to write that would take him all weekend to complete.

"Also," Jamie continued his criticism of his brother's reclusiveness, "your hair is getting a little on the shaggy side and I don't think it's a really good look for you."

Liam lifted his eyebrows and stared with sleepy green eyes at his older sibling. He was regarding him with his head resting on both forearms, his lunch left untouched before him. "Cut it in my sleep if it bothers you so much."

"I can't get into your apartment."

Liam took out his keys and slid them across the table.

Jamie frowned thoughtfully at him. "I really want you to meet Aaron."

He sighed, as if there were no greater punishment, and Jamie pushed on. "I like him, and we've been dating for a few weeks now."

And he's your rebound, Liam finished the sentence in his head.

As far as rebounds went, Jamie had shown little to no imagination or creativity in his selection. Aaron Johansson and Jamie Bennet had

had a sugary meet-cute, standing in line at Starbucks. One first date morphed into another, and another. And, as Liam was subjected to Jamie's gushing and the romantic photos smeared across Facebook, he found it difficult to ignore the striking similarities between Aaron and Jamie's lost love.

God, he nearly had the same exact hair color as Charlie, and his daily uniform was *also* jeans, a button-down, and a blazer. Plus, his first and last name rhymed, which gave Liam ample reason to dislike him before he even saw him.

He didn't dare discuss this with his brother. Instead, Liam looked up and shrugged. "Name the time and the place, and I'll be there."

Jamie immediately smiled. Liam relaxed. Who was he to cheat Jamie out of any happiness? At least he was moving on.

He met Aaron the following weekend, when the entire family was home for his mother's birthday. The family took to him immediately. Well, all but Liam.

"I don't understand," said Mrs. Bennet over the kitchen sink, "why you keep *grilling* him, Liam. It's like an interrogation room in there."

"I just want to know what his fascination with J.Crew is." Liam shrugged. He sat on one of the barstools, swiveling in it haphazardly. Nate kicked his chair, trying to knock him off. Aaron and Jamie were out on the porch, thankfully.

"I'm not a fan of the yacht-club look either," drawled Mason. To his right, Becca giggled. They were sitting very close together, and he would look over every few seconds to grin at her or kiss her forehead.

"The honeymoon stage," Mr. Bennet had told Liam in private that evening. "Just give it a few months before they start to chase each other with fire pokers."

He smiled sheepishly to himself now, recalling the memory.

"*That* young man is even more to my liking than Charlie whatshisface," Mrs. Bennet declared. She was wearing her apron now, and her cheeks were red from the steam. "Plus, he's got a *normal* job and makes a *normal* living; he's not this local celebrity we're all falling over ourselves for."

"Dear, the only person who fell over themselves was *you*," Mr. Bennet chuckled. He was leaning against the fridge, stealing a bite of lasagna whenever his wife happened to turn her back.

Mason turned to Becca. "When Jamie had Charlie over here for dinner a while ago, Mom face-planted rushing to greet him from the front door. Like, an *America's Funniest Home Videos* face-plant."

"That's terrible!"

"*Thank* you, Becca!" Mrs. Bennet simpered.

"Classic," Nate snorted, reaching for the lasagna. His mother swatted his hand with her spatula.

"Not until the second course, Nathan."

Mr. Bennet grinned, obviously victorious.

They went back into the dining room. Liam laid off the critiques and questions to appease his mother. During dessert, he decided to watch everyone instead.

At his right, Nate was trying to occupy himself without his brother (Ben was stuck at soccer practice). This usually consisted of texting, since he wasn't permitted to leave the table yet.

His mother was asking how Jamie and Aaron had met, and Aaron was launching into an enthusiastic, nauseatingly sweet account of it all. They were holding hands and, to their immediate left, Mason and Becca were practically necking on the table.

Liam felt a swell of loneliness, deep in the pit of his stomach. It surprised him that it felt so physical.

He turned to Nate. "So, how's school?"

Nate snorted at him without looking up from his phone. "Might as well ask me about the weather."

He took the bait. "How's the weather?"

"Bite me."

Liam sighed.

His father found him on the porch long after dessert had been cleared and the leftovers stowed away in the fridge. All guests had dispersed. Aaron was in the basement with Jamie, playing pool with his brothers. Mrs. Bennet was upstairs in the bedroom, "overtaken by the exhaustion of entertaining."

Outside, the air was dry and cold. Liam sat on the front step, looking at a snowbank. His father sat beside him and followed his son's line of vision. He cocked his head. "I hate to tell you this, but I don't think it's gonna put on a show for you."

Liam smiled faintly and wrapped his arms around his knees. Mr. Bennet chewed the inside of his cheek and looked toward the driveway. After a few moments of silence, he nudged Liam's shoulder. "What do you say we go dismantle Beckwith's treehouse?"

Maury Beckwith had been their neighbor for years, two houses down from Charlotte's home.

Liam turned. "What did he do this time?"

"He's held my toolkit hostage all summer," said his dad.

"Is that why everything's falling apart around here?" Liam prompted.

Mr. Bennet narrowed his eyes at him. "Smartass," he chuckled. Liam forced a smile and looked straight ahead again. "Is something bothering you?" asked Mr. Bennet. "You've been quiet."

"I'm fine—just tired."

"Also, Jamie tells me that he's barely seen you these past few weeks."

"School's been rough."

"Are your grades good?" he inquired.

"Yeah," answered Liam. "But it takes time and effort to *keep* them good."

Mr. Bennet nodded. "Yeah… but you always made it a point to get some semblance of a life on the side. Is this because Charlotte's gone? Are you having trouble making friends?"

Liam regarded his father with curiosity. Typically, his mother was the one who headed The Parental Inquisition. Which only meant one thing—his father was legitimately concerned. He opened his mouth and shut it.

Mr. Bennet was still looking at him. They were sitting shoulder to shoulder now. "You can tell me," he encouraged.

He selected his words carefully. "Would… would all this change if I was different, Dad?"

His father frowned. "What do you mean?"

"Would our *relationship* change…?"

"Different, as in… suddenly left-handed instead of right-handed?" he ventured.

"*No*," Liam chuckled, shaking his head. He sighed. "No."

Mr. Bennet removed his glasses and polished them with the sleeve of his jacket. "Did you get into some kind of trouble up at school?"

"No, I didn't."

"Well, then relax. Ease up. Whatever is bugging you can't be *that* important, son." He put his glasses back on and smiled.

Liam looked up.

Nate poked his head out of the front door then, obviously irate. "Dad, Mason and his girlfriend are eating each other's faces on the living room couch. It's a huge distraction from my gaming. Can you make them stop?"

Mr. Bennet sighed and got to his feet. He glanced at Liam before turning to the door. "You okay?"

He nodded. "Yeah, I'm fine."

When he was left alone once more, Liam shut his eyes. "Not that important."

CHAPTER TWENTY-FIVE

THE NIGHTMARES began soon after that.

They seemed random at first, dark shapes and threatening characters, strange noises and screams. On the third night, things began to take shape. It was often Darcy's face he saw, slack-jawed, hurt. Wickham would then appear.

They would be arguing in an alley, or a bar, or an abandoned warehouse. It would always be a violent argument. Occasionally Liam would spot a small girl off to the side, sobbing, screaming, begging them to stop.

Darcy would throw a strong punch and Wickham would recoil, beaten. And just as Darcy would turn to comfort the girl, Wickham would advance—a glint of steel, and then he'd lodge the knife between Darcy's ribs, and the girl would scream, and the hero would fall to his knees, blood gurgling out of his mouth, blue eyes glassy....

Liam came to, shouting. He was sitting up in his bed, his heart beating erratically, his ears ringing. He reached to turn on his lamp. The room flooded with light, and he fell back against the headboard and tried to catch his breath.

The TV was still on, blaring an infomercial in the wee hours of the morning. He rubbed his eyes, but flashes from his dreams sparked, so he opened them again. He was still trembling; his shirt clung to his body.

He got up and got a drink of water from the tap in the kitchen. The second bedroom door was closed. *Thank God*, he thought. He was grateful to have been spared the embarrassment of waking up his new roommate, an exchange student who had moved in only the week before. *Mauricio sleeps like the walking dead.*

After he had finished two glasses, he leaned over the sink and breathed deeply until he calmed down. Then he drank again.

Liam turned back to his bedroom, unplugged his laptop from its charger, and carried it with him back to bed. He checked his e-mails, looking for comfort or distraction—whichever came first. He clicked the first unread one.

From: charlotte.lucas@hartford.edu

To: lbennet1@hartford.edu

Hey, you. Sorry I've been flaky with phone calls. I'm switching providers. Meanwhile, there's this. We can also video chat, so tell me what your username is.

Are you okay? Fill me in.

He archived her message and scrolled on, not entirely motivated to respond, just yet. Then another e-mail caught his eye.

From: frank@travelgardens.com

To: lbennet1@hartford.edu

Dear Liam,

We hope you had a wonderful winter break! Your mother tells me that you went to England. Where to? We were hoping to use your new expertise on our next trip touring the English countryside. As I mentioned before, we're doing a summer feature on castles and estates. Jamie opted out—it's all on you, kid. We leave Sunday, March 3. When's your spring break?

Don't answer that. Maureen just did some snooping on Hartford's website. You're out of their clutches after classes, Friday, March 1. Ha! No excuses now.

The only question now is, do you want to?

All our love,

Uncle Frank and Aunt Maureen

Liam sank against the headboard, smiling. He suddenly felt overwhelmingly grateful, and stared past his laptop screen to the calendar tacked to his wall. Three weeks of classes, but after that....

He sat up and typed his response, enthusiastic. Now was as good a time as any for an adventure.

CHAPTER TWENTY-SIX

"SERIOUSLY?" CHARLOTTE'S voice sounded higher over the phone, heightened by her surprise. "The one week I go home, you decide to come here."

"Not exactly *there*," said Liam. "You're in London. This is in... well, not London."

"Same country," she said, mock-offended. "No, in all honesty, I'm glad you're going. You sounded a little bent out of shape the last time we spoke on the phone. Which was a millennium ago."

"It was not," he said coolly, zipping his suitcase.

"Have you told anyone about... your recent revelation?"

"No."

"No? Nobody?"

"I've told *you*," Liam pointed out. He did his best to sound as casual about it as possible.

"But nobody else?"

"Uh, my manager at work. But she kind of heard me mumbling to myself, so...."

Charlotte began to giggle.

His aunt and uncle would pull up any minute now to take him to the airport. He finally resorted to sitting on his bag just to get it closed. "I think I packed too much. I don't know how this happened."

"You should pack a lot—the weather is tricky here this time of year."

"You sound like my mother. Are you Mrs. Collins yet?"

A long, loaded silence. "Uh... that's partly the reason I'm calling. I'm going home because I called it off. I broke up with Collins. I mean,

I'll have to return to London after the holiday break because I still have to finish the semester. But I have to find a new place to live because Catherine the Great will want to chase me off her land with a pitchfork—"

Liam nearly dropped the phone. "Are you kidding?"

"No, I really will have to find a new place, or become a squatter. Doesn't that word sound disgusting?"

"I could *kiss* you, Charlotte! Thank God you broke up with him." He paused, suspicions arising. "Is Richard still there?"

"He left a couple weeks ago. That's another story I have to tell you for a different time."

"I hate that you share the most interesting things when I have the least amount of time to hear them."

"I would make a great TV writer," Charlotte said gleefully. "I'll see you when you get home. I love you! Have a safe flight. Oh, and try to visit the British manic-pixie girl. She lives there too, you know."

Liam suddenly remembered Ann for the first time all semester and thanked Charlotte for the reminder, growing more and more excited. "I love you too." He paused. "But you know that Catherine the Great was a *Russian* ruler, right?"

"Whatever, Liam."

Ten minutes later, he clambered into the backseat of the Gardiners' SUV, feeling happy and light for the first time in *weeks*. Maureen greeted him with a hug and a kiss, and Uncle Frank saluted him from the driver's seat.

Maureen, ever the hip aunt, had her black dreads pushed out of her face and secured with a red bandana. Frank was wearing mirrored aviators. "I think you're rubbing off on my uncle." Liam smirked.

"She is. Am I *cool* yet?" Frank lowered his sunglasses.

"Oh, honey," sighed Maureen. "Not even a little bit."

He pouted but gunned the engine anyway, pulling into traffic while his wife and his nephew laughed.

CHAPTER TWENTY-SEVEN

THE FLIGHT was a lot less turbulent than the one two months before. He was even able to sleep, in coach no less, lulled by his iPod. The landing at Heathrow, the train to Bath—all seemed much smoother than Liam had expected.

Perhaps because he had been actually looking *forward* to this trip, as opposed to the last one. He felt a sense of eagerness now, an anxiousness to be surrounded with the new and unfamiliar.

Frank and Maureen collapsed once in the hotel, of course. Liam loaded the camera ("I'm taking a film class this semester," he had explained to his uncle). He prepared his clothes in advance and went to bed restless. And then he was up by six the next morning, practically pulling them to their feet.

"You are quickly becoming my least favorite nephew," Frank told him crankily. "Which is pretty impressive because I always thought that Nathan would hold that title near and dear to his heart."

Liam grinned and settled into his bus seat. Frank took a swig from his coffee thermos and Maureen sighed, resting her head against the cool glass window. Liam framed a shot of them—then ducked when Maureen glanced up and swiped at him.

"*Nice* ones!" She scowled. "I said take nice ones."

"How do you know that wouldn't have been nice?" her nephew challenged.

"Because nobody looks attractive while they sleep."

"That's true." Frank nodded solemnly. His wife turned to stare at him, and he shrugged, unapologetic. "It's not the kid's fault—you told him to take pictures."

"I didn't know that he would obstruct traffic in the process."

Liam rolled his eyes. They had just been leaving Bath when he had accidentally held up the boarding line just because the light reflecting on the Circus was just "so, *so* breathtaking."

Maureen sighed and rested her head on her husband's shoulder. Frank kissed her hair. Liam framed the shot and snapped it.

Two hours into the trip, the bus had grown silent. Liam looked around to see that 75 percent of the tourists had fallen asleep, crammed against windows or their significant others like awkward sardines. The rocking of the vehicle was probably a contributing factor, but it had been helped by the weather—cold, gray drizzle pattered against the windshield.

Liam had a whole two seats to himself. He drew up the armrest, pulled down the hood of his sweatshirt, and propped his legs up on the seat beside him. He stared at the overcast sky outside the window opposite and closed his eyes.

They visited two country homes that evening, and were scheduled to see a famous estate in Lambton before the weather chased them back to the bus.

The tour guide, a woman with a cropped blonde bob and gray leather pants, told them over the PA system, "I'm afraid the way to the next estate has been closed off due to a weather-related accident." A chorus of moans, and then, "Wait, wait! We *have*, however, fallen into a bit of luck: the Pemberley estate in Derbyshire is open to visitors. The lucky part in this being that this is the final week before it closes for the public, due to scheduled renovations, I am told. You're in for quite the treat."

The Gardiners murmured their interest in front of him, but at that moment, Liam feared his limbs had become glued to his seat.

He began to clench and unclench his fists, and then he turned around. "Did she say… *Pemberley*?"

"I think so," answered his aunt.

Liam nodded, turning back. A moment later, he faced her. "So, these estates… are their owners ever home?"

"Well, a lot of them don't *belong* to the owners anymore," Frank told him, cheerfully oblivious to his nephew's anxiety. "Many have been sold off and are now owned by—"

"The ones that *are* still privately owned, though," Liam pressed. "They can't be living there *and* entertaining tours at the same time, right?"

"I doubt it," Maureen agreed. "Not that it matters anyway. Why do you ask?"

He shrugged, laughed a little too quickly, and turned back around.

Pemberley was gated, and the road beyond the gate and to the estate was canopied under bright green foliage. They drove past a babbling river and an abandoned cottage to a massive, white stone mansion perched high on a grassy hill. Winding elm trees lined stone pathways all the way down the property.

The bus emptied. The entire group pushed past him, but still Liam was rooted to a spot in front of the bus, immobile even when he was shouldered several times. He had his camera halfway up to his face, his mouth hanging open stupidly.

Frank and Maureen turned back for him and tugged him along. "Come *on*, son—I'm sure it's pretty inside too."

Liam was quick to lose the group. It wasn't intentional; it was just that his feet tended to lead him astray on their own. Pemberley was *astoundingly* beautiful, in spite of the scaffolding in the massive foyer and the sparkling chandelier that had been lowered to be cleaned.

It was all marble pillars, and stained glass dappling colors onto the floorboards, and golden domes, and winding staircase railings, and large, cavernous fireplaces.

Click. Click, click. After twenty minutes, Liam vaguely wondered how much film he had used on Pemberley alone. "*Shit*," he breathed.

He heard music, then—light and distant, a melody being drawn out of a piano. He turned out of the sitting room and walked down another corridor. Then down the portrait hall, where faces flanked by ruffled collars and naval uniforms seemed to trace his every step.

There was a door left open, and Liam peeped in to see the source of the music.

A girl was seated in front of a glossy, black grand piano. Her short hair was gathered into a stubby ponytail, and she wore overalls, though they were streaked with paint. Ann. *His* Ann.

Her features were hardened in concentration as her fingers nimbly coaxed music from the keys. Liam stared in disbelief. "Ann?"

She flinched, startled, and stared up at him with wide blue eyes. "*Liam?*"

She was up in an instant, knocking the wind out of his body with a tighter hug than her little body seemed capable of. "What in God's name…?"

"You *live* here?"

"What are you *doing* here?"

They had both asked their questions at the same time. Liam answered first. "I'm on vacation with my aunt and uncle. I was going to call anyway, but I didn't think… *here*… you live *here*?"

"Yes, since I was a little girl."

"But…." Liam stepped aside, scratching the back of his head in amazement. "*But.*"

An older woman entered the room, looking like she had just stepped out of a Brontë novel. Her reddish-gray hair was pulled back into an austere bun, and her pale face was humorless and lined. "Georgiana," she chided. "Are you interfering with the tours again? I haven't forgotten your prank during the summertime."

"*Never,*" his friend answered. She gave a pert little smile. "But that was classic, Cee, you *have* to admit."

"I'll do nothing of the sort."

"Georgiana," Liam echoed.

"My full name." Ann colored, crossing her arms over her chest. "Dreadful, isn't it? Cee, this is my friend from university, Liam. Liam, this is… oh, you look quite pale."

Cee, short for Cecilia Reynolds, he would learn soon after, was quick to come to his side. "Are you all right? Do you want to have a lie down?"

"No." Liam was shaking his head. He opened his mouth and shut it several times. "*Georgiana Darcy.*"

"Good God, Liam, as if it sounds better all at once."

"I always hated your nickname," Cecilia simpered. "Why you've spread it out to all your American friends is beyond me. Your proper name has a *legacy* behind it, miss—"

"But *you're* Georgiana," Liam interrupted. He stared at Ann wildly. "Why is this—you've—*how* could you not—*what?*"

Ann regarded him for a moment. "Are you having a stroke?"

It took him a minute. After he had calmed down, Liam cleared his throat. "I'm sorry for my rudeness." He extended his hand. "I'm Liam Bennet, a friend of Ann's from college."

"Pleasure," she responded coolly. "Cecilia Reynolds. I run Pemberley. Georgiana, are all your American friends this excitable?" she asked dryly, a hint of a smile pulling at the corners of her mouth.

Ann laughed and threaded her arm through Liam's. "Come on. I'll give you my own *personal* tour. Oh, I'm so glad you're here! I was dying of boredom."

They walked down the portrait hall. "Hey Ann," Liam asked slowly. "Do you have any other family home right now?"

Ann stared at him curiously. "No. My brother *was* here in the morning. We've started renovations on our own, you see, hence my terribly colorful uniform. He ran off a quarter to one, though. Why?"

He hesitated. "We've met."

"Who has?" Ann stopped in her tracks.

"Your brother and I."

"You and Will?" she snorted, eyebrows raised.

"Yes."

Georgiana's smile disappeared. "You're *joking.*"

"No." Liam pressed his lips into a straight line. They had stopped moving and stood in the center of the corridor, simply gaping at one another.

"*How?*"

"You know his best friend, Charles Bingley?"

"Yes, I adore Charlie," replied Ann.

"My older brother, Jamie, was dating Charlie for a few months. I met D—Will pretty often during that time," Liam said delicately.

Ann covered her mouth. "Did the Atlantic Ocean just shrink three times in size?"

"Yeah." Liam began to laugh. "Yeah, I think it did."

"*Oh.*" She stood on her tiptoes to hug him again, a gesture she was uncommonly fond of that day. Ann pulled back an inch or two. "He was nice to you?" Liam was silent, so she gasped, "*No.* He was horrid, wasn't he?"

"Not in so many words—"

"He's a moody little shit sometimes, but don't take it personally. He's *such* a good person. He just has the social aptitude of a fish. I'm sure he adores you, how could you not?"

Liam chose to be silent.

Ann took his hand and dragged him forward. "Come along, Liam. I have to show you the best feature of the house."

House seemed like such a tawdry term to describe the gloriously mammoth estate that was Pemberley.

The best feature of the house ended up being the kitchen. Liam frowned at Ann. "Don't get me wrong; it's impressive. I'm lovin' the marble counters but… it's kind of a letdown after everything else."

"I know." Ann cocked her head. "I'm just hungry." He chuckled, watching her pile a stack of cookies and cakes on the countertop. Most of them he had never heard of, English versions of wafers and Yodels and brownies.

"You eat all this?"

"Yes, I am a vacant black hole," Ann responded. "Wafer?"

"No, thank you."

He was standing rigidly in the kitchen, keeping very much to himself. He didn't feel comfortable at all. He didn't appreciate the reunion under these circumstances, though it was nice to see Ann—Georgiana. *Jesus*. His mind struggled to connect the dots.

If his aunt and uncle could turn up soon, they could all board the bus and he could pretend that this detour had never occurred. He would go on to tour less opulent, regal estates with *no* awkward acquaintances inhabiting them, and all would be wonderfully, blissfully—

"*Georgiana!* Your brother has just parked in the roundabout."

Cecilia Reynolds appeared in the doorway like some great, foreboding apparition, and Liam felt his breakfast threaten to return for an encore appearance. He clenched his fists.

Ann beamed, oblivious. "Oh good!" She took Liam's hand in her own. "Come on, Liam, come say hello."

He was rather desperate to avoid the freight train of mortification that awaited him. "I'd really rather not—that's okay."

"What, why?"

"My aunt and uncle are probably leaving soon and—"

"So? We'll be quick."

"*Ann.*"

"*Liam*, what's gotten into you?" she harrumphed.

He groaned in agitation and rubbed his eyes, feeling very much like he had left all of his courage back on the bus. And just as he was in the process of summoning it, Will Darcy materialized in the corridor.

He didn't get a good look at him at first, seeing as Ann was quick to give him a hug and a peck on the cheek. "I have a surprise for you! My friend has come all the way across the pond to see me."

"Is that so?" Darcy smiled. He shook his head and removed his scarf, tossing it over a barstool. "And pray tell, where is this f—"

The word died on his lips, and Will Darcy stared, in utter bafflement and disbelief, at Liam Bennet standing in his kitchen. His mouth fell open and his brow furrowed.

"Right." Liam clapped, nervous energy thrumming through his limbs. "Good to see you again. I think I—I'll get going. Pretty sure I just heard the tour group tail out of the foyer and I really wouldn't want to um—miss it, them. Excuse me."

"Liam," Ann said, affronted.

"I'll catch up with you soon."

Pemberley blurred as he made his way out, generations of Darcys muddling together into one prestigious, judgmental legacy. He burst out of the front door and down the stone walkway from the porch. Sure enough, he did spot some of his tour group idling about the bus, but they weren't all there—it wasn't time to leave yet.

His breath came out in bursts, and he realized he had been running, no, *sprinting*. Self-loathing rose indignantly in the pit of his stomach. He never ran away from anything—and here he was, frightened and shamed like some child.

He leaned his elbows against the white porch railing and closed his eyes.

"Hey."

Liam turned.

Darcy was standing before him. He was breathless too, clearly having just run after him. He laughed, nervous and abrupt.

"I'm sorry, that was rude," said Liam offhandedly.

Darcy shrugged, though his posture was still rigid. "I, um." His hand moved to the back of his neck, his eyes downcast. "It's good to see you again. I had no idea that you and my sister—"

"I had no idea she was *your* sister," Liam blurted.

Darcy looked up at him.

"I mean, I love Ann. Do you call her Ann? I don't know what's up with that. We became friends when she was studying at Hartford last semester, and she never told me that it was short for *Georgiana*." Liam found that his words came all at once, or not at all. He shut his mouth.

"I call her Ann, yes." Darcy smiled brightly.

The gesture was so disarming and genuine that Liam gaped at him in confusion for a couple of seconds, as if uncertain as to how Darcy's facial muscles could contort in a way that ended in anything other than a grimace. "And she spoke of a friend she made," he continued, "but I guess I never pressed the subject. Did you come to visit her?"

"No, this was en route for our tour. I'm vacationing here with my aunt and uncle. They run a travel journal and I'm helping them with photography," Liam explained.

"Oh, the Gardiners?" Darcy asked curiously.

"If you tell me that you know *them* too, I'm going to shoot myself through the frontal lobe."

"Relax, I just met them in the billiards room," said Darcy, but he was laughing. "Literally five or ten minutes ago."

"Oh," Liam murmured, straightening.

An uneasy silence met them, and the ample space between them seemed charged now.

Liam looked up apologetically. "I'm really sorry. I didn't think you would be home or else I would have never—"

"No, don't even worry about—"

"—I'm pretty mortified—"

"I'm really glad to see you. I mean it," Darcy insisted. He colored slightly then, and looked down.

Liam pressed his lips together.

The Gardiners met them on the porch shortly after, just as the stream of tourists exited and headed to the bus with their fearless, leather pants-clad leader. It was Maureen who noticed Liam first, whirling around with surprise and stopping her husband.

"Liam! We were wondering where you ran off to."

"Good to see you again, Will," Frank greeted the owner of the house.

"You too, Mr. Gardiner." Darcy smiled amiably and shook his hand.

"Oh, please—call me Frank."

Liam stared in bewilderment. He felt that at any moment, his head might pop off his body and spin on its axis and into the sun.

"Liam, I see you've met Will." Maureen beamed.

"We know each other, actually," Darcy said.

"Do you?" Frank asked, surprised.

"Yes, I had the pleasure of meeting your nephew when I was in Oakham County last fall," he explained. "My sister was studying at Hartford and my business partner was often in the area as well."

"Well then," said Maureen, resting her hand on Liam's shoulder. "Liam, you never told me that you made such important friends. I approve."

"I think I was the luckier one in making your nephew's acquaintance."

"*Our* Liam? He's all right," Frank snorted, clapping his nephew on the back so that he stumbled forward an inch, wide-eyed.

How is this my life right now?

"Actually, my sister and I were wondering if you and your family would be interested in staying for supper?" Darcy asked earnestly. "Mrs. Reynolds is an incredible cook, and she usually cooks *much* more than necessary. I'm sure Ann would love to catch up with you properly," he said to Liam, who wasn't quite finished being flabbergasted.

"Oh, that's really very kind of you," Maureen began, "but we have to stay with the tour in order to get back to our hotel."

"Where are you staying?"

"Derby Inn," answered Frank.

"That's no problem at all—it's not far. I'll give you a lift back myself tonight," Darcy insisted. "Or you're always welcome to stay here; we have more than enough guest bedrooms."

Liam opened his mouth uselessly, feeling very much like he was witnessing a train wreck that he was incapable of stopping. He gaped at his aunt and uncle.

Maureen broke out into a broad grin. "That's so kind. We would love to stay for dinner, but I'm afraid we have an early tour in the morning. But Liam, you're welcome to stay with your friends."

"Oh. Well, I wouldn't want to ditch you guys—"

"Please, we're *seasoned travelers*," Frank joked, straightening the lapels of his jacket and smiling. Liam stared at him, helpless.

Ann poked her head out of the doorway, smiling radiantly. "Hello! Liam," she said sternly, "you're staying over, or I'm never speaking with you again."

A beat. "*Fine.*"

Ann gave a girlish squeal and kissed him on the cheek before disappearing inside, and Liam couldn't help but grin. Darcy was having the same trouble. He smiled, seeming genuinely thrilled, and led the way back inside. Liam pulled up his hood and shuffled in after them with a sigh.

CHAPTER TWENTY-EIGHT

PEMBERLEY WAS mystical by night.

It must have been the history filling its halls, but Liam felt that each feature, every turn of a spiral railing and glint of a crystal candelabrum, seemed intensified in the evening.

Three of them sat in the living room now, cross-legged on the Persian rug with a gingham blanket set out before them. A fire danced in the hearth and Liam admired the display of food: the ahi tuna lettuce wraps with hummus, tomato mozzarella salad with basil, roasted chicken, and a pot of lemon-ginger tea. It had all been Ann's idea—some sort of warped, indoor, Middle Eastern picnic in the English countryside.

"*De*licious," she chirped, bringing a lettuce wrap to her mouth. "Is Cee an exceptional cook, or is Cee an exceptional cook?"

"She's an exceptional cook," Liam replied. He held his tea—too hot to drink but perfect to cradle with his sleeves.

The Gardiners had only left two hours ago, not realizing that their tour was scheduled an hour earlier than expected. They had barely eaten before they slid on their jackets and shoes, deaf to the protests of everybody else.

Just before they left, Maureen pulled Liam aside to have a word. "Are you going to be all right?" she asked, fixing her collar. "You have my international number."

"Yeah, I'll be fine."

"Such friends you have." Maureen grinned. "They're great."

"They are," Liam agreed.

Maureen wasn't listening anymore, but was peering over his shoulder and into the foyer where Will Darcy was fetching his keys and sliding on his canvas jacket. "He's a very *good* young man. I think he likes you."

Liam glanced up, armed with a defense against her joke, but he was alarmed by the sincerity on her face. Her hazel eyes seemed almost catlike, and he caught a brief smile before she leaned forward and kissed his cheek. "I love you, kiddo. I'll call you in the morning."

Darcy's inquiry to his sister brought him back to the present: "You're a little drunk, aren't you?"

"I might be." Ann pursed her lips, as if holding in a secret. She had finished a glass of white wine earlier and sat, drumming her fingers against the rim, humming. Darcy elbowed her gently and she erupted into giggles.

Liam watched the siblings carefully—watched them narrow their eyes at each other in challenge and then look away with identical smirks.

Months ago, he would never had imagined this at all. He would have thought that dinner with the Darcy siblings would be unbearably awkward and frigid. He had imagined something vaguely Stepfordesque—with harsh, clinical lighting, dry meat, and bitter red wine to wash everything down as they both stared at him stoically from their side of the table with mirrored movements like those twins from *The Shining*.

"More tea?" Darcy offered.

Liam shook his head with a short laugh. "No, thank you. I haven't even started this one yet."

"Weenie," Ann quipped.

"I'm sorry that we can't all down scalding beverages with alarming speed," he countered.

"Well, you should be—it's embarrassing."

He turned to her brother. "This one finishes her coffee while we're waiting in line to *purchase* the coffee."

"Yeah, Georgiana's impervious to extreme temperatures," Darcy replied archly. "That's why we make her do all the yard work in the summertime; she barely works up a sweat."

Ann elbowed him and Liam laughed. "Are you only calling her Georgiana to piss her off?"

"Pretty much." Darcy smiled.

"No, I believe he uses it more when he's home," Ann clarified. "I think Pemberley brings it out in him. Like I'm *Duchess* Georgiana, or a member of the landed gentry or something."

"Well, we *were*—generations ago."

Liam listened intently and brought his cup to his lips.

"Where are we putting you up for the night?" Ann asked him. Liam shrugged, so she looked at Darcy. "The Middle Room?"

"It's kind of cold in there."

"It's got the nicest bed."

"I'm comfortable wherever," Liam insisted. "It's nice enough that you guys are letting me stay over."

"Oh, shut *up*." Ann rolled her eyes. She got to her feet. "The Middle Room; it's decided. We'll turn on the space heater. I'm going to the kitchen for some sweets. Anybody want anything?"

"No," they chorused.

After she left, it was silent for a few moments. Darcy looked into his cup. Liam opened his mouth and, feeling a knot form at the base of his throat, shut it again. He didn't know how to begin.

"Sorry," he blurted.

Darcy looked up, puzzled.

"New Year's." Liam shrugged. "I made an ass out of myself and I made judgment calls without knowing the facts. Without your letter, I would have never known—so thank you."

Darcy regarded him slowly. "I'm glad you read it. But it's not your fault. I didn't exactly act in a way that encouraged you to assume differently."

"No, you didn't." Liam primly took a sip.

Darcy began to object, but then saw that the other man was smirking. He chuckled and shook his head. Liam cracked, smiling back.

"I heard your friend didn't marry Collins."

"No," confirmed Liam. "Apparently she's homebound now."

"I know. My aunt called me in hysterics. I left her on speakerphone in the kitchen and went outside to walk my dog." Liam broke into laughter and Darcy smiled. "How thrilled are you that they separated?"

"On a scale of one to ten?" Liam said. "Seventy-four."

Darcy grinned, and Liam found that it was contagious. "You have my cousin to thank."

"I hoped Charlotte would come to her senses naturally, but it definitely helps that she was into Richard," Liam agreed. "Maybe that was the push she needed."

"Mm," Darcy agreed, setting his cup down. "Probably saw what she would be missing out on."

There was another gap of silence, and then Liam asked, "What kind of dog do you have?"

"German shepherd," said Darcy, smiling. "She lives with me in New York. My neighbor watches her when I'm not in town."

"Shepherds are beautiful," Liam murmured.

"Yeah, she's something else. I love her."

Darcy began slowly and methodically to gather empty dishes. Liam leaned in to help, and he drew the stack of plates back. "No. Sit and relax. You're a guest—act accordingly."

"You're... extremely bossy and uptight."

"I know," Darcy said casually. "Someone has informed me before."

Liam laughed in spite of himself, coloring. Darcy smiled.

Liam watched him work and looked down self-consciously, his smile disappearing. It was eerie how at ease he felt with Will Darcy now. He wondered if it was because he was witnessing him at Pemberley, where he was free to open up and relax, where he had grown up. But he couldn't shake the feeling that it was something else—that he was watching this great man peel off his armor for the first time.

And he liked what he saw.

"I'm gonna go see if Ann needs help in the kitchen." Liam cleared his throat and got to his feet. Darcy watched him go.

CHAPTER TWENTY-NINE

THE SPACE heater, originally provided to help him, only succeeded in making the guest bedroom swelteringly hot. Agitated, Liam swung his legs to the side of the bed, leaned forward, and punched the heater off. Without its whirr, the room seemed eerie, silent, and dark.

He was still restless. Nervous energy wrenched his stomach into knots, and his mouth felt dry. Liam rose and ran his hands through his hair, conscious of it getting too long, conscious of it twisting in all sorts of directions.

He moved heavy maroon curtains out of his way and peered out the bay windows, though they didn't afford much of a view. The entire property seemed shrouded in blackness, and he could just make out the edge of the woods. Had his room faced the front of the estate, he would have seen the vast lake stretching wide like a canvas, reflecting the moonlight.

"Well, such is life," said Liam with a snap of his fingers; he stepped backward and the curtains resumed their job of concealment.

Liam pulled his sweatshirt over his head and slipped on a pair of jeans. Pausing in the doorway, he reached back to snatch his gray beanie from the dresser, and pulled it on, concealing his unruly hair.

Pemberley was no longer mystical by night; it was *creepy*. The halls were endless, and the spiral staircase seemed particularly sinister, as if designed to make him trip and rocket through the landing and out the fiberglass door. Unfazed, Liam jogged down the steps like a child on Christmas morning, filled with an uncalled-for eagerness.

He stopped in the foyer, found his shoes, and went out into the night.

The view from his guest room had not done the property justice. After a few moments of walking, Liam glanced over his shoulder at the sprawling estate and froze. Pemberley was awash in a golden glow, landscape lights shooting up in pillars from the stone pathways that crisscrossed to the entrance.

The estate itself sat on the east bank of a river; Liam didn't know why he had imagined a man-made lake in its place. The stream that ran right beside Pemberley was inky and mesmerizing in the moonlight. There was nothing artificial about the property, he realized. A small footbridge arched over the river and connected to the west bank, where the path ran a few hundred feet before disappearing into country roads and finally to the wooded hills.

Liam stood in the center of the bridge.

He drank it all in, forgetting that he had grown cold, forgetting that this was an hour where he was meant to be sleeping. It had been so long since he had marveled at anything. He pulled his hood up and laced his fingers behind his head, staring up at the night sky. Then he closed his eyes.

"What are you doing?"

"*Shit.*" He jolted. Darcy's face was a surprise and it wasn't, and he couldn't help himself from biting back, "Do you *always* wait for the perfect time to sneak up on me?"

"That would require a pretty keen insight into your sleeping patterns," Darcy admitted. He had been walking across the bridge from the opposite bank, and stopped to lean against the rail. "But no, I was on my way back in."

"From where? It's a quarter to midnight."

Darcy's shoulders rose in a delicate shrug. "Cee mentioned a pest problem out in the barn. I thought I'd have a look."

Liam's brow furrowed. "Barn?"

"Yeah. It's over there." Darcy pointed somewhere off into the distance, where a gravel path turned behind another stone outhouse and a wooden barn adjacent to it.

"This property never ends. Did you take care of the pest?"

"Not exactly. Turns out it's not a pest, just a stray cat and her new litter. She gave birth under one of the tractors."

"If anything, that should solve any future mice problems." Liam paused, leaning back against the bridge's rail. "They're cold, huh?"

Darcy shook his head. "No, that barn is insulated. They'll be all right."

They regarded each other for a while, still and alert. Then Darcy broke into a big grin. "Come on. I wanna show you something."

"Pardon?"

"Let's go." Darcy jerked his head to the left and set off. Liam stared after him for a few dumbfounded moments, then sprinted to catch up to his long-legged strides.

"Why are you so fast?" Liam demanded, following him as they walked onto the west bank and into further darkness. He was practically jogging to keep up now, and had ascertained that they were going nowhere near the barn as the path grew more rocky and uneven.

"I ran track in school," said Darcy.

"I thought you didn't grow up in the States."

"English people run too."

"You're hilarious."

"Right turn," Darcy warned.

"What—shit, *ow*."

Liam had swerved too sharply, to avoid ramming into Darcy's shoulder, and stumbled before catching himself. When he looked up, Will Darcy was standing just before him, where the ground seemed to stop suddenly.

He approached slowly and froze, staring past the cliff and the jagged rocks below at a view of a ravine and treetops that seemed to stretch on for miles and miles. And then even closer....

"Jesus Christ," Liam breathed, staring down at the hopeless black abyss. He felt his insides lurch and staggered back.

"*Whoa*." Darcy chuckled under his breath, and caught the crook of his elbow. "You're okay—you're okay, I promise."

"Bet this is more of a view for the daytime," Liam muttered. He tugged his beanie off and ran a hand through his hair anxiously before putting it back on.

"It's for anytime," Darcy replied. Liam looked at him, green eyes keen in the darkness. Darcy stared into the distance; his breath came out in cold, wispy puffs. "I come out here to think."

Liam was quiet for a few moments. "Does Ann?"

Darcy looked at him. "I don't know. I've never talked about it with her. It's always been a personal space for me since I was a kid—somewhere to go to clear my mind and find peace alone."

Emboldened, Liam took a step closer so that he stood at Darcy's level now. He lifted his chin. From this perspective, the treetops were more visible. He imagined how lush and green they would be when the seasons turned. He felt privileged then, to view Darcy's coveted square of Pemberley.

"This must be gorgeous in the summertime."

"Yeah, it is," Darcy murmured. "I'm glad you can see it now."

Liam watched him, noted the way his shoulders squared rigidly and his fists clenched and unclenched as he stared out across the wide terrain. His nearly black hair was windblown and his jaw set in concentration. Darcy turned and met his gaze evenly, curious. And for a moment, Liam knew exactly what he was going to do before he did it, knew exactly what he *wanted* to do. A brief inhale of frigid air, and then he took a step forward and kissed him.

Darcy grew very still for a moment, as if paralyzed with astonishment. It seemed to take a moment for him to realize that Liam was kissing him, actually kissing *him*, and when Liam felt Darcy's hands settle at the small of his back and pull him in close, he smiled against his mouth.

The knots in his stomach smoothed out, and he felt heat rush through his limbs again, calming and dizzying. He was vaguely aware of his fist curling into the fabric of Darcy's sweatshirt, and his other hand at the nape of his neck.

When they separated, the cold wind seemed jarring and unforgiving. Darcy stared at him, mildly breathless. Liam's hat had fallen off, and they both noticed it on the ground at the same time. A second passed and they lunged for it. Darcy was the quicker of the two.

"This is a ridiculous hat," Darcy said. He was smiling, his blue eyes impossibly bright. "C'mon Liam, you can do better."

"Shut up." Liam laughed and shoved him on the chest. "Give it back."

He held it just out of reach. When Liam lurched for it, Darcy kissed him swiftly on the mouth and turned to the bridge. "Gonna have to move faster than that!"

Liam watched him disappear onto the bridge, grinned, and drew up his hood. *Bastard*, he thought, smiling, before he broke into a sprint.

CHAPTER THIRTY

THEY STUMBLED inside, laughing and shushing one another. Darcy slid the door closed, shook the dirt off of his boots, and looked into the kitchen. It was shrouded in darkness.

Liam had not been as careful. "*Oww*" came a low hiss.

Darcy chuckled. "What did you hit?"

"Rammed into the kitchen table," he muttered low, arching his back. Darcy found the light switch, and Liam raised the hem of his sweatshirt, inspecting a hipbone that would be bruised by morning.

"Don't be such a baby." Darcy was laughing, shrugging out of his coat.

"I am *not* being a—hi." Liam's voice grew quiet, as Darcy was suddenly very close. He bent his head and trailed his cool fingers gently over the smooth patch of pale skin.

"You need ice?" Darcy murmured with concern.

"No," Liam breathed.

Darcy tilted his face up, and they exchanged glances for a moment. Then his touch was gone and he retreated to the sink. "Make yourself comfortable," Darcy said airily.

Liam straightened and relaxed his shoulders.

While Darcy washed dishes, Liam gaped at the corkscrew board of kitchen utensils, useless and otherwise, that ran between the granite counter and the stainless-steel stove. "You own a strawberry huller," he said, bemused.

Darcy looked up, smiling. "I do."

"Who owns a strawberry huller?" Liam mumbled. He took a spatula off its hook and sliced the air with it, as if he were wielding a broadsword.

"It's to de-pit strawberries," Darcy tried to explain, concealing a laugh as he filled a glass with water from the tap. "It was a *gift*."

"Well, obviously the gifter was well aware of the abundant patches of strawberries on your property," said Liam, replacing the spatula.

"Aunt Josephine was a little senile last Christmas, but I'll let her know what you think of her purchase."

"Very kind of you, I appreciate it."

"Oh, no problem."

Liam missed his last remark, caught up again in the grandiose luxury of the kitchen itself.

It was among the first of the renovations—he could see that now. The cabinets were teal and the faucet was polished chrome. Brass pots and pans dangled from panels of hooks above the stove. Nothing seemed out of place on the counter, and glass shelves showed rows and rows of fine bone china, glinting beneath spotlights.

It made him think of his own home: the chipping paint on the white cabinets and the gas stove that always needed igniting, the pizza boxes shoved clumsily to the side, dough from his mother's latest baking endeavor drying in a crusty smudge along the cutting board, dozens of cracked glasses over the years, and plastic cups with each boy's name on it from Disney World....

"Here." Darcy interrupted his reverie and handed him a cup.

Liam regarded it slowly and took a sip. "Mm—cider?" When Darcy nodded, he shook his head. "Tastes homemade. What *can't* Cee make?"

"Very little; she's incredibly talented," Darcy answered automatically. "Tell me about your aunt and uncle."

Liam turned his head. "What about them?"

"Well, you seem close."

"We are," he murmured, tracing the rim of his cup with a fingertip. "I'm their favorite nephew," he added with a cheeky smile.

Darcy smiled back. "Are you really?"

"Probably not." Liam shrugged, leaning back against the counter. "But they're both very good people, and I've been fortunate enough to get spoiled by them over the years. They're more well-off than my parents; I think my mother resents Uncle Frank a little for being the wealthier sibling."

Darcy was nodding, pensive. Liam pressed his lips together, unsure of what had compelled him to share something so private. But Darcy was not being judgmental; he made a surprisingly attentive listener.

"I liked them before I found out that they were related to you," said Darcy. "And then I found out you're their nephew—"

"—and your opinion of them *instantly* soured," finished Liam with a half smile.

"Not quite." Darcy chuckled. A beat, and then he said, "You know, my sister is thrilled to have you here. She thinks really, really highly of you."

"I think the world of her. She became a really good friend of mine when everybody else in my life was just—" He thought for a moment. "—well, going nuts."

"If she cares about you, she'll do anything for you," Darcy explained. "She has a good heart—she's just too naïve and trusting with it sometimes."

"Well, she seemed pretty cynical when I first met her," Liam insisted. "Sweet, obviously, but there was definitely a layer of jadedness to her. Very world-weary. You would be proud," he added, with an attempt at levity.

Darcy shrugged, set his own cup down in the sink, and hiked up his sleeves. "I'm not proud," he murmured. "She got hurt badly, and at a really young age."

Liam felt a knot rising in his throat, and felt compelled to apologize for the second time that evening—though this time more for his blindness concerning Wickham.

The thought of them together made his stomach churn. *I loved her like my own sister*, Wickham had sworn over the phone. It made him feel sick now, and he relived his embarrassment all over again, reddening.

He didn't even realize it until Darcy called attention to it. "You all right?"

"Yeah," Liam said quickly. He rubbed his jaw. A minute passed.

"You should probably go get some sleep; no doubt she'll be showing you around town tomorrow—" Darcy smirked. "—among countless other excursions."

"I'm not tired," Liam responded.

"Oh yeah?"

"Yeah." He yawned.

"Bullshit." Darcy grinned, and Liam found himself smiling with him.

It alarmed him. He looked down at his hands and slid nimbly off of the counter. "I should go to bed," Liam agreed.

They walked upstairs together, and Liam thought that the dark halls were much easier to navigate, and a lot more comforting to walk through, with Darcy beside him. Simultaneously, he felt unnerved and calm in his presence. They both stopped at the door of the guest bedroom.

Liam's bravado outside had long since waned, and he felt foolish now. He couldn't even muster the courage to make eye contact. He felt something slipping, slipping away….

"You going with us tomorrow?" he asked Darcy before he could stop himself. "On the *excursions*," he clarified.

Darcy hesitated. "If you want me to."

"I want you to," said Liam.

The change on Will Darcy's face was almost imperceptible. His face lit up boyishly for an instant, and then it was gone so suddenly that Liam worried it had been a figment of his imagination.

"Good night," said Darcy softly. He lingered for a moment. Then he turned down the hall.

"Night," Liam murmured to the darkness.

Later that night, hours after they had reluctantly parted ways, Liam lay awake in bed with his head cradled in his arm and his eyes fixed on the ceiling. His mind raced.

When he closed his eyes, he saw himself staring down past that rocky ledge again, into the beautifully dark abyss, the reality of what lay beneath shrouded and concealed from view.

CHAPTER THIRTY-ONE

CECILIA REYNOLDS, despite her protestations, was forced to take Sundays off. Liam witnessed the weekly dispute with a fair share of amusement, as the Darcy siblings tried to politely hustle their caretaker out the front door.

"But I was going to make *crepes* for breakfast," Cee insisted, securing a yellow beret over her graying curls. "How can I deny Liam a delicacy that *you* two have been enjoying for years?"

"He'll survive, I can assure you," Ann insisted, tying her housekeeper's scarf for her. "Americans are far too spoiled as it is." She stuck her tongue out at Liam and he grinned.

"I'm *serious*," the older woman protested.

"Cee, we don't want you here," Darcy said coldly. "Out of this house this instant."

"I ought to slap you, William Darcy."

"When you come back, at least," he teased.

When the door finally clicked shut, and the three stood in the foyer, watching one another, Ann clapped her hands gleefully. "All right! Breakfast is on me. Let's go, gents."

Ann was a horrific driver. Liam was spared the difficulty of holding his tongue about it when his aunt called him. He answered, gripping his seat belt tightly while Darcy criticized his sister's swerving as gently as he could—which was to say, not very successfully.

"Hi, Maureen," murmured Liam. His aunt was one of those staggeringly *cool* aunts who refused to be acknowledged as "Aunt

Maureen" and would only settle for a first-name basis. "We're on our way to an inn for breakfast."

"Oh, good, you slept in," Maureen replied cheerfully. "You got a little cranky toward the end of yesterday." She didn't wait for him to refute this statement. "Are you sure you don't want to join us for the Bakewell tour this afternoon? Apparently we're all getting free dessert. Frank is delirious with excitement."

"Of course he is," Liam chuckled. "Yeah, Ann told me about it. And I hate pudding, so I'd only be holding you back on the excitement—"

"You hate *pudding*?" Ann gasped wildly. "What kind of humanoid *are* you, Liam Bennet?"

"Clearly alien," Darcy agreed lightly.

"Probably hates red velvet cupcakes and happiness as well," Ann mumbled.

"Unicorns and starlight."

"Joy in general."

"All right, that's enough out of you two!" Liam paused, turning his head. He asked Maureen, "How much of that did you hear?"

"*All of it,*" Maureen chuckled. She told him to enjoy breakfast and use up his film, and that they would be in touch about dinner plans.

Ann's favorite breakfast spot was full, and they had to wait for a table for twenty minutes. Liam looked to Darcy, expecting a complaint, but Darcy said nothing and kept up his infectious cheerfulness.

When they finally crowded around a table and were poured coffee, Darcy got a phone call from the Nerve headquarters in Manhattan. He excused himself politely and stepped outside.

Liam watched him go, perhaps longer than he should have. When he glanced back, Ann was watching him, blowing on her coffee cup. She took a sip and leaned back in her chair, smirking furtively.

"What?" Liam arched an eyebrow.

"Nothing, nothing, nothing."

"As if those last two *nothings* are supposed to reassure me," he fired back, the corner of his mouth pulling upward.

Ann fiddled with the rings on her fingers and avoided eye contact. "Will told me everything," she finally said.

Liam wasn't surprised, only concerned as to what would become of their friendship now. His lips pressed together in a thin, grim line, and he held his cup awkwardly, hovering above the surface of the table.

"He," she started, hesitating. "Well, he's *really* secretive. Dreadfully so. But Will usually confides in me, especially when he feels that he can't speak with anybody else. Which has been quite frequently over the past few years."

Liam set down his cup.

"But when he came back from Rosings—" Ann began to smile. "He was completely shut *down*, Liam. I couldn't get a word out of him, edgewise. I visited him in New York and he was beyond preoccupied; he was really cut up."

"Am I supposed to apologize for that, Ann?" Liam asked quietly, beginning to feel uncomfortable.

"No! No." Ann smiled quickly and covered his hand with her own. "I don't doubt that Will made an ass out of himself, because he *can* actually do that from time to time. What I'm saying is that nobody has ever affected him quite like that before. And I didn't realize it was *you* who had until… let's say, twelve hours ago."

"I didn't put two and two together at first either," he murmured.

"I think he's in love with you," Ann said, and when Liam glanced up sharply, she cut in. "I'm *serious*. It's like he's walking on air when you're around, and I catch him smiling at you and it's just *ugh*, disgustingly cute in the best way possible."

Liam rested his chin in his palm, covering his mouth with his hand.

"So please," she said gently. "I know there's something there, and it's not ordinary. I can feel it between you two because it's kind of its own magnetic *vortex* where casual bystanders get unconsciously sucked in." Liam couldn't help but smile as Ann continued. "And I *know* that he messed up, and maybe you're not ready to let go. It was horrible. But please give him a chance. He's the *best* person I know."

"Ann," Liam started, unsure of where to begin. "It's really, *really* complicated. Apart from Will, I have to think about my parents, and my brother Jamie. I haven't... I didn't *know* this about myself and I'm not sure how my family will react or how it's going to change things. This is a brand-new situation and it scares the living *shit* out of me. I don't think I'm handling it well at all."

"Everybody else would be fine, Liam. It's your own happiness you should be concerned with," Ann said pointedly. "How you handle your own life is up to your *own* judgment, and I'm sure you're doing fine."

"My happiness depends on others as well. Just like you're speaking with me now because you want to see your brother happy."

"And you," she interjected. "You don't think I want to see you happy too? I wouldn't even say anything if I didn't think that this is something that doesn't happen often, and that you two are pretty much perfect for each other."

"In what way?" Liam laughed in disbelief.

"Well for starters, you challenge him. You keep him grounded and not quite so guarded. You make him question himself, and better himself."

"And what does he do for me?" he asked curiously.

"Well, he *does* make you blush a lot, which is damn near adorable if I may say so myself."

"*Ann.*"

She giggled despite herself, and Liam covered his face with his hands, shaking his head but chuckling. This was surreal.

"Who else knows that Will is—?"

"Oh." Ann waved her hand. "Me, of course. Mom did. Dad never knew. Richard Fitzwilliam, our cousin. Charlie, obviously. *Not* his sister, though. Poor thing. I believe she's had her sights set on him for quite some time."

Liam snorted, recalling Caroline's clinginess.

"That's it," she said. "But it's not like he's the sort of man who would go public with it."

"Why, is he worried that it's too controversial for his reputation?" Liam asked warily.

"No. It's not exactly a problem. Charlie handles it just fine. But they're two different people. Will was *always* private with his personal life, regardless of whom he was dating. He only discusses business; he's pretty strict about it."

"And what about Catherine de Bourgh?"

"Oh, that's right. You've met her." Ann grinned wickedly. "*So* sorry about that. She knows, though she refuses to believe it. She's been trying to set him up with heiresses and actresses since he was seventeen. Blames it on the divorce, any traumatic childhood experience, actually."

Liam's lip curled. "That's—"

"Ridiculous," Ann agreed.

Darcy walked in again and shrugged out of his coat. Ann sat up, and he slid into the booth again. "Sorry about that," he sighed.

"What, they couldn't wait for you to return on Monday? You're on holiday," Ann reminded him.

"Not in times of crisis. There was a server crash a few hours ago."

"Somebody spill coffee on a keyboard?" Liam quipped.

"Not exactly," Darcy replied.

"All fixed?" Ann asked.

"Nearly. It should be up and running in ten minutes or so." Darcy glanced at Ann. "In case you want to use the app on your phone again."

"Oh, I don't have a Nerve account."

Darcy opened his mouth, shocked, and looked to Liam.

"I don't either," he said sheepishly. When Darcy continued to assault him with his unfaltering, ice blue gaze, Liam snapped, "I'm sorry! Your interface is really convoluted and busy. I had trouble with the search feature too."

"But that was nearly three versions ago. Check out how clean it is now." Darcy defiantly showed him the screen of his phone.

"Oh." Liam's shoulders slumped. "That's very... Zen?"

Ann snorted. "You should see his apartment in New York. We would call that very *Zen* as well."

"I believe the term is *minimalist*," Darcy argued.

"It's only minimalist if you do it on purpose, not if you're too busy to buy proper furniture," countered his sister.

Darcy sat back, dejected, and Liam laughed. Ann met his eye and smiled a slow, genuine smile. They held each other's gaze for a few moments and then both looked away. Darcy watched the exchange with some curiosity, and then their waitress arrived.

The rest of the day was spent exploring and shopping. Ann had planned to take them to the Peak District National Park, until the weather turned for the worse and it began raining. ("*Poo*," she had said quite firmly, squinting up at the gray sky.)

The Gardiners arrived at half past five o'clock, having deviated from their tour. The farewell with Ann was particularly bittersweet. With Darcy... it was almost disappointing. His aunt and uncle hovered in the foyer, repeating their warm wishes and peals of gratitude, so Liam and Darcy simply smiled at one another from a distance, wavering and uncertain.

Liam walked down the main trail toward the car, a few paces behind his aunt and uncle, with his collar raised against the rain. He turned at the sound of his name to see that Darcy had run out after him in a T-shirt. His dark hair was already a mop of a mess, hanging in his eyes.

"You're an idiot!" Liam called out. "You're gonna get sick."

"Who are you, my mother?" Darcy demanded, but he was smiling. He halted in the middle of the path. "Come visit me in New York next weekend. Well, the weekend *after* the next."

"Excuse me?" asked Liam, laughing.

"I'm serious. There's a party at our headquarters for hitting six million users."

"Big shots," fired Liam. "Why should *I* go?"

"Charlie will be there."

He buried his hands in his jean pockets. "I might ream him out."

"Yeah, I know. Maybe he needs to hear it from you," said Darcy. "I've already apologized to him, but we're not on really good terms right now. Which I *deserve*, I know," he said quickly, when Liam threatened to argue.

Liam hesitated and looked over his shoulder, where the Gardiners had already reached the car.

"It could give you the opportunity to network with people," Darcy offered, half-serious.

"I don't *need* help networking, D—" Liam began impatiently, but stopped himself. Yes, he did. He just didn't want to admit to it. He stared at him. "You really want me to go?"

"*Yeah*, I really want you to go. And preferably reach this decision before I catch pneumonia—"

"*Fine*," Liam laughed. "Yes, I'll go. Now get back inside!"

Darcy grinned, shuddered against the cold, and broke into a sprint back to the house. Liam got into the car and buckled up.

"What was the holdup?" Frank asked.

"Just making plans," Liam replied.

He caught Maureen half smiling in the passenger seat. Liam turned his head. The engine roared to life, and he stared wistfully at the massive Pemberley estate, cutting an impressive silhouette even in the downpour.

CHAPTER THIRTY-TWO

SUNLIGHT FILTERED through the curtains, and when Liam opened one eye, he could see dust particles swimming languidly in the air. In the corner of his room, a cluster of half-deflated balloons dangled listlessly from their knot on a closet door's hinge—remnants of his twentieth birthday the week before, a weekday event that had come and gone with a family dinner and some much-needed cash. His nightstand was still littered with cards. And also tissues. And mugs.

In the back corner of his mind that was still clinging to sleep, he wondered when he had last cleaned his bedroom.

His mother wondered the same. The door swung open, and she stood on the threshold with a laundry basket resting against her hip. "Are you getting up, or are you just *completely* ruined by the college lifestyle?"

Liam groaned and rolled over so that his face pressed into his pillow. "The second option." His voice came out distorted and muffled.

"Do you have anything that needs washing?"

"*Mmfgh.*"

"Fascinating, Liam," Mrs. Bennet drawled.

He heard her maneuvering around his room, opening drawers and shutting them. By the time Liam glanced up, she had already found a miniature pile of clothes to toss into the washer. He propped himself up on his elbows and squinted at her.

"Oh—thank you."

She smiled. "Did you know that Charlotte is back in town? She flies back to England on Monday."

"How'd you know that?"

"She's been sitting on our living room sofa playing chess with your father for the last half hour."

When Liam finally staggered into the living room, Charlotte couldn't help but laugh. He had been in the process of pulling on his T-shirt, and it somehow got tangled up, twisted inside out over his head. "Goddammit."

"Language," cautioned his father, smirking over his coffee cup.

Charlotte untangled him. "You have been unleashed."

"Much appreciated," said Liam. He looked at Mr. Bennet. "We have more coffee in the pot, right?"

"Nope."

"*Dad.*"

"It's a quarter to one. You don't get morning coffee."

"An afternoon pot, then." Liam shuffled to the kitchen, halting only to ask, "You want a cup, Charlotte?"

"Yeah, I'll meet you there. No cheating, Mr. B," Charlotte warned, leaving the chessboard untouched on the coffee table. Mr. Bennet smiled.

"Here, I know you like the pink Mother's Day mug," Liam told her in the kitchen. He handed her the ceramic cup.

Charlotte hopped up to sit on the edge of the kitchen counter. Her blonde hair, longer than he remembered, was gathered into a messy fishtail braid over her shoulder. She watched as Liam emptied the coffee grinder into a filter.

"So…," she began.

"So…," he agreed, raising one eyebrow.

"Happy belated birthday." Charlotte smiled warmly. She drew a small box from her sweatshirt pocket and handed it to him.

Liam smiled and opened it. It was a watch with a smooth, silver face and a black leather strap. Charlotte pushed up his sleeve for him and fixed it on.

"Thanks, Char—I love it." He kissed her cheek.

She shrugged. "I saw it in this vintage shop in London and I thought of you."

Liam looked at it in admiration.

"Are you gonna tell me what happened in England?" she asked innocently.

"Are *you* gonna tell me what happened in England?" Liam laughed. "I'm still waiting to hear how things started."

"Oh, that's right."

"What happened between you and Fitzwilliam?"

Charlotte said, "You're on a last-name basis with him?"

"No, not at all, but he has a *really* cool last name," Liam rationalized.

She sighed and ran her hand through her bangs. "Well, I told you that on New Year's Day I wasn't... really with Collins at all."

"Yep," said Liam.

The coffee machine started to groan and shake. They both glanced at it, and Liam slapped it with the palm of his hand. It settled down and the pot began to fill.

"It's old." He shrugged. "Continue."

"Okay." Charlotte straightened. "It started innocently enough. I crept out of our room because I was still pretty drunk, and I texted Richard. I went up to his suite and he was just—" She started giggling. "A *total* goofball. I found him digging through the minibar because he just had to find potato chips. It was his quest."

Liam leaned against the fridge, listening.

"So, we flirted. His suite had a Jacuzzi, and we spent some time in there. Nothing happened, despite the fact that we were both in our skivvies and pretty drunk and... attracted to one another."

"Two things," Liam interrupted smoothly. "Well, one thing. *Skivvies*? Who says that?"

"Shut *up*." She shoved him, and he grinned.

She went on to explain that she had felt terrible about it in the morning and had tried to rectify her behavior by being overly affectionate to Collins. Bill Collins on the other hand, in all his slicked-hair glory, had decided to be cold and untrusting.

"Well in his defense," Liam said, "his fiancée disappeared with another man in the middle of the night."

"True." Charlotte winced. "Which is why I didn't really hold it against him and tried for the next few days to be The Perfect Girlfriend."

"Fiancée."

"Whatever." She waved her hand.

She hadn't seen Richard Fitzwilliam for the next week or so, when he showed up at the Rosings estate on a Saturday afternoon looking completely flummoxed. Charlotte recalled how messed up his hair had appeared, as if he had been running his fingers through it for hours. He had brought her a bouquet of daisies, and the whole exchange had been maddeningly awkward.

"What did he say to you?" asked Liam.

"He said that he had been *thinking* of me and decided to bring me flowers." Charlotte arched an eyebrow. "And then I reminded him that I was engaged. All he did was nod. Several times."

"Wow, you broke this boy."

"I'm not finished! So he left…."

Richard had left Rosings, and Charlotte hadn't seen him for another stretch of days before she ran into him at a bistro, while she was grabbing lunch between her classes. He was with a friend and had warmly insisted that Charlotte join them.

"So I did. It was really, really nice. He was completely back to his old self."

"Because his friend was there as a buffer, Charlotte," Liam pointed out. He stopped to pour them both coffee.

She mulled this over and nodded. "You're probably right. So when I finally left to go to class, we said good-bye and he kissed my cheek and told me that he'd visit Rosings that night. His aunt needed him to look over something apparently."

"Bullshit," he said quickly.

Charlotte smiled slowly.

Collins had been out tending the garden at the time; apparently he was obsessed with governing Rosings' landscape and dictating directions to the hedgers and gardeners who were paid to maintain the property. Richard found Charlotte in the kitchen and behaved "only half as awkward this time." He flirted a little more, kissed her, apologized for the kiss, and confessed that he really, really liked her.

"And, of course, I obviously really like him. And he's twenty-one. And I'm nineteen. And I realized—" Charlotte tilted her head. "What the hell was I *doing* with my life? Why was I rushing *anything?*"

Liam raised his eyebrows and smiled. He suddenly understood his parents' frustration, how you could tell someone a truth over and over again until you were blue in the face, but it would have no value to that person unless they discovered it on their own. He slumped his shoulders and took a sip of his coffee. *What a waste of breath.*

"So I broke off the engagement. Catherine de Bourgh called me a *brazen hussy*—stop laughing, she really did—and I squatted at a friend's apartment for the rest of the time," she said. "As for Richard, he's meeting me at the airport on Monday and I'm... pretty happy about that."

"So where are you staying for the remainder of the semester?"

"Richard said I could—"

"*Charlotte.*"

"*—stay as long as I needed to,*" she emphasized, narrowing her gray eyes. "What are you, my mother? I'm still apartment hunting; this is temporary, don't worry."

"I worry. But I'm happy for you."

"So tell me about your spring break!" Charlotte crossed one leg over the other and leaned forward to listen, smiling brightly.

Liam had to laugh. "I ran into Will Darcy."

"I had a *gut feeling* you might."

"Ann is his sister, by the way," he deadpanned. "Ann Darcy. Georgi*ana* Darcy."

Charlotte's brows knit together. A few seconds passed. "Boom, there's a plot twist."

He recounted the whole story to her. The surprise stop at Pemberley, the awkward but warm reception, Cecilia Reynolds' stiff loyalty and extraordinary culinary skills, the kiss above the ravine, Ann's secret plea, and Darcy being so... *so....*

"*Nice,*" Liam concluded, perplexed. He lifted the coffee cup to his lips.

Having listened intently to his story without interrupting, Charlotte set down her cup and looked him in the eye. "You're going to go for this, right?"

"No," he said hesitantly.

"*What?*" Charlotte demanded.

"I don't know." Liam passed a hand across his face.

"I agree with Ann. If I thought that Will Darcy was just playing games or *having fun*, I'd talk you out of it. But—" She laughed shortly. "Liam, this is someone who has such intense feelings for you that he *tried to talk himself out of them*. And failed—spectacularly."

"Yeah, but I hate that. What, like it's so terrible to like me? That's not exactly a compliment."

"I think it was mostly because you're a few years younger than him," she said, taking a brief sip. "And also, it's not entirely encouraging when you're attracted to someone who pretty much dislikes you. Not that he knew the extent to which you didn't like him."

Liam looked into his cup. He hadn't. Liam recalled how stunned Darcy had looked that night in the hotel room, astonished and mortified at his error.

"Face it," Charlotte said, seemingly on cue. "He's smitten."

"But doesn't anybody care about what *I* feel?" Liam asked hotly. "Yeah, maybe he's not who I thought he was. But when push comes to shove, he's responsible for ruining Jamie's relationship. I don't know if I could ever forgive him for hurting my brother like that."

Charlotte shook her head. "*Charlie* is responsible for your brother's heartbreak. If a man has a weak character, those closest to him can easily turn his head, okay? Call his shots for him. If Charlie really loved Jamie, he wouldn't have let *anybody* talk him out of it."

"Darcy is persuasive," Liam countered.

"And Charlie is gullible." Charlotte shrugged. "At least Darcy admitted his mistake and tried to correct it. He's only human.... I think you're just determined not to like him as much as you really do."

"Why would I do that?" he murmured. He wasn't looking at her anymore, but down at the counter, drumming his fingers on the edge.

"Because whenever something good happens to you, you always wait for the bottom to drop out."

Liam quickly glanced up at her. Charlotte gave him a small smile and touched his cheek fondly. "Think about it."

He did think about it. He thought about it all day, long after his best friend left. He thought about it as he sat in the living room for hours, watching and not watching his younger brothers play video games. It was difficult for anybody to catch his attention the first time around.

"*Hey!*" Liam finally flinched when Ben tossed a sofa cushion at him. "Finally."

"He zoned out." Mason smiled, turning back to the game.

"What do you want?" Liam hurled the cushion back at his younger brother.

"Nothing," Ben said, dodging it. "I was just testing your reflexes."

Liam stared at him for a few moments. "Where's Nate?"

"Probably hanging out with George again," Mason answered for him. "Dammit. I asked you to *defend* that line, Ben."

"I can't be everywhere," Ben mollified, tilting his controller.

"Who's George?" Liam cut in.

"Oh, right." Ben paused the game and turned to look at his brother from over his shoulder. "George Wickham. He came by a few days ago asking to see you."

"Wait, *what?* Then why the hell is Nate hanging out with him?" Liam was sitting on the edge of his seat now.

"He's really into that one band he was in," Ben said. "It's fruit-related, that much I remember. George was really nice."

"Of course he was. So, they're what, *hanging out?*"

"George promised to give him free guitar lessons because he's your little brother," said Mason. "It's pretty cool, if you ask me. He played for us and he's really talented."

"*Nate* is?" Ben asked.

"George."

"Oh."

Liam sat mulling this over, and then he sprang up and stepped out onto the porch, dialing Nate. This didn't sit well with him at all.

"Hello?"

"Hey Nate."

"Oh, you're home," Nate said breezily. Liam could hear the twang of an electric guitar in the background, then a muffled voice. "Wickham says hi, by the way."

"Yeah, that's what I'm calling you about. Why are you hanging out with him?"

"He's mentoring me. I want to play the guitar as well as he does."

"And don't you find it a little suspicious that he's doing that for free?"

Nate started to say something, and then sighed. "Here, he wants to talk to you."

"Wait—"

"Hey, Liam!" said George sunnily.

Liam sighed. "What's up?"

"Pity I missed you the other day. I was in town. I'm seeing this girl who lives a couple miles away so I thought, I'll swing 'round, see if Bennet is still in the neighborhood—"

"George, why are you mentoring my younger brother?"

"Well, I still owe you one, don't I? From backing out of the Netherfield gig."

Liam hesitated. "You don't have to do that. In fact, I insist that you don't do that."

"It's my pleasure. Nate reminds me of myself at that age. He's very passionate about music. He has great instincts as well. Listen mate, we're learning chord progression so I have to go."

"George—"

"But let me know when you're free and we can hang out. Bye!"

The line went dead. Liam sighed and pinched the bridge of his nose.

CHAPTER THIRTY-THREE

CLASSES RESUMED that Monday, and Liam found himself more impatient for the weekend than he had been in a while. He jogged his leg nervously beneath his desk, and he was prone to staring vacantly out the third-story window. Something about campus now triggered anxious thoughts.

He felt alone, though he had been at Hartford without Charlotte for quite some time. Jamie's phone calls had grown more and more infrequent since he transferred divisions at his new company. Liam had last spoken to him two weeks before, when Jamie called to say that he had broken up with Aaron. He didn't include particular details, but Jamie seemed rather blasé about the ordeal, chalking it up to being too busy at work to sustain a relationship.

Whether it was true or not, Liam couldn't say he wasn't relieved.

Charlotte, of course, disappeared back to London. He had a smattering of acquaintances from the café, his classes, and some clubs he had dropped out of after the first semester, but Liam couldn't shake the feeling of isolation.

Nobody that he *really* wanted to talk to was anywhere in the University District.

"Mr. Bennet, can you tell me the second accusation that Socrates was charged with during the trial?"

Liam snapped his head forward. The professor had lowered his glasses and was openly smirking.

"He was accused of atheism. He explained natural phenomena scientifically, so the people of Athens assumed that he didn't believe in the same gods that they believed in." Liam set his pencil down upon his desk with a click.

Dr. O'Connell hesitated, and then turned on the balls of his feet. "Correct. Can anybody tell me what his rebuttal was?"

His shoulders relaxed. *Asshat.*

After class was dismissed, he decided to barricade himself in the library. He was just in the process of chaining his bike, loaned from Jamie, when his phone started vibrating in his sweatshirt pocket.

"Hello?"

"So you are definitely coming up this weekend, right?" asked Will Darcy.

"Not if you're going to be that bossy about it."

"There's a difference between being bossy and insistent." He could hear his smile through the phone.

"Not to you, there isn't," Liam challenged. He added, "I'm taking the Amtrak from Trenton. The train's at 4:10 p.m. last I checked. Uh, if you can text me the address, I can just take a cab from Grand Central—"

"Nah, I can meet you there. I live six blocks from the station."

"Works for me." He sandwiched his phone between his ear and shoulder, twisted the last dial of his lock, and stood up straight. "So, the dress for this party—"

"Is casual, don't worry."

"I'm not worried."

"You sounded worried."

"Just curious, not worried."

"Well, what else are you curious about?"

"The catering," Liam joked, smiling. "I'm not so good with seafood."

"I'll be sure to relay your concerns to management."

He grinned and shook his head. "God, you are such a—"

"Yes?" Darcy asked smoothly.

"Never mind. I'll see you Friday, Will."

"Bye, Liam."

For as sparse as his attention was on Monday, Liam could hardly concentrate on the two classes he had Friday. If class ended on time, he would have just a *sliver* of time to make it to the station. As soon as he was dismissed from Statistics, Liam slung his bag over his shoulder and pushed through the masses. "Excuse me, pardon me, I'm *that* kind of douche bag right now, I know, *yes*, sorry!"

His car needed a little more encouragement, and he turned the key repeatedly in the ignition, coaxing until it roared to life.

Liam relaxed on the train. He liked trains, though he imagined they would lose their charm around the second day for commuters. Still, he liked watching men in crumpled suits reading the paper and children stealing their mother's tablets to play games he hadn't even heard of yet. He hooked in his earbuds and let himself drift off.

Darcy was waiting outside in a cluster of people and uniform cabs. He brightened when he spotted Liam, and Liam, so calm on the train, was once again overtaken with nervousness pin-prickling his fingertips. He licked his lips, gripped his bag a little tighter, and walked toward him.

He stopped three feet short. "Hey."

"Hi."

"You didn't have to meet me," Liam said offhandedly.

"Don't worry about it," Darcy insisted.

As they walked down Lexington Avenue, Liam noted Darcy's clothes and decided that he couldn't tell whether or not the man had gone to work that day. His black button-down was pressed, but the sleeves were rolled neatly to his elbows—also, no tie.

"So, this is how the great entrepreneur William Darcy dresses down," Liam challenged.

Darcy paused for a moment, exhaling evenly out of his nostrils. Then he continued walking. "There are so many things wrong with that statement."

"Yeah? Like what?"

"*Entrepreneur*, for one. What a terrible term—"

"It's French," Liam added.

"Well, they should have kept it."

When they reached Darcy's building, they boarded the elevator, and Darcy punched the *PH* button and leaned against the railing. Liam stared at the button, blinking.

"You own the entire top floor, don't you?" he asked in a monotone.

Darcy hesitated. "Yes."

"Of course you do," Liam sighed. The elevator stilled with a *ping*, and he stepped across the threshold.

The apartment was empty, for the most part. The furniture that was there was very functional and sleek. Glass partitions separated rooms, and when he peeked around the corner, he saw that the kitchen seemed to be stainless-steel, state-of-the-art everything.

"More strawberry hullers in there?" Liam asked innocently.

"All right, smartass." Darcy smirked. "We have a few minutes, so make yourself at home. I have to send a couple of e-mails."

"'Kay."

After Darcy had retreated into the den, Liam turned quietly about the room. It almost seemed like Darcy had just moved in, judging by the building of cardboard boxes neatly stacked against the wall. An armchair and a coffee table were the only items of furniture in the living room. He wandered to the corridor, glanced over his shoulder, and entered the master bedroom, leaving the door ajar behind him.

There was a queen-sized mattress on the floor, without a frame. The bed was made very carefully, with its blue pinstriped sheets stretched across the mattress and tucked tautly under the sides. Liam smirked—he suspected Cecilia Reynolds' influence here.

Liam strayed to the dresser, and trailed his fingers over belongings. He picked up a hairbrush and set it down, then an old novel from a secondhand bookshop. Then he moved, and something brilliant and iridescent caught the light streaming between the blinds.

It was a round, gold locket. Liam regarded it for a moment and then took it off its peg. An engraving of a crane standing among reeds and water lilies was raised against the gold setting. Its slender neck looped downward, wings spread before flight. It grasped a diamond in its beak. Liam flipped it over, moving his fingers over the inscription: *APD.*

The floor creaked and he flinched.

"*Not* sneaking up on you," Darcy cautioned. He was in the process of unrolling his sleeves. "And I see you've found the locket."

"It's beautiful," Liam murmured, replacing it. "Looks very old."

"It is. It was in my father's family for a couple hundred years. I think it's from the Regency Era." Darcy was perusing his closet now, picking out a new shirt.

"Who's APD?"

"My mother—Annabella Parker Darcy. My father had it engraved for her as a gift after their engagement."

"And yet you came to own it?" Liam asked curiously. He sat on the edge of the bed.

"Yeah," Darcy said quietly, still facing the closet with his head bent low. "After my dad died, I think it hurt my mother too much to see it in her jewelry box."

He slipped the shirt off and eased it onto a hanger. Liam watched the muscles of his back tauten with his movements, broad shoulders tapering down a long torso to a narrow waist. Then Darcy slipped on a different shirt—pale blue. He turned and Liam quickly lowered his eyes.

Darcy stared at the dresser now, adjusting his collar. "Ann didn't want it. I took it home. I really like family heirlooms. It's like a direct link to the past."

Liam smiled to himself. "I wish I made it a point to treasure family as much as you do."

"Well, it's easy to take them for granted when you have many people in your life," Darcy murmured, sitting beside Liam. "But growing up, it was mostly Ann, my father, and I. When you lose one person… the whole ship seems to capsize."

He grew silent. Liam stared at Darcy's profile—his jaw set and his eyes fixed on a distant point in the room. Liam reached forward and fleetingly touched his cheek. The moment passed, and he moved his hand to mess up his hair; Darcy pulled back with a laugh.

"Cheer up," Liam told him, smiling. He got to his feet. "We have a party to go to."

CHAPTER THIRTY-FOUR

TWO HOURS into the Nerve celebration, and Liam was wandering around the top floor of the sleek Manhattan high-rise wearing three leis and a pair of neon-green eyeglasses that weren't his. He was also carrying somebody else's beer—and that somebody shrieked his name as he rounded the corridor.

Chandra Marone, a stunningly pretty black girl, raced to snatch her bottle back. She held on to his shoulder as she slipped her red pumps back on. "Did you get lost *again*?"

"*Yes*," Liam laughed. "This place is a maze."

She smiled. He didn't know what he had been expecting from the cluster of employees celebrating six million users of a nascent social media platform. Perhaps the spatter of socialites at the Netherfield party had left a bad taste in his mouth. But everyone Liam had encountered at Nerve thus far was delightful: friendly, down-to-earth, and *not* dressed to the nines in tuxedos and designer gowns.

"The building is confusing," Chandra told Liam, tucking a strand of dark hair behind her ear. "I'm glad I found you, though. Will was asking around—they're doing karaoke soon."

"Oh, no. I'm not doing that. No, no, *no*."

"Yes!" Chandra grinned. She faltered, and then touched his glasses fleetingly. "Are these Bob's? From accounting? He never lets *anybody* touch his stuff."

"Well, I'm really, really special, so...."

"I mean, you would have to be, if Will Darcy brought you here."

"What do you mean?" Liam cocked his head, losing his levity.

Her ruby lips spread into a slow smile. "As incredible of a boss as he is—and he really is one of the most genuine, kindest individuals I've ever worked with—he's never brought *anyone* to work events." She tapped his nose fondly. "So you must be pretty special, kid."

It would have been natural for Liam to blush, but then he got stuck on Chandra calling him *kid*, which seemed odd. She was William Darcy's newest assistant—and a recent college graduate. They couldn't be that far apart in age.

"But I have to ask." Chandra hesitated. "Is he seeing anybody? Because he is *so* cute, I actually can't handle it."

"There you are." Darcy finally found them. Liam and Chandra jolted apart as he met them in the hall. Darcy opened his mouth, and then stared quizzically at Liam. "Those are Bob's."

"Yes." Liam took the glasses off and handed them to Darcy. "Please give him my apologies when you return them. I might have taken them without permission."

"He's pretty buzzed; I doubt he'll mind." Chandra waved her hand. She smiled at Darcy. "I left the Lowman reports on your desk this afternoon. Did you get my text?"

"Yeah, and I ignored it. Because it's *Friday*." Darcy smiled patiently. "Go have fun, Chandra. Kenny's trying to loop you into a karaoke duet."

"Well, lucky for him that I'm a phenomenal singer." She beamed and turned back down the hallway. "Pleasure to meet you, Liam!"

"You too." Liam smiled. After she had gone, he leaned in close and mock-whispered, "Your receptionist is in love with you."

"No...."

"*Yes*," he chuckled, scratching his nose. "Just asked me if you were available."

Darcy rubbed the back of his neck. "Shit."

Liam snorted and then took Darcy's hand in his. "Come on. Show me where Charles Bingley is hiding."

Charles Bingley was hiding in his office, beyond the closed, frosted-glass door with his name on it in gilt letters. Darcy knocked and entered, and Bingley raised his head with a brief grunt of acknowledgement before turning back to his computer—then he did a double take and stood up.

"Liam! *Hi*."

"Charlie." Liam smiled politely. His smile wavered.

As terrible as Bingley had left things with Jamie, it was difficult to be cross with him now. Bingley looked thin and *exhausted*, with dark circles rimming his eyes and his shirt hanging a little too loosely on his body. He ran a hand through his hair and smiled wide. "So good to see you!"

"I'm gonna go check out the Lowman reports." Darcy cleared his throat and excused himself. The door clicked shut behind him.

"Uh." Bingley maneuvered himself around the office, touching everything and then setting it down. He picked up a mug. "Do you want a cup of coffee or something? I just got this espresso machine last Christmas. I've actually never *used* it, but I'm sure I could figure it out."

"No, that's okay."

Bingley pressed his lips together and nodded. "How have you been?"

"Good," answered Liam. "I guess Will told you about... Pemberley and running into his sister."

"Yeah. Yeah, he has. It's good to see you again. I'm glad you two are on better terms."

"Yeah," Liam said quietly.

"How's...." Bingley paused. "How's Jamie doing?"

"Good—busy at work. He transferred departments at his new company, so he's more involved in the design process now."

"Oh, good. He was always really talented in graphics. I'm happy for him."

A loaded silence passed between the two of them. Bingley tapped his fingers against the edge of his desk. Liam glanced up and shook his head. He asked quietly, "Why did you leave without telling Jamie? Or me? Any of us?"

Bingley looked up. He looked unbearably upset now. "I don't... I don't know," he sighed, removing his glasses. "If you hate me, I completely understand. I would too."

"I could never hate you, Charlie. I hate what happened. There's a difference," said Liam.

"I hate it too," Bingley murmured. He glanced up at him, opened his mouth, and then shut it. Liam got the impression there was a *lot* Bingley wanted to ask, but nothing he would allow himself to. He finally worked up the nerve to say, "If you could just tell Jamie that—"

Liam cut him off. "I guarantee you that whatever you want me to say to him will be fifty times more appreciated if it came out of your mouth." A beat, and then, "If you don't have his number anymore, I can write it down for you."

"I have it," Bingley said softly. "I guess he's probably seeing someone else now? It's hard to imagine that he wouldn't be; he's... well, he's pretty wonderful."

"He is pretty wonderful, make no mistake about that," Liam said firmly. "But you never know. Give him a call."

Bingley gave a small smile. Liam turned to the door.

"Hey, Liam?"

"Yeah?" He looked over his shoulder.

"Thank you."

As Liam wandered out among the party guests, he felt as if he were encased in his own bubble. He couldn't imagine telling all of this to Jamie—would he? *Should* he? He stopped and drew his phone from his back pocket. The battery was almost dead. With some hesitation, he put it back.

God, he wouldn't even know where to begin. It suddenly made him feel *sad*, as if there were a rift between him and his brother, and he couldn't account for when the split had happened, and how wide the fissure had cracked.

"Hey." Darcy caught up with him, and touched his elbow fleetingly. "You all right?"

"Yeah," he muttered. "I just have a bad headache. Do you mind if we head back soon?"

"No, not at all. I'll go get your jacket."

CHAPTER THIRTY-FIVE

THE VIEW from Darcy's penthouse made him feel infinitely small, and Liam crossed his arms over his chest and rested his forehead against the cool glass, watching cars zip by intersections.

"You're not okay," Darcy murmured behind him.

Liam glanced over his shoulder. "No, I am. I had a really good time tonight. Much better than I expected." He smiled for good measure. "It's just this whole business with Charlie and Jamie...."

"What specifically?" Darcy asked politely.

Liam sighed. "I wish I knew how to fix it."

"Liam," said Darcy. "I think you did a lot more tonight than you give yourself credit for. Don't be so pessimistic."

"Something you shouldn't say to an eternal realist," Liam responded.

Darcy smiled, warm and genuine. Liam fixated on him. There was this side to him, the part he had kept so carefully hidden before, that everybody else seemed enamored with. Chandra, Richard, Ann....

Had it been there all along? Had he been ignoring it?

"And you *are* hell-bent on sleeping on the sofa," Darcy confirmed with a drawl, displeased.

"Yeah." Liam smiled. "I'm not turning you out of your bed. Hospitality be damned."

"It wouldn't be much of an inconvenience. I don't sleep much anyway."

Liam raised his eyebrows, amused. "Why?"

Darcy shrugged. "I have trouble drowning out the sound of the city. You could say that growing up in Derbyshire sort of ruined me."

"Really? I think it did the opposite," he said. When Darcy looked up, Liam smiled faintly at him.

Darcy stilled, then took three steps forward. He laid his palm flat against the glass beside Liam's head. Liam didn't tense this time, but regarded Will Darcy calmly, anticipation a quiet, steady hum in his fingertips.

A moment of hesitation, and then Darcy leaned forward and brushed his lips against Liam's. They shared breaths for a moment, and then Liam's fingers curled around Darcy's collar and pulled him in closer. His lips moved; he kissed the corner of Darcy's mouth, his jaw, the base of his throat. Darcy's eyes fell shut, and a low, nearly imperceptible noise escaped his lips—almost like a sigh.

Liam closed his eyes and pressed a kiss to the side of Darcy's jaw. His fingers slid down his shirt, nimbly undoing buttons as he went.

CHAPTER THIRTY-SIX

HE WOVE in and out of sleep, well aware that it was time to rise but physically fighting it. His dreams faded and scattered, and when Liam finally sat up, it took him a few seconds to remember where he was. The sun was just beginning to rise, filling the vast room with light. He squinted.

Darcy slept soundly. Liam studied his face in the pale morning light—the smooth brow, the curve of a cheekbone not pressed into his pillow, his dark hair mussed and unruly from sleep. The corners of his mouth lifted, and Liam thought momentarily to reach out and touch him—but then he stilled his hand and slipped off the bed quietly, afraid to wake him.

His cell phone was dead on the dresser, long forgotten. Stifling a sigh, Liam unwound his charger and plugged it in. His gaze flickered up when Darcy stirred, but he gave no indication of waking. Liam powered on his phone and waited.

(11) Missed Calls. Five messages.

Liam frowned. He dialed voice mail and listened.

Darcy seemed to note the lack of warmth beside him, propped himself up on an elbow, and rubbed his face. He looked sleepily at Liam, who was crouched beside the outlet, one hand covering his mouth. When Liam looked up, his green eyes were wide with alarm.

Darcy's smile disappeared. He sat up, looking concerned. "Hey."

Liam hung up and rose fluidly, looking around for his backpack. He began to methodically stuff it with his belongings. His lips were pressed together in a thin line.

"Liam," said Darcy.

"Yeah?" he asked, clipped.

"Where are you going?"

"I, uh." Liam ran his fingers through his hair. "I don't know where I put my jacket last night. Do you have it? Maybe you put it in the coat closet; I don't remember."

Darcy opened his mouth and then shut it.

Liam met his eye. "I have to go. It's my brother, Nate. He's been in an accident."

Darcy straightened. "When?"

"Late last night. Around two in the morning."

"Is he okay?"

"No, he's been hospitalized," Liam said mechanically.

"Jesus." Darcy got out of bed and hunted for his sweatshirt. "What happened?"

Liam felt as if he had just swallowed a handful of marbles. "I just—I don't know. Jamie left me a voice mail. He was with George Wickham at the time it happened. Or just *before*, I don't understand—"

"George *Wickham*?"

"Yeah."

"I'll drive you home."

"Don't be ridiculous." Liam brushed him off. He zipped up his bag and slung it over his shoulder. "I'm taking the train."

"Well, when's the next one?"

"I don't know!" Liam snapped. He took in a breath and pinched the bridge of his nose. "I'm sorry," he muttered. "I'm sorry—"

Darcy was shaking his head. "Stop apologizing. I'm driving you. Get your things together. I'll have the car ready outside in five minutes."

"Will, you're not driving me—"

"Yes, I am," he said coolly.

"*No*, you're—"

"Shut *up*," said Darcy. Somehow, Liam had missed the entire process of him getting dressed, because he stood before him now completely clothed. Silently, Darcy took Liam's bag and shouldered it.

"Will?" said Liam quietly.

Darcy paused, lingering now in the doorway.

"Thank you."

He pressed his lips together. "Don't forget your watch on the bureau."

IT WAS a garishly beautiful Saturday morning, not that either of them seemed to notice. As Darcy pulled onto I-95, Liam finished the phone call with his father. Mr. Bennet had sounded calm but uncomfortably quiet, detailing the events of the night before.

"So, what happened?" Darcy murmured, glancing quickly at him before he changed lanes.

Liam was shaking his head. "Wickham went to a friend's house party in the city—thought it would be a big *laugh* to bring an underage kid. Got drunk. Let *Nate* drink. There was some argument, and George pushed Nate into the street. He was hit by a car."

"Jesus," Darcy breathed.

"And Wickham panicked and left him there. The driver called 911."

"How badly is he hurt?"

"He has a broken leg and a possible concussion. Dad says he's having trouble moving his neck...." Liam covered his face with his hands. "God*damn* it, this is all my fault."

"No, it isn't," Darcy said patiently.

"Yes, it is. I didn't tell *anybody* what I knew about Wickham. I let things unfold on their own—terrible things, and I didn't step in." Liam turned, nearly hysterical in his imitation. "Nate's hanging out with George Wickham? Oh *cool*, that can't end well! Here, let me do *nothing* to stop that."

"There's only so much that you can do; people will do what they want."

"Yeah, but he's just a kid," Liam murmured. He glanced out the window, jaw set. "A stupid, stupid kid."

Luckily, traffic was sparse that Saturday morning, which allowed them to make good time. Darcy pulled into a rest stop around thirty miles in, to get coffee. Liam stayed in the car to answer a phone call. When Darcy walked out of the convenience shop, he scoffed and propped his sunglasses on his head. "*Seriously?*"

Liam had moved the car to a gas pump. He had just finished pumping gas and placed the nozzle back. "It's the least I can do. You were down three-quarters of a tank."

Darcy sighed and handed him his coffee. They sat in silence on the trunk of the car. Liam sipped coffee from the Styrofoam cup and gazed into the distance. The blue sky was nearly blinding in its brilliance.

"Who drinks their coffee black?" Darcy teased.

Liam shrugged. "Real men." A beat, then, "Though this is the shittiest cup of coffee I've ever had—"

"It *is* some truly phenomenal shit," Darcy agreed, laughing. A few seconds passed, and he asked, "Who called you?"

"Mason. I asked for an update. Nate's still getting tests done. He's concussed. But he's spoken to Mom, so he's pretty lucid and coherent."

"A good sign."

"Mmm," Liam agreed, finishing his coffee. He slid off of the trunk and trashed his cup.

Darcy remained seated on the trunk, watching him very carefully. Liam did his best to conceal his distress; every movement was quick and mechanical, and his face was smoothed into a mask of tight composure except for brief moments. But when he thought Darcy wasn't looking, his resolve would crack and show just how worried he was for his brother.

He was just opening the passenger door when Darcy slid off the trunk and caught his hand. Liam glanced up. "It's going to be okay; *he's* going to be okay," Darcy assured him. "I promise."

Liam's lips quirked up, sardonic. "I don't know if that's up to you to promise."

"Have a little faith," he commanded firmly.

Liam lifted his head. "Okay."

Darcy leaned forward and kissed him. "Get in the car."

CHAPTER THIRTY-SEVEN

LIAM ROUNDED the corner outside the waiting room and spotted Jamie leaning against the wall, checking his phone.

"Liam!" Jamie started. "Oh, thank God. Where have you…?" He stopped in his tracks as Will Darcy caught up with them.

"Parked the car," Darcy explained to Liam.

"Great."

The three of them stared at one another awkwardly until Liam cleared his throat and broke the silence. "Jamie, you remember Will Darcy? Will, my brother."

"Of course," said Darcy smoothly, shaking his hand. "Good to see you."

"Hi." Jamie stared, faltered, and looked down at his shoes.

"Listen, I'm probably going to take off," Darcy told Liam. He held himself uncomfortably, his shoulders squared again. Liam was reminded of their first meeting. "Let me know if you need anything else."

He turned and retreated down the hall. When he was a few feet away, Jamie said very calmly and very quietly, "What on God's green earth is William *Darcy* doing here?"

"He drove me back," Liam said, breathless. "Hold that thought?"

Before Jamie could respond, his brother sprinted down the hall. Liam pushed into the exit stairwell and gazed down, spotting Darcy already jogging quickly to the ground floor. "Hey!" he shouted.

Darcy stopped and gazed up. "Hey." When Liam met up with him, he couldn't help but laugh. "And you say you're not a fast runner."

"Only when provoked," Liam clarified. "Don't do that."

"Do what?"

"Disappear before I can say good-bye or *thank you* or anything that I wanted to say."

Darcy smiled. "Well, what did you want to say?"

Liam paused. "Well, all that, essentially."

"You're welcome. But it's not like there was any alternative," Darcy murmured. "I'm not the type of person to sit idly by when bad things happen to people that I care about."

"I know—I'm beginning to grasp that."

"Well, good." Darcy chuckled.

They lapsed into silence. The shock of the situation was starting to catch up to Liam, and he spent quite a few seconds staring down at the floor, his brow creased. He opened his mouth uselessly.

And then it was unclear who had embraced whom, but Darcy's arms linked around Liam's waist and Liam held Darcy's shoulders, eyes closed. It was fleeting but almost desperate, and Liam heard Darcy's voice, a soft hum near his ear: "Don't worry. It's going to be okay."

Darcy's lips brushed against his neck and Liam clasped his hand, and then with a brief quirk of his lips, Will Darcy disappeared down the stairwell. Liam heard the door shut, and then silence.

CHAPTER THIRTY-EIGHT

LIAM BURST into the room and shrugged out of his jacket. "Hi," he greeted. "Someone give me an update."

Most of the Bennets looked up at the intrusion. Ben was glued to his phone, exhausting every social media platform available. Mason put down his issue of *Sports Illustrated*. Behind Liam, Jamie moved to the window and crossed his arms over his chest. Mr. Bennet did not bother to leave his chair, but stared at Liam as if he could see through him. Empty cups sat stacked on the coffee table, along with a plate of bagels—poppy seeds littered the floor.

"Where's Mom?" Liam asked Jamie.

"With Nate. They tried chasing her out, but she won't leave."

"Where were you?" Mr. Bennet suddenly asked Liam. His face was white.

"New York City," answered Liam.

"What's in New York?"

"Does it matter? Tell me about Nate."

"His leg is broken in three places," said Mason. "He has trouble turning his neck and he says that his back really hurts. He's going to need a lot of physical therapy. Nobody can find Wickham, but we're gonna file a police report. Endangering a minor, et cetera…."

"Did you just *say* et cetera?" Ben looked up from his phone, incredulous.

"Liam," Jamie interrupted smoothly. "Can I talk to you outside?"

"Not now. Dad, you look *really* pale." Liam ignored his older brother and sat by his father; he took his hand in his. "Have you had anything to eat today?"

"No. I'm scared to death," Mr. Bennet confessed. He cupped his son's cheek with his palm, and Liam saw genuine fear lining his father's face. His hand dropped. "I don't know when your mother and I reversed roles. But there's a reason she's in there instead of me."

"You've always been a little squeamish," Jamie reminded him. "And any hysteria that Mom has subdued will just rebound at a later hour."

Mr. Bennet shook his head. "They said that he couldn't get up afterward. What if his spine is damaged? He looked white as a sheet. So goddamn pale...."

Liam gripped his hand. "Nate is going to be okay."

"You kids don't get it, do you?" Mr. Bennet said seriously. "We have no health coverage—not even for his rehabilitation."

There was a pause, and then Jamie and Liam chorused, "*What?*"

"Dad was laid off two months ago," Mason explained quietly. Ben stared at his phone again.

"And you were going to tell us this *when?*" Jamie demanded. Liam straightened, shocked.

"You and Liam weren't home for the last few weeks and it's a stressful enough situation without burning up the phone lines with it," replied Mr. Bennet.

"No severance package?" Liam frowned.

"Nothing. Thirteen years there, and *nothing*. Some young kid took my place." Mr. Bennet stared down at his shoes. Liam had never seen him look so devastated. "And now I can't even help my boy."

"We'll figure something out," Jamie said quickly. He squeezed his father's shoulder. "Dad? You have to be strong. It isn't like you to fall apart like this. We'll make it work."

"I wish you would have told me," Liam murmured.

"Liam, you've been in your own little world for a while now," Ben suddenly said. Liam looked at him in surprise. "If you really wanted to know, you could've called home and figured it out."

"Ben, it's not like I'm *uninvolved* or something."

"No," he agreed, faltering. "But you've been distant for months."

The room grew quiet, and he became aware of his brothers and his father staring at him. Liam sighed heavily and raked his fingers through his hair. "I'm gonna go get some coffee," he mumbled.

Jamie was waiting for him in the hall when he came back from the cafeteria. He gave him a short smile, his attempt at being comforting.

"Here comes the inquisition, I imagine?" Liam drawled. He leaned against the wall.

"What Ben said was harsh," Jamie started. "I mean, you could say the same about me. I've been swamped with work, and I've been coming home pretty infrequently. Every two or three weekends."

"But?" Liam prompted with a sigh.

"*But* it's been a physical distance, Liam," Jamie explained patiently. "You've been closed off since you came back from England. Emotionally distant. Everyone's noticed."

Liam looked at him but said nothing.

"I don't see you for weeks and then you come here with Will Darcy. It's... well, it's surprising. Can't I at least know what's going on?" Jamie asked in earnest. "As your brother, don't you think I have a right to know? I *care* about you, for Christ's sake."

"Yeah, I care about you too, Jamie," Liam interrupted. "God, of course I do. But it's complicated."

"Try me."

He met his eye and chewed the inside of his cheek, thinking. "I don't know where to begin," he said helplessly.

"I'll help you. Why were you in New York?" asked Jamie patiently.

"Darcy invited me. His company was having a party."

Jamie faltered. "Did you see Charlie?"

"Yes," Liam mumbled. "Which is why I didn't want to tell you. I'm the last person who wants to burden you with past issues. Especially when you seem so moved on and well-adjusted now."

"Just because I don't talk about it doesn't mean it's not there," Jamie said. "Doesn't mean I'm not thinking about it."

"You should know that Charlie looks *shitty*," Liam piped up, and Jamie laughed. "Seriously, a complete wreck."

"That doesn't make me feel better," said Jamie.

"Not even a little? Come on, man. If you can't revel in your ex-boyfriend's misery, what *can* you enjoy in life?"

"A lot, and stop deflecting," Jamie warned, pointing at him. "What I want to know is what's going on between you and Will Darcy. What, are you friends now?"

"Uh." Liam rubbed the back of his neck. "Sort of."

"Sort of?" Jamie echoed doubtfully.

"Look, he was at Rosings, and I never told you. He was there in England when I visited Charlotte. I didn't bring him up because I didn't think he was important, and I didn't want you thinking about Charlie again."

Jamie's eyebrows were raised, but he leaned closer, goading Liam to continue.

Liam turned his head to look levelly at his brother. An even intake of breath, and Liam confessed what had happened. He revealed everything except the events of the night before, which seemed too private and too intimate to divulge. It took a few minutes, an uncontested few minutes with Jamie listening in silence. His face was unreadable until Liam finished, and when he looked over to gauge his reaction, he found that Jamie was smiling slightly to himself.

"I had my suspicions," he finally admitted.

"About?"

"About you... and about Darcy. I knew there was something bubbling beneath the surface. You spark off of each other."

"Meaning we *argue*?" Liam asked, bemused.

"Yeah, but...." His mouth quirked up. "He keeps up with you. And you put him in his place. And it's kind of electric."

"And infuriating."

"They go hand in hand, I find."

"I suppose you're right."

"But Liam, you're an *idiot*," Jamie said impatiently. When his brother bristled, he continued. "Me. You couldn't tell *me*, of all people, what you were feeling and going through? What made you think that it was even an *option* to carry it all on your own shoulders?"

Liam tried to work past the knot in his throat. He lifted his shoulders in a noncommittal shrug. "I didn't see a different way to handle it."

"Were you ashamed?" Jamie asked quietly.

"No, not at all. Just completely confused. Maybe if it were someone other than Will, I would have felt more secure. But Jamie, I really disliked him at first," said Liam.

"And now?"

"I… don't. I misjudged him. He's not proud…." Liam faded off in thought. "He's socially *fucked*, I'll give him that. But it's not so much out of arrogance than just a lack of trust, unless he's with the people he cares about." He turned to his brother, almost enthusiastically. "Because, Jamie, when he's with the people he loves, he just *lights up*. And he's so nice to be around."

Jamie listened to him with a pensive look on his face.

"I realize it's something to be worked on, opening up to people who are *not* in your immediate circle of friends or family," Liam said mostly to himself now, scratching the stubble on his chin. "But he's getting better, so it seems promising, huh?"

"I think so," Jamie agreed, his smile broadening.

"What?" Liam said after a moment, coloring.

"You *like* him," Jamie laughed. "A lot."

"I mean, not *really*—"

"You really, really do."

"Shut up." Liam straightened and walked back toward the waiting room.

"*Finally!*" Jamie chuckled behind him. "Someone you care enough about to blush over. I'm glad you have a pulse, Liam Bennet."

When they entered the waiting room, the doctor was speaking to the huddled Bennet clan, who were hanging onto his every last word. Ben looked palpably relieved, and Mr. Bennet almost burst into tears, conveying more emotion than Liam had ever seen him display in the last twenty years. Mrs. Bennet kissed the doctor stoutly on the cheek. When she saw Liam, she shrieked and pulled him in for a hug.

"No spinal cord damage," she said tearfully during the embrace and peppered his face with kisses. Liam laughed and scrunched his nose.

"What's the worst of it, then?"

"The broken leg, but it's a clean break and should heal properly," she said. "Also his head injury, but he's cussing like a sailor in there, so all the nuts and bolts are screwed in properly."

"He *will* need physical therapy," the doctor reminded them. "For a few weeks, for his leg. But we can release him within the next two days, assuming he will have proper attention at home."

"Of course he will. I won't leave his side," Mrs. Bennet declared.

"He'll be thrilled, Mom." Ben grinned.

Liam's phone went off and he excused himself into the hall. He was smiling when he picked up. "Hello?"

"Hello! It's Ann."

"Ann—hi."

"Hi darling. Will's told me everything that happened. Are you all right?"

"Yeah, yeah. Nate's going to be okay." He explained the rehabilitation and nitty-gritty details.

Ann sighed heavily. "How awful. I was livid when I heard. What a complete and utter bastard. If you need help tracking him down, I have a few ideas—"

"No, that's okay." Liam shook his head, though she could not see it. "Honestly, the time will come to track Wickham down. In the meantime, we're more focused on getting Nate back up and running, and paying off his medical bills. Apparently my dad's been laid off, which adds a little more stress to the situation."

"Oh no!" Ann cried.

"Yeah. I feel terrible. Like I haven't been focused on my family at all."

"Don't be so hard on yourself. Show me a person who can manage their attention equally on all areas of life and I'll show you a fraud," Ann declared. "One thing always gives way for another. It's just the eternal seesaw of life."

He had to smile. He had missed her light, punchy optimism.

"I think we'll be all right. We're resilient. My dad is pretty spooked about it. Mom has little-to-no knowledge of expenses; she's always been pretty loose with our finances…." He was suddenly conscious of his rambling and shut his mouth, embarrassed.

"Please move to England; you wouldn't have to worry about this sort of thing, and you could live with me and have brunch constantly. Win-win."

"I'll be on the next flight over," said Liam.

"Liar," crooned Ann. A pause and then, "What hospital are you at, love?"

"Um… Meadowford Memorial. Why?"

"Curious, is all." She hesitated, then said, "Will is very worried about you. I'll be happy to tell him about Nate. I can't imagine the state you must be in—I would be a mess if something had happened to my brother."

"I hope you never have to know," Liam replied. "You're very close."

"Yeah, he's my insides. I adore him," Ann said simply, genuinely. "Except for a time when we were kids. There was one year he convinced me that kangaroos didn't exist."

Liam laughed. "Are you serious?"

"Yes! He thought it was hysterical. Didn't anticipate a seven-year-old traveling to Australia to prove him wrong, but luckily I did own an encyclopedia."

"Always a good student."

"Always. Bye, darling. Keep me updated. Take care of yourself."

"Take care, Ann."

CHAPTER THIRTY-NINE

NATE'S SPIRIT wasn't much hindered by the accident—though this could have been because the entirety of the household waited on him hand and foot as soon as he was discharged from the hospital.

"I'm gonna get *loads* of girls," he said triumphantly, gingerly touching the cut and bruise now purpling above his left eyebrow. "Sympathy tail."

"You're incorrigible," Mr. Bennet said dryly.

"Mom always encouraged the power of positive thinking, Dad," Nate retorted. "Glass half-*full*."

"Glass half-horny," Mason muttered under his breath. His mother glowered at him and walked out of the room. Beside him on the couch, Jamie snorted.

They camped out in their living room. Liam sat on the floor with his back against the couch, the laptop open in front of him. This was the second weekend he had spent home, having requested time off from the café to spend with his family. He had his reading glasses on, and his brow furrowed in concentration. Occasionally, his eyes flickered to his phone.

He had texted Darcy an update about Nate the day before, and had followed up with another a few hours ago. But Darcy had not answered, and Liam felt the unease of rejection gnawing in the pit of his stomach.

He decided to ignore it—at least for now. In the meantime, he was browsing for possible rehabilitation clinics for Nathan, instead of finishing the fifth page of a paper for class.

The Gardiners had ended up pitching in for the medical bills. ("And so they should," Mrs. Bennet had simpered. "He's their *favorite* nephew and they have no children.") But physical therapy was a different beast to tackle.

"I have a solution." Ben wandered into the living room from the kitchen, snapping open a soda can. "How about we just throw things at him until he grows stronger?"

"Wow Ben, if your good ideas were pennies...," Jamie began.

"We'd be destitute," deadpanned Liam.

"I'm in no rush for physical therapy," said Nate. "Do you *know* how many girls have texted me since I showed up at school on crutches? God, I may keep the cast on even after I heal."

Mason uncapped a marker from his school bag, leaned forward, and wrote *DICK* on Nate's cast.

"Hey!"

Liam glanced over, grinning. Mason smirked at his brother. "What are you going to do, chase me?"

Nate looked helplessly at his mother. "Mom!"

Mrs. Bennet poked her head around the corner from the foyer. "Sweetie, I'm going to go buy groceries for dinner. If you need anything, ask your father." She turned. "*John*, be nice to your son."

Mr. Bennet folded his newspaper, exposing his face. "I'm always nice," he said in a voice that strongly suggested otherwise.

Liam was grateful for the levity, and especially grateful for Nate's lightheartedness. He had been very much a shadow of himself when they first saw him in his hospital bed, pale and beat-up, a myriad of cuts and bruises on his body. Nobody had the heart to berate him for his behavior the night of the accident. After all, he had suffered the consequences.

Liam hadn't been able to handle it. He clenched his fists. God, if he ever saw George Wickham again—

"I would rearrange his face," Jamie said simply that night. They sat on the porch, staring at the empty street. "He's a coward—a spineless excuse for a man."

"He changed his phone number," muttered Liam.

"Of course he did. He's petrified."

Liam took out his phone. After a couple of moments, he sighed and pocketed it. Jamie turned to face him.

"Have you heard from Will?" he murmured.

"No."

"Give him a call. It's been almost two weeks."

"*No*. I already left him a couple of messages. I don't want to come across as—"

"Needy?" Jamie finished. "Wasn't it you who always encouraged me to speak my mind? Say what I'm feeling?"

Liam rolled his eyes. "*Maybe*. But I'm much better at giving advice than taking it."

"Naturally. But it only takes practice," said Jamie.

He recalled his conversation with Darcy then, while he had been plucking out scales on the piano at Rosings. Liam half smiled. God, that seemed like centuries ago. He looked at Jamie. "Well thank you for the wisdom, *Bro*da."

Jamie snorted.

They watched a familiar minivan pull up the street then, headlights blinding. Their mother parked crookedly in the driveway, and both boys got up to help her unload groceries from the trunk.

CHAPTER FORTY

A WEEK went by and nothing. Liam returned to school, distracted and disengaged. The weather took a turn for the worse too, drawing in tropical storms named after minor Disney characters. He often cycled in the rain.

"Don't you own a car?" Callum asked him, handing Liam his apron. Liam shook his hair dry and his manager scowled. "Thanks for that, buddy."

"Car is in the shop," Liam sighed, slipping the apron around his neck. The engine had died, sputtering out a week before as he was making a right turn in an intersection.

Nothing fatal had occurred, thankfully. But his mother had burst into hysterics when he told her over the phone that night, practically hiccupping. *"Goodness gracious, is the universe out to leave me childless? Does nobody have compassion for my fragile nervous system? Two children in one month—"*

"Not injured," Liam had reminded her. He was sure to treat her with gentle patience, as anything else these days seemed to be inflammatory.

His shift passed without much business, allowing him to fool around in the manager's office, snoop over payroll clipboards, and play around with office supplies until Callum chased him. By nine o'clock, the rain had stopped. As Liam unchained his bike, he stopped to check his phone.

Nothing from Darcy.

He had called him last night too; it had gone to voice mail.

Liam felt the sting of rejection and swallowed, slipping the phone back into his pocket. Something had changed.

Had he screwed up?

Been too indifferent?

Reacted too late?

Maybe the entire ordeal was just too dramatic for Darcy. Maybe it had scared him off. *But he had acted so sincere....*

His phone went off, and Liam answered it a little breathlessly. "Hello?"

"Liam," said his mother. "I have such good news!"

He perked up. "Oh yeah? Please tell me it's about Nate."

"As if anything else can occupy my time right now; of course it's about your brother. The doctor said that he is healing properly. Also, we've had a mysterious benefactor settle the physical therapy costs."

Liam's brows knit together in confusion. "Benefactor?"

"Yes."

"Do we have a wealthy great-uncle in hiding or something?" he asked suspiciously.

"No. I know the identity of the person; I'm just not allowed to tell you," Mrs. Bennet said slowly.

He laughed aloud. "Not allowed to tell *me*?"

"No! And I plan to make good on my promise, given what's been done for us in our time of need."

He ignored the tinge of melodrama. "And you were given instructions not to tell me, specifically."

"Well, specifically, nobody is supposed to know. But especially you," she clarified.

"Do you know this person?"

"I know of him."

"Why accept charity from someone that you don't know *personally*, Mom?" He started to grow concerned for her, worried that she had fallen into a scam of some sort.

"Because he wouldn't take no for an answer," Mrs. Bennet replied. "It put me in quite the awkward position, Liam, and I swore that I would repay him. But even then, he would not accept it being a loan. He also called to say that he settled the last of Nathan's medical bills, those that your uncle Frank couldn't cover. How we are indebted to this man, I cannot even begin to tell you."

Liam's mouth was hanging open. He shut it. Darcy instantly sprang to mind. Though he struggled with the *why* and the *how*, he had a gut feeling. A steely certainty.

"Mom?"

"Yes?"

"Was this person William Darcy?"

Dead silence met him on the other end.

"Oh my god." He passed a hand over his face.

"I didn't say it was him!"

"Of course you didn't." Liam muttered.

"But how do you know him?" his mother asked quickly.

"Who?" Liam smirked.

"William Darcy. Mason tells me that he's an entrepreneur." She let the word roll off her tongue like it was exotic.

"So what you're saying is that it *is* William Darcy."

"No, this is a different subject we're starting now." Mrs. Bennet was all innocence. "But hypothetically if it were William Darcy, how exactly did you two meet?"

"Through Jamie's ex, Charlie Bingley. Will Darcy is his best friend and business partner," Liam explained as sparsely as he could. "We, uh, we've been thrown together a few times. He knew Collins too."

"Oh?"

"I also knew his sister here at school."

"I'm a little confused."

"I will explain everything to you in due time, Mom." Liam smiled. "I promise. But everything is all right and you don't have to worry about anything."

"That's what all of you boys say to get me to stop pestering you."

"Well, for a reason, I would imagine."

"You're a horrible child, Liam Bennet," she mock-scolded, and then added, "but you seem to have some excellent people in your life, so I can't fault you there."

He smiled. "Thank you, Mom."

CHAPTER FORTY-ONE

LIAM WITHDREW his key from Jamie's door, cranked the handle to the left, and shoved his weight against it until it gave way. Then he flicked on the light and set his brother's mail on the coffee table. Finally, he stowed his bike in the narrow hallway between the bathroom and the coat closet.

He paused, smiling. Jamie's apartment was pristine and spotless; it bore no comparison to his own. Liam sighed, removed his cap, and ran a hand through his unruly hair. He helped himself to a can of soda from Jamie's fridge, sat back on the couch, and turned on the TV.

It was the second night he would be staying with him, given how much closer Jamie's apartment was to the Oak Café. Then Jamie would obligingly give him a ride to his campus in the mornings—at least until his car was up and running again.

"Three weeks of pay until I can afford that fix-up," Liam had complained to his father over the phone.

"Let me help you, son. We have Nate's medical expenses paid off—"

"But you have many more. I can handle it, Dad. How's the job search going?"

Mr. Bennet's answers had grown increasingly monosyllabic, and Liam knew that his father's pride had taken a significant blow by the termination. His mother was quietly optimistic, gently pushing her husband each day to send out his resumes.

Liam rested his head against the back of the couch and let his eyes fall shut. He imagined that he would have to send out his own resumes in a couple of years, find himself a job, build a future. It was terrifying. Sometimes it all occurred to him at inopportune times, like when he was running. He would freeze in his path, sweat cooling the space between his shoulder blades, and feel the icy crush of future responsibility. His chest would constrict, and his mind would whirl on.

And then he would call Jamie, because Jamie was always the logical side of their coin, and Jamie would assure him that there was *always* a solution somewhere, and there was no point in worrying about things he couldn't control. That sometimes fate had a way of working things out.

Liam wasn't sure if he believed it—but that didn't mean it wasn't comforting to hear.

He felt indebted to William Darcy, and this alone caused an uneasiness in the pit of his stomach. He felt that he could never pay him back, for *everything.*

And he didn't like having debts. Being Darcy's charity case, well, that was pathetic, wasn't it? How would Darcy view him now?

Liam opened his eyes and stared at the ceiling. He imagined Darcy's face then—the steely blue eyes and the strength in his jaw. And then the change when he would smile, and his entire *being* would lighten, and everything would somehow seem just a little bit better.

Liam found he was smiling now, the uneasiness replaced with something else. He *missed* him. He missed him a lot. It gnawed at him. Liam sat up, surprised at himself. He swallowed.

The doorknob jostled and Jamie walked in, smiling as he shrugged out of his leather jacket. "Hey there. Did your shift end early?"

"Yeah, they're trying to save payroll." Liam shrugged. "Which is a little annoying considering that I'm looking for *more* hours, but what can you do?"

"Intern at the company for the summer," Jamie suggested, opening the fridge. "I'm pretty sure they're looking for new hires."

"What would I do at your company?"

"Scan files and send e-mails, probably. Answer phones, be a wiseass. You should have no problems there."

"*Hmm*," Liam smiled, stroking his invisible beard. "Sorry for squatting. I'll return to my apartment eventually."

"You're fine." Jamie plopped down beside him. He laced his hands behind his head and stretched. "There's no shame in saying that you don't want to be alone."

"Well, technically I don't live alone," Liam pointed out.

"Mauricio can't be very good company. He barely speaks English," Jamie said. "And just because you're not physically alone doesn't mean that you don't feel alone."

"And what indication do I give of *feeling* alone?" Liam asked coolly.

Jamie turned. "Give me some credit. I've been your brother for over two decades; I think I can tell."

Liam pressed his lips together and looked down. He couldn't help but laugh. Jamie touched his shoulder.

"I think I went about this the wrong way," said Liam quietly.

"What do you mean?"

"I mean, there's a reason that Will hasn't contacted me at all. He cleaned up my family's mess and trashed the paper towels, and now he wants nothing to do with our ridiculousness—*my* ridiculousness."

"I think you do him a disservice by assuming he would be so judgmental," said Jamie. A moment passed, and he added, "I still can't believe what he did."

"He's a really good man," Liam murmured. He was fastening and unfastening his watch, preoccupied. "He's sort of perfect. I realized it too late."

Jamie watched him with concern. Then his phone began to ring. "I'm sorry," he mumbled, as he rose to get it from the coffee table. He reached forward and froze.

"What's wrong?" asked Liam.

It continued to ring. Jamie said very quietly, "It's—it's Charlie."

Liam stared at him. "Pick *up*, Jamie!"

He did. Liam slid to the edge of the couch and sat up straight, listening intently to the one-ended conversation.

"Hi," Jamie murmured. He paced nervously, and Liam raised his eyebrows, amused. "I've been well, thank you."

He was proud of Jamie, who was polite but clipped, obliging but reserved. His brother seemed to listen for a long time, then opened his mouth and closed it. Occasionally, he colored.

"Charlie...," he started slowly. "I don't think that's such a good idea. What you did... I didn't take lightly." A beat—Bingley's rebuttal, Liam guessed. Then Jamie sighed. "All right. How about that Chinese restaurant near my apartment? Yeah. That's the one."

"Holy shit," Liam murmured.

Jamie turned. He dipped his head low. "Tonight is fine."

He ended the conversation and sank down to the sofa. He stared at his phone. "So...."

"So?" Liam egged him on.

"He wants to talk to me. Even if I can only give him ten minutes." He smiled. "I agreed on fifteen."

"Cold-*blooded*," quipped Liam.

"Is this a good idea? I'm not sure this is a good idea," Jamie began anxiously, cracking his knuckles—a nervous habit. "Fuck."

"You never say 'fuck.'"

"Might be a good time to start," he muttered.

Liam grinned.

He lingered around the apartment as his brother got ready to leave that evening. After Liam suggested a shirt change and wished him luck, Jamie left and Liam stood in the foyer feeling strangely sad and optimistic at the same time. He rubbed the back of his neck and glanced around.

Catherine de Bourgh called while he was helping himself to Jamie's leftovers. He had just removed a carton of lo mein from the fridge when his phone buzzed on the countertop—he answered it without glancing at the screen.

"Hello?"

"Is this Liam Bennet?"

"Last I checked, yes," he said whimsically, twirling lo mein around his fork.

"Clever," the caller deadpanned. "Good evening, Liam. This is Catherine de Bourgh. We met—"

"I remember." He closed the fridge warily and set the carton down. "How are you, Mrs. de Bourgh?"

"I hope to be much better by the end of this conversation," she responded coolly. "I hope you don't mind; I got your number from my niece, Georgiana."

"Not at all," he lied.

"I wouldn't dream of calling you otherwise, but I simply wanted to clarify a matter or two. I've recently heard that you and my nephew, William…" She cleared her throat. "You and William are—"

"Yes?" Liam said.

"Whatever relationship you seem to have fostered with my nephew can't be anything serious, but I wanted to take precautions. Whatever you have assumed about William is wrong."

"Is it really?"

"As I understand it, young people today are awfully curious, having flings with whomever happens to stroll along. We live in a fairly liberal, progressive era that I do not necessarily approve of, but I don't presume to be ignorant of its existence. I'm still waiting for Charles Bingley to emerge from his phase, which I'm sure was a publicity stunt, though you didn't hear it from me."

"Excuse me?" Liam gaped.

"I implore you to put an end to it now before it tarnishes our family legacy." Catherine cut down to the chase. "Will is very soon to be engaged to my stepdaughter, Violet."

"Violet de Bourgh," Liam echoed in a monotone.

"Yes."

"That is some truly messed up *Brady Bunch* shit, Mrs. de Bourgh. Also, I've never seen two people less interested in each other than Violet and Will."

"I'll have you know that they have been seeing each other for two years now—"

"Is that the story you panned out to the press?" Liam retorted.

"Listen to me," Catherine said sharply, and Liam thought that he had never heard her sound quite so shrill before. "Will is not—"

"He's gay."

"I assure you, he is—"

"Very gay."

"Excuse me—"

"So gay."

"I'll have you know—"

"The gayest."

"If you care about him, you will leave him alone!" Catherine countered sharply. "Their marriage would mean joining his fortune with Violet's, securing the longevity of this family. It will not be disrupted because of some poor, perverted English major—"

"Oh my god, is this really happening?" Liam demanded. "Are you serious right now? Did you just tumble out of the wrong century?"

"I am extremely serious, Mr. Bennet. What do you have that could possibly benefit my nephew in any way? What are your connections? I've heard that your family is the sort to acquaint themselves with George Wickham, as if your situation weren't bad enough. William does not need any such company in his life. Wouldn't you agree?"

Liam faltered, speechless with indignation.

"Besides," Catherine continued smoothly, "I've also heard about your brother's relationship, and his designs on getting Bingley's fortune. I can't imagine that your motives are much different, no matter what you tell yourself. Lord have mercy if Will's name is to be polluted with such a scandal. His father would surely rocket out of his grave."

"I—"

"Promise me that you will stop seeing him."

"No." Liam clenched his jaw. "No, I promise you nothing."

A loaded silence, then, "You're a very selfish young man, Liam Bennet."

"And you have no respect for your nephew's happiness, Mrs. de Bourgh. You obviously know nothing about Will, which is really pretty sad," Liam retorted. "But also, you know absolutely nothing about *me*, nor my family. You have no right to insult us."

"I see that I have to resort to Plan B." Catherine cleared her throat. "Very well. I imagined that this might happen. How much do you want?"

"What?"

"How much money would it take for you to stay away from him? Don't be coy. Student debt is nearly crippling these days. Or so I hear. My family isn't burdened with such trivial concerns, but I may be able to help yours."

"Wow," Liam breathed.

"Take the opportunity while it's still hot, Mr. Bennet. Would ten thousand be enough? Of course it would. Who do I make the check out to?"

"You can make it out to Fuck You," Liam said. "And then deposit it up your arthritic sphincter. Have a *fantastic* evening, Mrs. de Bourgh."

And with that, he hurled the phone onto the couch.

CHAPTER FORTY-TWO

"JUST GIVE him a nudge."

"I don't want to wake him; he looks so peaceful."

"*Peaceful?* He's drooling a little."

Liam opened one eye blearily and was confronted by three truths.

#1: He had an audience. Bingley and Jamie were smiling at him, the latter sympathetically. They both had their jackets on.

#2: He had fallen asleep in his hoodie and jeans, under Jamie's fleece blanket on the living room sofa.

#3: He had *over*slept.

"Tea?" Jamie thoughtfully placed a mug on the coffee table.

Liam sat upright. "What time is it?"

"Quarter to nine." Bingley put his phone back in his pocket.

"Crap. My shift started fifteen minutes ago," said Liam miserably.

Jamie nodded. "I thought that might be the case. Well, given the fact that you're already late, there's an egg-white and turkey-bacon omelet waiting for you on the kitchen table."

"And coffee," added Bingley.

"Right, coffee too. Also, you may want to hit the shower first because your hair is doing this thing again where it has its own zip code."

Liam touched his head self-consciously, rose, and closed himself in the bathroom. Ten minutes later, he was eating breakfast while Jamie cleaned the kitchen.

Bingley fumbled with his keys. "I'll just uh… wait outside in the car."

"Okay." Jamie turned. There was a palpable tension between them. "We won't be much longer."

"Okay," Bingley said quietly. He smiled, faltered, and then showed himself out.

"So," Liam started hesitantly. He took a sip of coffee. "You and Charlie, huh?"

"He did *not* spend the night."

"But it obviously went well."

"Well enough," said Jamie cryptically. He turned on the faucet.

"Well enough for him to stop by again in the *morning*? Yeah, I would say so. You gonna tell me what happened?"

Jamie turned and leaned against the counter. He sighed. "Well, we talked a lot. And it's kind of difficult to pick up right where we left off. I don't know if I can trust him again."

"Right," Liam agreed. "So?"

"*So* we're just going to start off with a blank slate. As friends," he added quickly.

Liam narrowed his eyes.

"I mean it," Jamie laughed.

"I know *you* mean it, but I'm not so sure that's his intention." Liam smiled and got up. He rinsed his plate and set it in the dishwasher. "Thanks for breakfast."

"Anytime. Get your jacket on. Charlie's giving me a ride to the office, and Oak is on the way."

"Good—I did not feel like biking," Liam sighed.

He pulled on his jacket and slung his backpack across his shoulder.

He was halfway out the door when Jamie stopped him. "You all right?"

"Yeah," Liam answered slowly. "Why?"

"You were muttering in your sleep. Last night when I came home and this morning too."

"Oh."

Jamie pressed his lips together, watching him. Years of sharing bunk beds as boys had made them quite conversant in the other's sleeping patterns. "You don't do that unless you're upset."

"*Or* just having a weird dream," Liam suggested breezily.

"*Liam.*"

He pulled up his hood. "Charlie's waiting for us. We better go."

Jamie sighed but allowed his brother to pass. He locked the door behind them.

Against all odds, Rosemary was running the café for the day. Naturally, he was reprimanded. But he found solace in the business of the shift. The flow of customers was consistent, and before he knew it, it was dark outside.

"Good work today, Bennet," said Rosemary as they were closing. Liam looked up in shock. She cleared her throat. "Don't be *late* next time."

"Yes, ma'am."

His walk home was slow. The air was brisk. He hooked in his headphones. By the time he made it to Jamie's block, his body ached from working all day. But at least it had kept his mind off of—

He froze. "Will."

Darcy had been sitting on the stoop of the building, staring at his phone. He smiled when he saw Liam and stood up. "Hey."

"Hey." Liam took out his headphones. "What are you doing here?"

"Well, Charlie wanted to talk with your brother," he explained. "I guess I came by for moral support, but then I felt like I was *intruding* so I decided to wait outside."

"Oh." Liam suddenly started to laugh.

"What's so funny?" Darcy rubbed the back of his neck, seeming self-conscious.

"Nothing. I just pictured Jamie and Charlie talking and you standing awkwardly near them, with your arms glued to your sides. Quiet. Will Darcy, the awkward sardine."

"I'd be lying if I said that wasn't pretty much what happened."

Liam sat next to him. Briefly, their knees touched. They were silent, staring at a fixed point in the street.

"So," Liam said slowly. "What do you think the verdict is on these two?"

Darcy glanced back at the door. "Wish I knew. But I don't think he's worked his way back into Jamie's good graces yet."

"No," Liam agreed. "It's going to take time."

"But they have a chance?" Darcy murmured.

"Yeah. I believe so. I don't think Jamie ever got over him fully. But he would probably hit me if I revealed that in front of him."

"Is your brother capable of that?"

"I've only seen it happen once, but he throws a pretty solid right hook." Liam looked down at the asphalt.

"I see."

"Why didn't you call?" Liam asked suddenly.

Darcy stilled. He didn't speak for a few seconds. "I'm an altogether flaky, disagreeable person."

"Which is what *I* thought." Liam played along. "But seriously: was it something that I did?"

"*No*," Darcy insisted. "I just wanted to give you space with your family, Liam. Plus, the last time I pursued you, it was an absolute disaster. It was a train wreck."

"It was a car crash at the site of a train wreck," he agreed.

"You're... really not a very encouraging person," Darcy said dryly.

Liam chuckled. He felt a swell of relief.

"Did you want me to call?" Darcy baited.

"Maybe."

"And instead you got a call from my aunt."

Liam looked at him. "Maybe."

"I'm really, really sorry, Liam," Darcy said genuinely. "I found out this morning and I was furious. There's no excuse for what you had to deal with."

"I handled it. It isn't your fault. I was pretty disrespectful, though."

"Yeah," Darcy said slowly. *"Arthritic sphincter."*

"Oh god," Liam laughed, burying his face in his hands. "I'm *so* sorry."

"Ann and I got a laugh out of it. You always did have a colorful way with language."

"Regretfully."

"She's…." Darcy sighed. He ran his fingers through his hair. "Catherine's a pill. And a bigot. She's pretty deluded about Violet as well. That girl has been seeing the same man for the last three and a half years."

"Violet?" Liam echoed. "Wow, good for her. Do they have actual conversations?"

"Yes. Maybe. You know, I'm actually not sure." Darcy laughed. "But she also disapproves of that relationship, so she refuses to acknowledge it."

"Well." Liam shrugged. "You can't choose your family, can you?"

"No. But I was worried that you would hate me for it."

"You paid off Nate's expenses when my family couldn't," Liam said abruptly. He was looking down. "Don't think I could hate you even if I tried, Will—and believe me, I have tried."

Darcy had grown silent.

Liam smiled at him. "Did you really think my mother wouldn't tell me?"

"Realistically, I guess not."

"Why did you do it?"

"What else was I supposed to do?" Darcy blushed and looked at the ground. "You were miserable, and your family was struggling. I couldn't stand by and do nothing."

Liam hugged him. Darcy pressed his face into his shoulder and wrapped his arms around him.

"Thank you" came his muffled voice.

"I found Wickham too."

Liam pulled back, astonished. "What? *Where?*"

"Don't worry about that."

"You are *really* shady." Liam laughed.

Darcy grinned. "It wasn't a pretty conversation. But your brother will get a check in the mail in a few days. I encouraged Wickham to sell all of his instruments and gig supplies. Also to set your brother up with a *proper* licensed music tutor. Or else your family would press charges for endangering a minor."

"You *encouraged*?"

Darcy hesitated. "Gently coerced. With force."

"That's not gently."

"Well, he's pretty weak."

"Oh god." Liam shook his head. "Will, how am I ever supposed to repay you? For any of this?"

"I don't want you to."

"But you've done so much for my family. If they only knew."

The door behind them opened, and they both turned. Mr. Patrizio, Jamie's middle-aged neighbor, walked out with a garbage bag.

"Good evening, Liam."

"Hi, Mr. Patrizio."

They watched him walk down the sidewalk, then turn to the clearing behind the parking lot. Darcy stood abruptly and zipped up his jacket. "I'm hungry."

Liam stood up as well. "I'm without my car right now. But there's a good diner two blocks out. We can walk."

A pause. "Let's do it."

CHAPTER FORTY-THREE

LB: You're probably sleeping. But Charlotte, you picked a horrible time for international travel. Charlie is trying to win back Jamie and I'm having late night pancakes with Will Darcy. And I think I'm in love with him. And I can't form logical sentences. HELP. ME.

Two minutes passed before his phone vibrated against the tabletop with a reply.

CL: Man up and tell him how you feel! I was already awake.
LB: No, you weren't. And I can't do that. I'm afraid.
CL: Don't be. Also, what kind of pancakes?

Liam put his phone away and slumped in his seat. Darcy stirred his coffee absent-mindedly, reading yesterday's paper. He glanced up.

"Whatcha doing?" he asked with a smile.

Texting my best friend about you even though it's almost four in the morning in the United Kingdom and I probably just cost her a fortune because I'm childish and desperate and afraid of what you might do to my heart.

"Responding to an e-mail," Liam said breezily. "It was Charlotte. She had a minicrisis. She can be so *needy* sometimes."

Darcy smiled politely.

Liam lowered his eyes. God, what was he so afraid of? It seemed to be the most natural thing to do—he knew exactly what he would say. But each time he opened his mouth, his heart thundered in his chest and his fists clenched. When the bill came at the end of the meal, Liam yanked it out of his hand with misplaced aggression.

"It's the least I can do," he mumbled, taking out his wallet. "At least let me buy you breakfast for dinner."

"This is what I was afraid of," Darcy sighed.

"What, me buying you a meal? You're right, it's pretty terrifying."

"No, you feeling like you owe me something. That's why I didn't want your mother to tell you; I was afraid of you getting weird about it."

"I'm not weird about it. It's a *diner bill*. I could never even come close to the debt you paid—"

"See, right there!" Darcy sighed and sat back in his seat. "Can we just forget about it?"

Liam paid their tab and tipped their waitress, and they walked in silence back to the apartment complex. The atmosphere had changed, and Darcy walked with tension in his gait. As they neared Jamie's block, Liam spoke up.

"Will, I'm not hanging out with you because I think that I owe you anything." He had stopped walking, and he laughed despite himself. "For God's sake, those were pancakes. Let me repay you in pancakes!"

"I know," Darcy muttered, shoving his hands into his pockets. "But I don't want you to think that what I did was a big deal. I just want things to be normal between us."

"But it *was* a big deal," Liam insisted.

"No, it wasn't. I did it for you, Liam. I know it was helping your family and I'm happy that I was able to help, but I did it for *you*."

They had stopped walking entirely now, and Darcy was looking at him in earnest, his eyes wide and bright even in the darkness. "And I didn't call you because I was afraid of screwing up again. Because the thought of losing you actually makes my insides hurt. I swear, it's an actual physical *ache*—"

Breathlessly, Liam closed the gap between them and kissed Darcy on the mouth.

"You won't lose me."

CHAPTER FORTY-FOUR

JOHN BENNET'S den was, surprisingly, the cleanest room in the entire house. Liam always marveled at the neat rows of books, the alphabetized files, and the dust-free shelves. His father maintained his room like a pristine palace. There were elements of the eccentric too—a Norman Rockwell painting, a box of untouched cigars, and a bottle of brandy that was only broken out on special occasions.

Mr. Bennet lowered his glasses when Liam entered and closed the door behind him. "Hi, Dad."

"Take a seat, son. What's on your mind?"

Liam sat on the couch. He wet his lips before speaking, nervousness working its way into his stomach. He ignored it. "I invited somebody over for dinner tonight. I've already told Mom."

"Okay," his father replied with some hesitation.

"His name is Will Darcy."

Mr. Bennet cocked his head, intrigued. "Oh yes, I've heard about *this* one. He's Public Enemy Number One, correct? You ranted about him your entire fall break."

Liam did his best to subdue a laugh. "Yeah." And then he explained to his father what Will Darcy had done for Nathan, and the family, watching slowly as the smile faded from his face and was replaced with fresh alarm.

"Good God. I have to pay him back."

"Dad, he wouldn't accept it. He doesn't even want to hear about it." Liam smiled and looked at the floor. "He's *very* stubborn, and relentless, but he has the best heart. I've given the wrong impression of him. Because I *had* the wrong impression of him."

Mr. Bennet fixated on him for a few moments. "You care a lot about him?" he asked quietly.

Liam sat upright. "I…."

His father leaned forward and rested his elbows on his knees. "Do you really think that I didn't know what you wanted to tell me that night in February, son?"

Liam's brows knit together. "I thought…."

His father sat back in his chair. "Well, I'll be honest. I *didn't* know what you were going to tell me back in February. But I mulled it over quite a lot and tried to figure you out. And then I spoke to Jamie—"

"Oh god," Liam muttered, raking his hands through his hair. "And here I thought *you just got me*. Jamie told you everything."

"Give me credit. I knew something was up," Mr. Bennet said. "But as the months went on, you closed up more and more. And I hate to think that it was because of me."

"It was and it wasn't. I didn't know how else to deal with it."

"That's what family is for. We help you carry your weight, Liam. We are there to ease your burdens. What other function would we possibly have? What good would I be to you boys? Lord knows I've failed in the past, but I want to change that now."

Liam half smiled. He glanced down. "You haven't failed."

"I could have prevented what happened to Nate if I were more responsible as a father," Mr. Bennet said gravely. "And the answer to your question is 'no.'"

"My question?"

"You asked if our relationship would change. And it won't. It doesn't matter to me who you love, Liam, as long as you both respect each other."

Liam rose and took his father's hand in his. "Thank you, Dad."

"You better tell your mother too."

"I will."

"Though she may not care very much now that your brother is back with Charlie," said Mr. Bennet. "All she can talk about is how rich Jamie will be now. I don't have the heart to tell her that your grandfather's inheritance was already awarded to someone else."

"No kidding." Liam laughed. "Who was the lucky grandson?"

"One I've never met," said Mr. Bennet. "Turns out Collins has a half brother living out in Montauk. Tied the knot three weeks ago. I should send him a bottle of wine."

"Collins must have been furious."

"Serves him right, the little shit."

CHAPTER FORTY-FIVE

LIAM STARED wistfully out the window as the setting sun dipped below the brilliant Manhattan skyline. Writing this article was just *not* happening—not on a gorgeous day like today. His hands were fixed over the keyboard, sleeves rolled neatly to the elbows—but he wasn't typing.

He looked at the white envelope, torn open and jagged, by the computer monitor. He smiled, excitement quietly bubbling in him.

"Hey." His colleague, Kristen, peeped over the cubicle partition. "Weren't you supposed to get out of here at three?"

"Yeah, but I'm still not done the second blog entry. I don't want Hank to hate me."

"Hank *loves* you," she scoffed. "You're the only editorial intern he's keeping around for the fall term. Which is *suicide*, if you ask me, since you'll be commuting to New York twice a week."

"On top of going to school full-time." Liam smiled. "But I have other reasons to be here."

"You mean your handsome boyfriend? Yes, we've met."

"It's his birthday today. We're meeting in Central Park. I'm really excited. His sister will be there, my friend Charlotte and her boyfriend are coming—"

"Then get *out* of here." Kristen smiled. "I'll cover for you."

He grinned.

The cab ride was slow, wedged in bumper-to-bumper traffic. He didn't mind. It was difficult for him to mind much these days, especially in the sultry June weather.

They met at the Boathouse in Central Park. Ann greeted him with a shriek, and he hugged her, lifting her off the ground. She kissed his cheek.

"God, I've missed you!"

An hour later, their table was crowded and abuzz with conversation. Jamie had recently returned from a business trip to China and was showing everyone photos on his phone. Bingley looked at him with adoration.

Darcy did his best not to mock him, and Liam grinned.

To his right sat Charlotte and Richard, on and off again within the past year and currently on again. Charlotte, in a string of part-time jobs, was able to loan her mother enough money to keep her creditors at bay. Richard had recently taken a position with Nerve.

"Nepotism? What's that?" Richard joked, stretching his arm out behind Charlotte's shoulders.

"It is *not* nepotism," Bingley clarified, "if you're a skilled software engineer and you were hired for your expertise."

"It was nepotism," said Darcy dryly. Liam laughed.

"Oh yeah?" Ann asked coyly. "Then where is my position at the company?"

"Finish school and we'll talk."

Jamie laughed. "I'm not so sure you want to work with your brother. Last summer, Liam interned at my company and we fought like cats and dogs."

"Only because I *hated* that internship," Liam pointed out.

"Are you happier at this one?" asked Richard.

"Oh yeah. I fetch a lot of coffee. But I'm writing articles—now that the editor knows I don't suck."

"Moving on up." Charlotte raised her glass.

"Liam's a brilliant writer," said Darcy. "Did you tell them that you're the only summer intern they've agreed to hold on to for fall? They like him that much."

"Liam, that's wonderful," Jamie exclaimed. "Tell Mom and Dad."

"I will next weekend," Liam responded. "Mom wants us both there for Saturday's potluck dinner."

Jamie wrinkled his nose. "It's that time of year already?"

"Yeah. Mason already called me complaining. I'm bringing Will with me. Mom asked him to make penne alla vodka."

"He makes *amazing* penne alla vodka," Ann agreed.

Charlotte turned. "My mom is trying to get me to go to that. She's bringing casserole. Stay away from it… it's repugnant."

"Thanks for the warning," Darcy chuckled.

Ann hit her fork against her champagne glass. "I would like to raise a toast!"

Everyone lifted their glasses.

"To my brother, Will," she continued, smiling. "The best man I know. May you have a healthy, happy year. And may you continue to be surrounded by those who love you most."

Darcy smiled. "Thank you, Ann."

Liam clinked his glass with Darcy's.

When it was time to leave, they clustered outside the restaurant talking for at least another fifteen minutes, laughter ringing into the air.

Jamie hugged his brother. "I'll see you next weekend, okay? Get back safe."

"I will. Bye, Charlie!"

"Bye, Liam." Bingley grinned. He took Jamie's hand. "Come *on*, slowpoke."

Jamie kissed his knuckles. "Lead the way."

They made it back to Darcy's apartment at a quarter to midnight. Darcy stumbled a little, mildly buzzed, as Liam held the door open and withdrew the keys from the lock.

His German shepherd lifted her head from her perch on the sofa, tail whipping back and forth. She ran to greet them. Liam scratched behind her ears. "Hi Sadie."

Darcy walked into the kitchen, loosening his tie. Liam shrugged out of his jacket and unbuttoned the top button of his dress shirt before he plopped down on the couch. The TV was turned to a muted *Law & Order* episode, and he closed his eyes. Sadie rested her head against his knee, and Liam looked down. He leaned forward to stroke her slick black and tan fur.

"I'm putting the kettle on. Tea?" Darcy called from the kitchen.

"Please and thanks."

Darcy was back in the room two minutes later. He put two mugs on the coffee table and poked Liam, imploring him to scoot over.

"*Fine*. So bossy."

"That I am." Darcy lowered onto the couch and Liam curled up beside him, linking his arm with his. "You're tired," he murmured.

"Yeah." Liam rested his head against his shoulder. "But I'm glad I'm not commuting back tonight."

"You can stay as long as you need to," promised Darcy. "But I'm worried what you're going to do when school starts up again in the fall."

Liam turned. "What if I could go to school here instead?" he asked quietly.

Darcy started. "What do you mean?"

His lips curled into a smile. "Well, what if, *hypothetically*, I had applied to transfer to NYU back in January and what if—*hypothetically*—they had accepted me?"

"Are you joking?" Darcy asked coolly.

"Nope."

"You waited until *now* to tell me."

"I'm nothing without my delivery."

"I hate you," Darcy groaned.

"You *love* me," Liam said smugly.

"I do," Darcy sighed, pulling him close. He kissed him, and laughed.

"I mean, there's still the matter of affording it. But NYU is giving me a grant, and it makes sense given how my internship is going," Liam explained, mildly breathless. He smiled wider now. "And I would be close to you."

"I don't think that you could have given me a better birthday present than that."

"Oh, that reminds me," Liam muttered. He turned and reached for his laptop bag, then fished until he pulled out a gift-wrapped parcel. He handed it to Darcy, smiling coyly. "Happy birthday."

"*Why?*" Darcy tore the paper off, revealing a black, leather-bound copy of *Far from the Madding Crowd*. Carefully, he opened it. "First edition," he murmured. "This is from—"

"Netherfield," finished Liam.

Darcy looked up, blue eyes wide. "How did you get this?"

Liam shrugged airily. "I saved up."

"Liam...." Darcy kissed him, and Liam linked his arms around his neck; he felt him smile against his mouth.

"Love you," Darcy murmured, cupping his chin.

Liam smiled. "Love you back."

AJ MICHAELS lives in the greater Philadelphia area and is an avid Jane Austen junkie. She has an immense appreciation for the universal themes in classic English literature and believes in finding humor in every situation. She runs primarily on coffee and terrible puns, and can often be found convincing her German Shepherd that he is not actually a lap dog (though he has yet to be convinced).

You can e-mail her at prideandmodernprejudice@gmail.com.

Also from DREAMSPINNER PRESS

Also from DREAMSPINNER PRESS

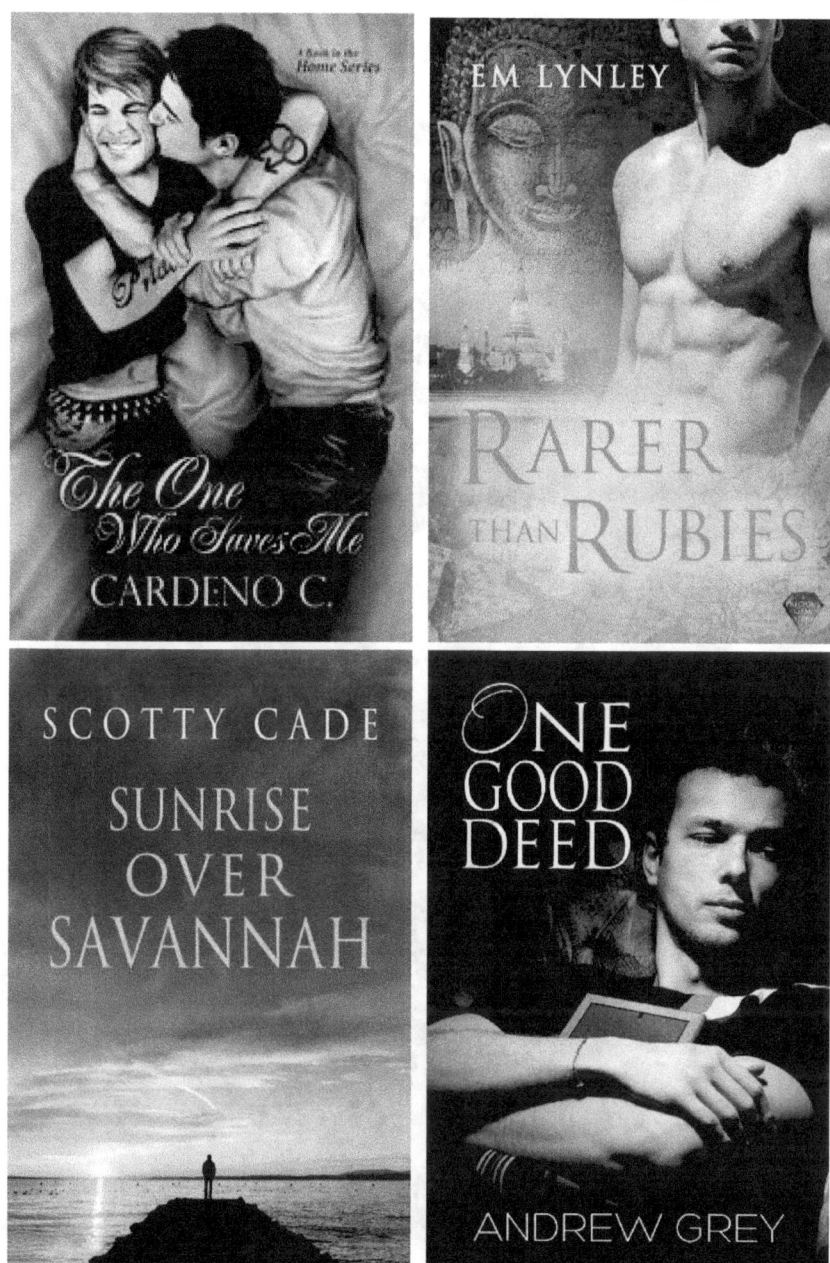